The Bitch and the Bastard

Flynn looked strikingly attractive and it bothered me that I'd become conscious of it.

'You followed me,' I accused him.

'Relax,' he said, plucking up one of my blonde tresses and twining it around his finger. 'You're in a crowded bar. What are you trembling for?'

'You make me nervous,' I admitted. 'Keep away from me, Flynn. That's all I came to say.'

He shook his head. 'No it isn't.' He yanked the bell-rope of my hair, forcing my face close enough for his lips to caress my cheek as he murmured into my ear. 'What you'd like me to do is to hook my finger into this ring-pull thing and slide your zip down to your navel. Then, right here, in front of everyone, you'd have me plunge my hand inside.'

I was so mesmerised by his seductive voice that I barely noticed his finger trailing down beyond the end of the zip until, bang on target, he pressed my throbbing clit. Even through my clothes, his touch was electric.

The Bitch and the Bastard

WENDY HARRIS

BLACK
lace

Black Lace novels contain sexual fantasies.
In real life, make sure you practise safe sex.

First published in 2001 by
Black Lace
Thames Wharf Studios,
Rainville Road, London W6 9HA

Copyright © Wendy Harris 2001

The right of Wendy Harris to be identified as the
Author of this Work has been asserted by her in
accordance with the Copyright, Designs and Patents Act
1988.

Typeset by SetSystems Ltd, Saffron Walden, Essex
Printed and bound by Mackays of Chatham PLC

ISBN 0 352 33664 1

Chapter One

My back was to the door but I knew she was there; the cloying stink of her cheap perfume had wafted into my nostrils and I could feel my hackles rising like a rash of prickly heat as I readied myself for her first bitchy comment of the day. But I wasn't prepared for the sudden slap of hot coffee on my shoulder.

'Fuck!' I exploded, leaping from my chair.

'Ooh sorry, Pam. I tripped,' she cooed, her voice oozing syrupy contrition. But, as I spun to confront her, I noticed the residue of a crafty smirk loitering on her lips.

'You clumsy cow!' I hurled at her, my eyes shooting spikes of pure malice.

'It was an accident,' she lied. 'And on your new blouse too. What a shame!' She dabbed ineffectually at a splodge of muddy liquid on my collar.

'You've ruined it, Janice,' I seethed.

She shrugged. 'I've probably done you a favour. Let's face it, Pam, acne would have been kinder to your complexion than this awful bilious yellow. What on earth possessed you to buy a colour that makes you look sick?'

I felt sick. Sick to death of Janice Becker who had

1

blighted my life since childhood, from my very first day at playschool when she'd tried to scalp my pigtails.

All through our formative years, we'd been bitter rivals; enemies in the playground and on the streets, forever picking at the scab of our hatred to keep it raw and festering.

Our fiercest fights had taken place in puberty when, snapping and snarling like pit bull terriers, we would lunge into battle at the slightest provocation. But, as we'd blossomed into womanhood, we'd brawled with words and speech, biting with tongues instead of teeth as we'd turned from fighting dogs to spitting cats.

Our vendetta might have ended with our school-days but for the cruel misfortune that had seen us enrolled at the same secretarial college for a further two years of bickering and sparring. Only the dismal prospect of us ending up in hell together and bitching our way through eternity had stayed my hands from throttling this monstrous Siamese twin whom fate had welded to my hip. But, with stubbornness in common, we'd survived to graduation, and our paths had parted at last.

I thought I'd seen the last of her after that. But five years on and here we were again. Back at each other's throats and vying for position at VoiceCom plc.

Although I'd joined the firm six months after Janice, it still seemed as if she was dogging my footsteps and I loathed her as much as ever.

In addition, I now despised her for spreading a rumour that I'd slept my way up from general office. It wasn't true. I'd only bedded my boss in lieu of a love affair that had never quite materialised. But I'd actually wanted romance, and if Tom had put more than his dick on the table, I would have jumped at the chance of something more substantial than the furtive fucks I'd ended up with. With this impeccable motive, I was reasonably convinced that I'd won my promotion on merit. Whereas Janice had earned hers on her back, like the slapper I knew her to be. She was a nasty, vindictive slut who'd stop at nothing to get what she wanted. Plus she was shit at shorthand. Knowing her as I did, I was pretty sure she'd spilled that coffee on purpose.

'What are you doing in my office?' I demanded.

'Tom wants to see me,' she said, poking at my rubber plant with a scarlet talon.

'What for?'

'You don't know?' she asked pointedly. 'You're slipping, Pam. I wouldn't allow Roger to fart without telling me about it first.'

'Always? Or just when you've got your head between his legs?' I retorted, making a mental note to kick Tom in the balls for keeping me in the dark.

She smiled like a crocodile. 'It takes a man-eater to know one.'

She sat down and I turned back to my keyboard, intending to ignore her. But she spoke to the back of my head. 'I needed to speak to you anyway.'

'What about?' I growled at my screen, in which her face, Medusa-like, was reflected.

'Bethany's hen-night. Did you book the stripper?'

I softened at the mention of our mutual friend and swivelled to face her. 'Yes. But he can't do the officer and a gentleman routine. Apparently, some pissed-up WI veterans ripped his whites to shreds last week.'

'Damn,' Janice grumbled. 'Beth loved that film. What have you asked for instead?'

'*Braveheart.*'

'Hmm.' She seemed satisfied. 'Good choice.'

I studied her sceptically. She was being unusually friendly today and I didn't like it. 'Your roots need touching up,' I commented. 'Or were you thinking of going back to black?' She glared at me and I knew that I'd touched a nerve because she'd always envied my natural blonde hair and had only bleached hers several shades lighter to make mine look dull. 'I suppose you know that too much peroxide can make your hair fall out?'

'I suppose you know that my fist can make your teeth fall out,' she threatened caustically.

This was more like it. 'They're crowns,' I reminded her with a dazzling smile. 'You'd only break your knuckles.'

Her eyes narrowed. 'I still say your money would have been better invested in chest implants.'

I winced. She knew I was jealous of her big, wobbling tits, which somehow made my own ample bosom seem a lot less ample. I think it went back to our school-days, when she'd had full-blown boobs long before the rest of us.

'Pancake Pam,' she reflected, reading my thoughts.

'Not any more,' I said, thrusting out my chest. 'But I bet you're still called "Jodhpur Thighs".'

Tom walked in. 'Now then, girls, miaow miaow,' he said. 'Why are you always sniping at each other?'

'Just a bit of fun,' I answered sweetly.

Tom perched on the edge of my desk. 'I have radar for animosity,' he said. 'Just remember, we're a team here, girls. So, you'd better learn to get on with each other or you'll both be out of a job.'

Janice simpered. 'Pam and I go way back, Tom. There's nothing in it, really. Just a bit of schoolgirl rivalry.'

He was looking at her breasts. 'Well, you're big girls now.'

It annoyed me, the way he was staring at her. He'd had me, and now he wanted her. I could see it in his eyes.

I suppose she was attractive in a piggish kind of way: small piggy eyes, snub nose, thick lips. But I considered myself to be prettier. And I had much the better figure for clothes. Janice, with her soft blancmangy curves, looked rubbish in skintight trousers. But she had the kind of figure that made men's eyes pop from their sockets and I could see why Tom was gaping at her.

4

I crossed my legs to draw his attention to them. They were four inches longer than hers, and I knew Tom admired them. 'So, what's this all about?' I asked him.

He took the bait and moved his eyes to my thighs. 'The director of our French operation is coming over in a couple of weeks on a fact-finding mission. I'd like you to act as his PA during his stay with us, Pam.'

This was excellent news. A prestigious assignment, which was bound to earn me Brownie points in my quest to take over from Beryl, our managing director's personal assistant, who was due for retirement soon.

The trouble was, Janice had Beryl's job in her sights as well. She pulled a sour face. 'I should have been selected for this,' she moaned. 'I've much more experience than Pam.'

'Only in the sack,' I uttered cynically.

Tom's eyes were back on her bosom again. 'That's probably true, Janice. But Pam speaks a little French and although Monsieur Planquet is fluent in English, it might make him feel more at home if he hears his native tongue now and then.'

'Don't you wish now that you'd spent more time in French class and less time French kissing behind the bike sheds?' I baited her.

She scowled at me but didn't rise to the jibe. 'What's his first name?' she asked Tom.

'Pierre-Nanu,' he supplied.

'Pierre the Gnu?' she queried. 'He sounds ugly.'

'On the contrary, I hear he's a bit of a ladies' man,' said Tom. 'I want you to organise an official welcoming party, Janice. Roger thinks we should make it a promotion thing. Invite our prestige clients – females in particular. Nothing too fancy. Wine and cheese will do.'

'I still think I should have been given the job of looking after him,' grumbled Janice, heaving a sigh that jiggled her breasts.

I chuckled to myself. Tom already had his wine and

cheese party: Janice was whining, and I had a cheesy grin on my face. I knew my boss's expression. He'd made up his mind and all the tit wobbling in the world wasn't going to change it.

'Off you go then,' he instructed Janice, giving her arse a slap that made it ripple like a jelly.

She made a wanking gesture behind his back and strutted from the room.

Tom put his hands on my shoulders. 'You know I should have given her that job, don't you?'

I nodded. I knew what was coming next. He placed my hand on his fly. 'You owe me a favour, Pam.'

I traced my finger down his zipper and smiled.

Chapter Two

*T*his is the moment I like the most: his cock in my mouth, his legs trembling, his eyes glazing over with euphoria. My power over him is absolute.

As I let my teeth graze along the rippled contours of his cock, he knows no fear. His trust in me is childlike. I am the vehicle of his pleasure and it does not enter his mind that I could harm him. He is oblivious to everything but the touch of my lips and the warm vacuum inside my mouth that sucks on his shaft like a vampire.

I feel him quaking with rapture. I feel the tension in his muscles as I grasp his quivering haunches.

'Oh God, Pam, this feels fucking great.'

If someone had seen me kneeling at his feet, they might think that I was worshipping him. But they'd be wrong. He was worshipping me. I was the angel of deliverance conveying him to paradise and his groans were songs of praise.

'I think I love you.'

It was touching how grateful a man could be on these occasions. I gave his balls a gentle squeeze.

I always knew when he was ready to come: he'd drill

his fingers into my skull and try to nail me to the spot. But I drew the line at swallowing his spunk.

'Please,' he begged, as the first salty drops of semen began to trickle from his glans.

I loved it when he begged like this. It made me feel so horny.

'Sweet Jesus, just this once.'

But I had already withdrawn and covered his cock with tissue. I was still finishing him off by hand when someone pummelled at the door. 'Mr Carson! Mr Carson! Are you in there?'

'I'm coming!' Tom shouted. And he was.

'Please hurry, Mr Carson. It's urgent.' The voice belonged to Darren, my trainee assistant. I wondered what on earth could be so urgent that he should think it necessary to bang on the door of the executive loo as if trying to break it down.

Tom, angry at having his ecstasy cut short, raked up his zipper and flung open the door. 'What is it?' he barked. 'Can't a bloke shit in peace?'

Ashen faced, Darren stuttered an explanation. 'It's your wife, sir. She's here. In the building.' He looked at me over Tom's shoulder, seeking my approval.

I nodded. 'Go and tell her Mr Carson's on his way.' Then I licked my lips slowly, so that he'd know what I'd been doing. Unconsciously, he copied me.

I'd been tormenting him for weeks: whispering words loaded with sexual innuendo, luring him with lascivious looks and teasing him with touches. I'd stirred him into a state of simmering expectation. But, like a stallion about to be broken, he was still wild-eyed and fearful of me.

As Darren bolted down the corridor, Tom fixed me with his steel-grey eyes and caught up my wrist. He'd witnessed the exchange. 'Aren't you a little old to play with toys?'

I glared at him defiantly. 'Don't start getting macho with me, Tom.'

It was as pointless as telling a fish not to swim. 'I don't want you flirting with that boy,' he insisted.

'And don't try dictating to me unless I'm holding my notepad,' I warned him, tugging my hand from his grip. But he caught it again and dug his fingers into my skin.

'Just remember who's boss.' He was pressing hard enough to bruise and if he'd thought for a minute that I'd let him get away with branding me with his finger-nails, he would have done it.

I shot him a look that dared him to leave his mark. 'Better not keep your wife waiting, Tom.'

I was fuming as I watched him go. But I loved his broad, powerful shoulders and the swagger of his walk. 'You pig,' I uttered softly.

Back at my office, I found Darren putting away some files. 'Is she still here?' I asked him.

He didn't look up. 'Mr Carson's taken her to lunch.'

I moved in on him, like a predator. 'You did the right thing, Darren. We have to protect the big man's arse at all times.' I slid my hand over his buttocks.

'Miss Roberts . . . please.'

'Please what?' I whispered, letting my fingers crawl to his crotch. He shuddered against the filing cabinet. 'Did you know what I was doing? I was sucking him off in there. Sucking him off.' My nails were circling his groin as I spoke. My caress was light as feathers. 'Would you like that, Darren? Would you like me to gobble your cock?'

His hand flew to his forehead. 'Oh please, Miss Roberts, I can't think.'

I lifted my hand to his shoulder and patted him benignly. 'You're not paid to think. Get me France on the phone; Monsieur Planquet's secretary.'

I could see the agony of frustration on his face as he slammed the file drawer and stomped out.

I sat down and rotated slowly in my chair: A smile of satisfaction played on my lips. Bugger Tom and his warning. This was sauce for the goose and if I wanted to play power games with Darren then I damn well would!

After I'd spoken to France, I summoned Darren on the intercom. He stepped warily into the room. 'Get the blinds, will you? The sun's reflecting on my screen.'

He walked over to the VoiceCom module on the wall, which was nearer to me than to him, and croaked the instruction, 'Blinds down.' When nothing happened, he tried again. 'I think it's broken,' he concluded after a third attempt. 'Shall I call Flynn?'

'No,' I said hastily. 'I'll deal with it.'

It was not unusual for the company's products to malfunction on a daily basis and the maintenance engineer was a regular visitor to the executive floor where most of the prototypes were installed. His name was Flynn and I hated him. Not least for the oily, insulting black eyes that stripped away my clothes whenever he looked at me. But there was also a hint of menace in his swarthy rough-cut features, which both repelled and fascinated me. And although I was not attracted to his rugged Mediterranean looks in a sense that I could recognise, there was something about him that reached into my deepest basest instincts and uncovered a sexual response. It was something that I needed to explore.

I was on the phone to Bethany when he entered the room, and I could sense his impatience as he waited for me to finish. I found myself laughing louder than I should have, and twiddling with the phone cord.

It unnerved me, the way he was prowling behind my chair, breathing in my perfume. And I was conscious of his scent: musky and feral, with a trace of tobacco but not the smallest hint of aftershave.

'We'll try that new wine bar in Sutton Street,' I babbled into the phone. 'I'll see you in half an hour.'

'Boyfriend?' he uttered huskily, as I replaced the receiver.

'I don't think that's any of your business.'

He leaned towards me, his rough-shaven chin almost scraping my cheek. 'What's your problem?'

'I beg your pardon?'

He twitched his jaw. 'Well, you didn't get me up here for my health now, did you?'

Already, he'd made me feel foolish. 'The blind isn't working,' I snapped.

'Uh huh.' He took a screwdriver from his pocket and rolled it between his fingers in a way that made me consciously grateful that I was wearing a bra. 'I'll take a look at it,' he said.

I watched his back as he worked, noticing things like the way his tight black boiler suit hugged his lean, sinewy hips; and how his unruly black hair clung in tendrils to his collar. He reminded me of a panther.

He suddenly turned and glared at me. 'Screw,' he said.

'What?'

'There's a screw missing from this panel. Do you know where it is?'

'No.' I went back to reading my e-mails, determined to ignore him. But he made it impossible by whistling the overture to *Romeo and Juliet*.

Presently, he commented, 'I can't see the point of these things. Are people too lazy to pull on a string?' He cast a look over his shoulder that condemned the entire executive breed.

'Maybe they're too busy pulling other strings,' I suggested. 'Someone has to run the puppet show.'

He dropped the module he was holding so that it hung from its wires. Then he flicked it with his finger to make it swing. 'Does Tom pull your strings, or do you pull his?' he asked insolently.

The question inflamed me. 'As well as being Head of Promotions & Publicity, Mr Carson has a substantial shareholding in this company. I think that gives him the edge, don't you?'

11

He moved to the side of my desk and, weighting his words like an accusation, murmured, 'It was the air conditioning last week, wasn't it?'

I stared at him in disbelief. Surely he didn't think that I'd manipulated these meetings? The idea was almost too absurd to warrant a response, but he was drumming his fingers, waiting. So I dropped my voice to a sultry purr and admitted to having sabotaged everything just to be near him. 'You wish!' I finished scornfully.

But my cynical laughter didn't faze him for a minute. He merely lowered his eyelids and continued to look at me through the longest eyelashes I'd ever seen on a man. Then he smiled in a way that didn't soften his cruel lips but made them appear even crueller. 'The light in the cupboard?' he reminded me.

He had a point there. Perhaps it hadn't been necessary for me to stay in the cupboard while he'd fixed it.

'Pure coincidence. Is it my fault if VoiceCom products are crap?'

He laughed, as if he'd been teasing me all along. 'Don't let Tom hear you say that.'

I hated his sardonic smirk. 'Get back to your work, Flynn.'

'It isn't easy to concentrate when there's a sexy woman in the room staring at your butt,' he observed.

I considered denying the charge but, since it was true, I opted to brazen it out. 'I make a hobby of studying men's bums,' I declared. 'Don't read anything personal into it.'

'Just let me know if, at any point, you'd like me to drop my trousers so that you can take a better look.' He turned back to the module and, after a while, I heard him say, 'Blinds down.' The venetian blind responded to his voice like a puppy to its master. After testing it twice, he strolled back to my desk and perched on a corner. 'It had some dust in its ear,' he reported.

I nodded. It was a common problem. 'You can go if you've finished,' I told him.

'I'll go when I'm ready,' he said. 'What happened to your blouse?'

I instinctively recoiled as he extended a finger towards my lapel. 'It's coffee.'

'Couldn't you find your mouth this morning?'

I knew I should have smiled at his joke but he was looking at my lips so intently that I grew nervous of him sitting so close. My voice came over as hostile. 'Look, I've work to do and you're cluttering my desk, Flynn.'

'Bullshit,' he uttered, leaning towards me.

He locked eyes with me, and a shiver of unknown origin whiplashed through my body. He was reading something in my gaze that I hadn't even acknowledged to myself and I sensed that he was light years ahead of me in unravelling the complexity of my innermost thoughts concerning him. I gave myself a mental shake. *Don't even think for a moment that you're attracted to this man.*

But, like a swaying cobra, he tantalised me, and I couldn't tear my eyes from his face. If he had touched me then, I might not have recoiled. But then Darren walked in and broke the spell.

'What is it?' My voice sounded brusque, as if he'd caught me with my knickers down.

Darren's mouth drooped sullenly as he flicked his eyes from my face to Flynn's. 'Do you want anything from the deli?'

'I'm going out to lunch,' I informed him.

'With him?' he asked jealously.

'Certainly not.'

This cheered him. 'I'll fetch your coat, Miss Roberts.'

Flynn shook his head gravely as the boy went out. 'That kid has the hots for you,' he stated sardonically. 'He must have caught you looking at his butt.' He leaned forward and, once again, drew my scent into the nostrils of his large Latin nose.

'Why do you keep smelling me?' I demanded.

This time his smile was disarming. 'I make a hobby of smelling women. Don't read anything personal into it.'

I came away from my encounter with Flynn more muddled than before. My nerves felt jagged and raw, and I was in no mood to receive Bethany's cheerful announcement that Janice would be joining us for lunch.

'Oh joy,' I groaned, as the blight of my life walked into the ladies' toilet.

Bethany, who was examining the coffee stains on my blouse, didn't notice the exchange of scowls between Janice and me. 'What happened to it?' she asked.

'Janice Becker,' I replied, expelling the name like a gobbet of spittle.

'It was an accident,' the bitch insisted, waving her hand dismissively. 'I'm going for a piss.'

'I'm sure it was,' Bethany assured me sweet-naturedly.

I sighed. She was such an innocent. And, much as I hated Janice, I wasn't prepared to upset Bethany who, for some weird reason, liked us both. I'd never understood why, for she was much too good for either of us. She was a non-smoking, animal-loving veggie from Wales, who cared passionately about the ecosystem and campaigned for the rights of endangered species. She was marrying her childhood sweetheart at the weekend and Janice and I were determined not to spoil it for her.

'Are you getting nervous yet?' I asked her.

'Not really,' she answered in her lilting voice. 'I'm more worried about what you've got planned for my hen-night. Did I tell you that Megan is coming up from Cardiff after all?'

I was pleased for her. She'd been hoping that her old schoolfriend would make it.

'That's great,' said Janice, emerging from a cubicle. 'I

hope she likes a laugh.' She joined us at the mirror and started teasing her hair into place with lacquer.

Predictably, Bethany said, 'I hope that's ozone-friendly.'

'Don't start, Beth,' Janice grumbled.

'But it ought to concern you,' Bethany insisted. 'The hole in the ozone layer is getting bigger every day.'

'Do we give a fuck?' Janice asked her own reflection. 'No,' she concluded. 'It seems that we are more concerned with this ruddy little pimple.' She flattened her nose to inspect a tiny blemish. 'Does it notice?' she asked me.

I made a gesture of irrelevance. 'Does a wart on a bollock?'

'Ha bloody ha.'

I dodged a vindictive squirt of hairspray and Bethany copped a mouthful instead. 'When there are icebergs floating up the Thames, don't say I didn't warn you, Janice,' she spluttered.

I patted her shoulder. 'That'll only happen when the hole gets as big as her gob.'

Janice rolled her eyes incredulously. 'This from someone who can eat a baguette sideways?'

'Oh, pack it up you two,' groaned Bethany. 'Anyone would think you were bitching for England.'

'She started it,' I said.

'No I didn't,' Janice contradicted me.

I squared up to her. 'Yes you did. You called me a freckle-faced cunt at playschool.'

She nodded, remembering. 'A *stinky* freckle-faced cunt.'

'You called her the C-word at playschool?' gasped Bethany.

Janice spread her hands. 'I didn't know what it meant.'

'I didn't know what it meant either,' I said. 'But I hated those bloody freckles.' I rolled up my sleeve to reveal a few stubborn speckles of pigment. 'Still do.'

15

Janice peered at my arm. 'Those are liver spots.'

Bethany sighed. 'But that was ages ago. You've both grown up and you've changed.'

'Pam hasn't changed,' insisted Janice. 'She's still a c–' Bethany's hand clamped over her mouth, muffling the expletive.

'And you're still a foul-mouthed butterball,' I parried.

Bethany shook her head dolefully. 'I give up!' she declared. 'Just promise you'll behave at my wedding.'

'Of course we will,' we chorused. But, as we went outside, we let her walk on ahead and, behind her back, continued muttering insults.

'Fat arse.'

'Tit head.'

I figured myself to be ahead on points by the time we reached the wine bar and magnanimously offered to buy the first round of drinks.

'Look who's serving behind the bar,' Bethany pointed out.

'It's Lion,' squealed Janice.

'Where?' I craned my neck, anxious for a glimpse of the man who, by virtue of utter gorgeousness, had occupied my fantasies for the better part of a year, before suddenly and mysteriously disappearing from the scene.

Despite my fixation, my knowledge of him was limited: I knew his name, Lionel Piers-Vaughn, and the fact that his father was a millionaire who sat in the House of Lords. I knew the size of his biceps – but only through exposure to his arms in short sleeves. Yet I didn't know why he had elected to earn his crust as a cocktail barman instead of languishing at Oxbridge. And, more importantly, I didn't know if he fancied me.

A group of us had discovered him working in a dreary little dive called the Singapore Sling, just a stone's throw away from the office. We had adopted the place and made it a regular haunt until Lion's sudden departure had seen its popularity plummet.

16

I recognised the eagerness with which Janice was muscling her way through to the bar. She'd been as hooked on him as I was but had used tactics far less subtle in her pursuit. I wasn't surprised to see her launching her breasts across the bar as she leaned over to greet him. Nor that her jacket had opened to reveal a crochet-top manifestly unsuited to the task of containing her mighty bosom which, like silly putty in a string bag, was oozing through the holes in fleshy globs.

Lion seemed happy to see her and kissed her on both cheeks. 'How marvellous, darling girl.' He was just as I remembered, with his sexy upper-crust voice, long tawny hair, and sultry amber eyes. Spotting Bethany and me, he reproduced his dazzling smile. 'I might have guessed you'd come as a posse. Am I to be lynched for running off as I did?'

'We ought to hang you upside down by your balls,' scolded Janice. 'You might have said goodbye before buggering off into oblivion.'

He winced. 'I would have, my darling, had I not been somewhat forcibly ejected from my previous place of employment in a manner suggesting that any attempt to return might pose a considerable threat to the well-being of my wedding tackle.'

'He was fokking the manager's wife,' explained a huge, ginger-haired Irishman who had sidled up beside him. He made a noise like a whistling projectile. 'Slung from the Sling, he was, and landed on my doorstep with a black eye and bruises on his nuts.'

'This is Matt,' said Lion. 'Proprietor and purveyor of baloney.'

Matt ogled Janice's cleavage. 'You're a big girl for your age,' he commented. 'You'll not be more than eighteen, I'm thinking.'

Flushed from the compliment, Janice turned to look at me. 'Did you hear that? He thinks I'm eighteen.'

'He means eighteen stone,' I said crushingly. I ignored her withering look to smile over her shoulder at Matt.

'There's a lovely smile,' he acknowledged.

'It ought to be,' Janice snorted venomously. 'She paid a fortune for it.'

Bethany intervened. 'Do you think we might have a drink? Pina coladas all round?'

'Sweet little Bethany,' mused Lion, as Matt turned away to fix the drinks. 'How are you, my angel of innocence?'

Bethany's elfin face turned strawberry. 'I'm very well, thank you.'

'She's getting married at the weekend.' Janice jumped in. 'I'm sure she'd love it if you came to the wedding. How do you fancy a trip to Wales? I wouldn't mind sharing my room.'

'But you're sharing with Pam,' Bethany reminded her. 'And all the other rooms are taken.' Janice pleaded with her eyes and Bethany relented. 'I suppose he could bunk in with one of Nigel's friends.'

'That doesn't sound half so exciting,' said Lion. 'But I might be tempted. God knows I could use a break.'

'Then it's settled,' chirruped Janice. 'You'll be coming as my guest.'

He looked at me. 'Do you think I should?'

I was gutted but determined not to reveal my feelings. 'If you need to think about it, then maybe you're getting too many offers.'

'Not as many as I'd like,' he replied, with equal ambiguity. 'Excuse me, darling, I have to serve.'

I was left wondering what he'd meant. Would he prefer that the offer had come from me rather than Janice?

'Three pina coladas,' said Matt, slamming them down on the bar. 'Now then, girls, did you ever try a pineapple up the arse?'

'Is that a new cocktail?' asked Bethany.

'Fokk no,' chuckled Matt. 'I'm just a filthy pervert.'

18

Bethany and I giggled, but Janice was still on tenterhooks and, when Matt had gone, said worriedly, 'I hope Lion is serious about coming to the wedding. Do you think I should have been more persuasive?'

'You must be joking,' I said. 'You did everything but hurl your panties into his face.'

'At least mine wouldn't stick to his face,' she retorted. 'You're just jealous because I had the bottle to invite him on a date and you didn't.'

Bethany sipped through her straw. 'I'd never have the nerve to ask a man out,' she muttered timidly. Just then, Lion's head popped up from behind the counter and startled Bethany into gulping pina colada into her lungs. Choking, she waved, trying to warn Janice.

'I was determined not to let him slip through my fingers again without dating me,' Janice reflected. 'Men like Lion are an endangered species.'

While Bethany spluttered and waved her hands, I kept silent, watching in amusement as Lion leaned on his elbows, listening.

'Of course, I always knew he fancied me,' Janice went on. 'He used to watch me all the time. In fact, he couldn't take his eyes off me.'

'I wonder if he ever watched you without your knowing it,' I snickered.

'We'd have been red-hot lovers, if he hadn't disappeared,' she continued obliviously. 'And who knows what could come of this date? I might end up as Lady Piers-Vaughn!'

It was cringingly embarrassing and I was enjoying every minute of it, until Bethany spoiled the fun by jabbing Janice's arm. 'He's behind you,' she blurted, like a kiddie at a pantomime.

Janice blanched as he confirmed his presence with a tap on her shoulder. 'Excuse me, your ladyship, but exactly how hot is red-hot?'

It was the first time I'd seen her speechless.

Chapter Three

My eyelids are locked in fear. I cannot see him but I know he is there. I feel his strong hands pushing my legs apart and his searing hot breath on my thighs.

I am powerless to stop him. Yet, despite my fear, there is a spluttering sparkler of lust in my loins and a groan, like distant thunder, rumbling in my throat.

His tongue, huge and heavy, is thrusting into my sex, slurping and licking from anus to clit. I can't breathe as it trawls up my belly, scraping my skin like a rasping cat's tongue.

Suddenly, I know this isn't a human and, tearing open my eyes, I see hair, black hair, like a lion's mane, and the muzzle of a beast.

I am terrified, yet horribly aroused, as roaring jaws scoop up my breast and teeth like needles clamp around my tender flesh in a teasing prospect of pain. I can no longer restrain the hunger inside me or hold back its desolate cry. 'Bite me, dear God, please bite me!'

I awoke with a start. There were goosebumps on my skin and an oily wetness seeping from my sex. It had been a dream, a nightmarish dream. So horrible and horny that I was almost ashamed of myself for inventing it.

I flopped back on my pillows and, after reviewing as much of the dream as I could remember, I arrived at the conclusion that my dormant brain had conjured this creature – this sphinx in reverse – as an erotic manifestation of Lion. But why the black hair? And why invest him with so much power over me?

My thoughts turned reluctantly to Flynn. Had my mind confused the two men? It rattled me that, even subconsciously, my brain could weave Flynn into my fantasy. It felt like betrayal and I was angry with myself.

My irritation disrupted my morning routine and at my third attempt to scoop my long hair into a chignon, I noticed that my eyes in the mirror were hostile and glittering like sapphires. 'Don't look at me like that!' I scolded my reflection. 'Look at Flynn like that.'

I was still in a foul mood when I arrived at the office twenty minutes late, and walked smack into Flynn coming out. He caught me in his arms and, for a moment, our bodies were pressed together, with only the buffer of my breasts between us.

Leaping back as if he'd clawed me, I struck his shoulder with my fist, snarling, 'Why don't you look where you're going!'

His eyebrows furrowed into a dark line of dissent. 'I thought I was.' Then he fixed me with his sloe-black gaze and insolently drew my scent into his nostrils. 'If I'm not mistaken that's "Eau de Sexual Frustration" you're wearing today.'

'Oh, go smell your own feet,' I huffed, shoving him aside.

As I slammed the door shut, I rounded on Darren. 'What was Flynn doing here?'

Darren's china-blue eyes registered hurt at my abruptness. 'My computer wouldn't boot this morning. But it's all right now. Flynn's fixed it.'

I felt awful. The poor boy seemed always to be on the

receiving end of my irascible moods. I sidled up to him and ran my hand across his close-cropped hair, stroking him like a kitten. Then, moving my mouth to his ear, I whispered remorsefully, 'I'm sorry I snapped at you, Darren.' I could see the tension in his body as my tongue grazed over his earlobe.

'I don't mind, Miss Roberts,' he gulped.

'In my office, Pam. Now!'

I jumped as Tom's voice slammed into the back of my head like a baseball. He sounded furious and, as I turned to face him, I saw that he was.

I went to him meekly and allowed him to drag me into his office by my elbow. As soon as the door was shut, he confronted me. 'I thought I warned you about that kid.'

'I don't know what you mean,' I said, brazenly meeting his stare.

'Don't give me that shit. You're all over the boy like a rash.'

I had never seen him so inflamed before. If this was jealousy, I needed to explore it. 'What if I am? You're the only one who's itching, Tom.'

He looked at me sternly. 'Keep it up and you could find yourself facing a lawsuit for sexual harassment.'

This was priceless coming from Tom. I laughed out loud. 'Why don't you call him in and ask him if he feels sexually harassed?' I suggested.

He didn't know how to answer my challenge and walked over to the window. Then, staring out, he muttered, 'I don't suppose there'd be much point in that. He's probably enjoying your sex games.' He swung round to face me. 'But what happens when he wants to play for real?'

I lifted my shoulders. 'You don't own me, Tom.'

He strode the distance between us and slapped a proprietary hand on my shoulder. 'Do you think I'd let a runt like that step on my toes?' he rasped.

I looked at his hand as if it was bird shit. 'What gives you the right to –?'

He stepped behind me and, quick as a flash, hooked his arm around my throat, choking off my words. Then his other hand forced down my head so he could ravish the nape of my neck, nuzzling, licking, kissing, until I was squirming like bait on a hook. I struggled feebly in his arm-lock, plucking at his sleeve. But he knew that he had me in his power, that I was in meltdown, even before he'd finished unbuttoning my jacket.

I could only whimper like a puppy as he plunged his hand into the 'V' of my sweater and, dragging down my bra cup, took possession of my breast, kneading and squeezing until, gasping, I spun in his arms and crushed my lips to his.

It was the first passionate kiss that we'd shared in a long time and I'd almost forgotten how thrilling his weaving tongue could be. Suddenly, it didn't matter if he was staking his claim or exerting his power. It only mattered that we were kissing like lovers at last. But then the phone rang.

Tom wiped his mouth and shunted me aside like a piece of clutter. I felt cheated by his ice-cool equanimity on the phone, and humiliated when, seconds later, he covered the mouthpiece and dismissed me with a perfunctory, 'That will be all, Miss Roberts.'

I slammed his door so hard that the glass in it shivered and threatened to break. Darren glanced up at the noise and I could see his eyes taking rapid stock of my dishevelled clothes, smudged lips, and furious expression. 'Can I get you something, Miss Roberts?' he asked, placatingly.

Give me your cock, I wanted to say. Let's show the boss that his minions don't need his almighty approval to fuck amongst themselves. But all I actually said was, 'Fetch me a coffee please, Darren.'

I was hammering on my keyboard when he returned with a steaming mug and placed it on my desk. But I stopped when I noticed that his fingers were trembling. All of a sudden, and without a word, he trailed his hand over the edge of my desk and dropped it onto my knee.

Shocked by his unexpected boldness, I could only stare in amazement as he slid back my skirt to my stocking top, revealing the button of my suspender. At which point, I came sharply to my senses and slapped my thighs together, trapping his hand. 'That will be all,' I told him firmly, unintentionally echoing Tom and bringing tears of frustration to his eyes. 'For now,' I added softly.

I felt sorry for the boy, but he had no call making a move off his own bat. If I couldn't be the dominant partner in this potential relationship then I wasn't going to play. I wanted his complete subordination. I wanted to wield as much power over him as Tom had over me.

As the day wore on, the atmosphere grew increasingly tense. I was avoiding Tom and Darren was avoiding me. But we still had to work together and, out of necessity, a line of communication was established through means of short businesslike sentences, delivered with minimum eye contact.

I found myself slipping out of the office as often as I could and, after several trips to the ladies, it became inevitable that I would bump into Janice Becker.

She was washing her hands as I walked in. We acknowledged each other in the mirror but, not wanting to talk, I hurried past her into a cubicle.

'I thought we'd start out at Matt's Place tomorrow,' she called out to me. 'I need to speak to Lion about the arrangements for the weekend.'

How typical of her to rub it in about her date with the man she'd practically stolen from under my nose! 'So long as we don't stay there all night,' I called back. 'It's supposed to be a pub crawl from the office to my flat.' I pulled up my panties and spoke the command 'flush' into the VoiceCom, but nothing happened.

'That one's on the blink,' Janice informed me, belatedly.

'Bugger,' I groaned. 'Nothing works in this place.'

'Try shouting "fuck" into it,' she suggested through the door. 'It's worked for me before.'

'Are you taking the piss?'

'No, honestly, Pam,' she insisted. 'Flynn told me that he and the boys had rigged it that way for a laugh.'

If Flynn was involved, it sounded plausible. But how had Janice learned the secret? Was she friendlier with him than I knew? For some reason the idea rankled with me and added vehemence to my expletive as I aimed it into the VoiceCom. Still nothing happened.

'Louder,' Janice prompted me.

'Fuck!' I shouted. 'Fuck!'

Incredibly, at my third attempt, a mechanism clicked. But, instead of flushing into the pan, a fountain of water belched up from the bidet spout and splattered all over my skirt.

'Oh megafuck!' I wailed. 'With a fucking bowl of fuck on the side!'

'Goodness gracious me! Is that you in there, Pamela Roberts?' came the horrified voice of Beryl Parker.

My heart sank like a stone and, splaying my hands against the door, I mimed the motion of banging my head on it. Of all the people to have heard me! Beryl Parker, to whom I'd been sucking up for so long in my bid to slide into her shoes, marked 'PA to the MD', just as soon as she slipped out of them. And, knowing how much she hated foul language, I'd been notching up Brownie points for months by pretending that I went regularly to church and didn't swear.

'Hello, Miss Parker. I didn't see you come in,' cooed the lying bitch who'd contrived my invective. 'Pam seems to be having trouble with the flush.'

'Then press the override button, dear!' Miss Parker instructed shrilly.

'What button?' I hadn't noticed a button.

'It's on top of the cistern,' said Janice. She laughed. 'Evidently, Pam isn't familiar with VoiceCom's sanitary products, Miss Parker.'

Locating the button, I pressed it and mentally visualised the last of my Brownie points swirling down the pan. Determined to salvage a few, I came out firing an apology. 'I'm sorry I swore, Miss Parker. It's . . . um . . . my time of the month.' I was pleased with my fabrication. Surely there wasn't a woman in the world who could fail to be sympathetic?

'That is absolutely no excuse for profanity,' she insisted, confirming herself to be a dried-up old spinster who'd long forgotten the horrors of PMT. 'And, by the way –' she made her voice confidential '– there's a damp patch on your skirt.'

Surely the shrivelled old bat didn't think I'd peed myself? 'It was the bidet,' I explained.

'Perhaps she needs instructions on how to use a latrine.' Janice chuckled. 'It isn't difficult, Pam. You simply raise the skirt and lower the knickers.'

'Not all of us are as practised in that as you are,' I seethed.

'Now then, Pamela, that was uncalled for.' Miss Parker intervened. 'If I were you, I would slip off that skirt and hold it under the hand-dryer.'

'I don't think I want to see this,' said Janice, grinning like a Cheshire cat as she strutted out of the door. Whereas Miss Parker stayed long enough to disapprove of my underwear. 'Those knickers are scandalous,' she tutted. 'You'll catch your death of cold in them.' But, as she went out, shaking her head, I called after her, 'Janice Becker doesn't wear any at all!'

As I stood there in my stockings and panties, holding my skirt under the dryer, I amused myself by formulating plots on how I could murder Janice, and was so engrossed in one particularly ghoulish invention that I didn't notice the shadowy figure standing by the door until he spoke. 'Miss Becker reported a fault.'

Leaping out of my skin with a squeal, I grabbed my skirt and, spinning round, clutched it in front of me. 'Flynn!' I exploded. 'How long have you been standing there?'

A sly smile spread across his features. 'Just came in.'

'And I suppose Miss Becker didn't happen to mention that you'd find me in my undies?'

He shook his head. 'Never said a word.'

'Don't lie to me, Flynn. I can see you've been running. You're out of breath.'

'I'm panting,' he agreed, tilting his head to one side. 'But who wouldn't be?'

Only then did I realise that he was looking into the mirror behind me. And, when a glance over my shoulder confirmed his perfect view of my half-naked arse, I gathered the shreds of my dignity. 'Get on with your work,' I commanded, deliberately turning back to the task of drying my skirt and so presenting him with a full-on display of the original.

Surreptitiously, I watched him in the mirror as he toured the contours of my legs and buttocks with his eyes. He was practically steaming through his nostrils, and I couldn't begin to imagine what was running through his mind.

'You're provocative, Pam. Do you know that?' he croaked.

I was suddenly fearful for the girl in the mirror who seemed strangely detached from me. 'You've to call me Miss Roberts,' I said, trying to keep the tremor from my voice. He took a step towards me. 'Don't come any closer,' I warned him.

But he advanced another step, and then another, like he was taking part in some slow motion porn on the Internet. I froze as he came up behind me and rolled his hand over the curve of my bum.

Had he pinched me or squeezed me, I could easily have rejected him with a slap. But this slow, confident possession of my flesh was horrendously stimulating. Yet, somehow, I found my voice. 'Fuck off, Flynn. I'm not interested.'

He locked eyes with me in the mirror. 'Is that what you think?'

I tried not to feel his fingers circling my thigh. 'It's what I know,' I insisted.

He brought his cheek close to mine. 'Then you don't know anything at all.'

I was mesmerised by his glittering black gaze and hardly noticed his groin rubbing into my butt until I felt the twitch of his cock through his clothes. It brought me sharply to my senses. 'Take your filthy hands off me!'

He stepped back apace and his fingers trailed from my flesh. 'How does that scene go? You say that and I say – what?'

I couldn't believe that he'd had the nerve to pull me up over a cliché. Furious, I jumped into my skirt, ranting, 'Go flush your head, Flynn – if you can get the bloody VoiceCom to work.'

'You think I'm the one who needs cooling down?' He laughed and repeated, 'You don't know anything at all.'

'I know I despise you,' I spat at him.

'Shall I tell you what I know?'

I tried to brush past him, but he steered me backward to the sink and leaned his weight on me. Then his words dripped huskily into my ear. 'I know that when you walk out of here your panties will be squeaking.'

I flung out my arm to strike him but he caught my wrist and, gripping it tightly, wrestled my hand to his crotch. I struggled to win it back as our eyes sparred with daggers of fire. But though we were a matched battle of wills, the uneven contest of strength had me gasping from exertion and wincing in pain, until I had no choice but to submit to his cock bulge. And the touching of it made me want it, just as he'd known it would.

'Now you know what I know,' he said, releasing my hand. 'I'd like to finish this but I have work to do. You can go now.'

I fled through the door with the sound of his dirty laughter echoing in my ears.

I walked slowly back to my office, trying to come to terms with what had happened. There was no question in my mind now that, while I still loathed Flynn, my body was working to an entirely different schedule and on some bestial plane that had nothing to do with my conscious thought. Nor could any doubt remain that Flynn knew exactly how to source this primeval swamp of darker needs and draw them to the surface. For, whilst not actually squeaking, my panties were undeniably damp from the encounter and it repelled me to think of my vagina drooling for more when all I'd wanted was to flee.

It irked me that someone other than Tom was creating so much havoc with my senses. It was bad enough to be enraptured by *his* power without succumbing to the sexual drug of Flynn, which was nothing but detrimental. For, where my relationship with Tom had proved congenial to my ambition, there was nothing to be gained from fucking the maintenance man. I resolved to avoid him.

With this clear in my mind, I entered my office in better spirits than I'd left it, for I had settled on the idea of letting my boss appease me in the best way that he knew. But as I approached his office to convey my intention, I heard the sound of giggling from within. Not a girlish giggling, but the donkey-like braying of Janice Becker – a sound that was anathema to me.

I barged in without knocking and caught them red-handed: she, perched on the edge of his desk; he, with

29

his hand up her skirt. But he, at least, had the decency to look guilty as he snatched his hand from her snatch.

'I'm sorry to barge in,' I uttered coldly. 'I was looking for Darren.'

'He went home sick,' Tom replied, narrowing his eyes. 'Any idea what's wrong with him?'

'Did he look flushed?' asked Janice, snickering behind her hand. Tom snorted with laughter and looked down at the floor.

'You told him, didn't you?' I hurled at her.

She made a gesture of innocence. 'He asked me if I'd seen you. What could I say?'

'Oh lighten up, Pam,' chuckled Tom. 'You have to admit it was funny. I can just imagine Beryl's face. "A fucking bowl of fuck" – that was priceless.'

Joyful at having diminished me, Janice cranked her fat arse from the desk. 'Anyway, Tom, I'll let you have that guest list as soon as I've typed it.'

'Good girl,' he said, reaching out to pat her thigh but thinking better of it when he noticed my barbed-wire stare.

She smiled sweetly as she sauntered past me. 'I'll see you tomorrow, Pam.'

And I'll see you in hell, you smug-faced harpy, I thought.

'I don't know what you've got against Janice,' said Tom. 'It seems to me that the two of you have a lot in common.'

'We appear to have you in common,' I levelled at him sharply.

'That was nothing, Pam. Just a bit of fun.'

'Oh yes? I bet it wouldn't sound half so funny in a courtroom. Why is it one rule for you, Tom, and another for me?'

He came over and wrapped his arms around me. 'I was jealous, okay? Now, why don't we get back to that unfinished business from this morning?'

I was pleased by his admission of jealousy, but I wasn't ready to forgive him his flirtation with my enemy.

'I'm going home,' I said, unravelling myself from his arms.

He gave a casual lift of his shoulders. 'Suit yourself. But I'll be working late if you change your mind.'

As I collected my coat and walked down the corridor to the lift, my head was spinning from the day's events, which had started with a dream that now seemed a premonition, and had ended with Tom's confession.

But there was more to come and it was waiting for me inside the lift. 'Good evening, Miss Roberts,' said Flynn as I entered.

Alarmed, I jumped out again. 'What are you doing here? Is the lift out of order?'

He shook his head. 'I'm running a maintenance check.' Then he leaned against the wall, a picture of nonchalance. 'Well? Are you coming in or are you just going to stand there?'

All my instincts prepared me for flight, but it was five floors to the bottom. And, besides, there would be too much traffic in and out of the lift to afford him the opportunity to molest me again.

As I walked in, he spoke into the VoiceCom. 'Close door and activate maintenance override twenty-one.' Then his face broke into a wicked smile, and my stomach flipped as I heard him say, 'Going down?'

Chapter Four

*H*e looked like a panther, standing there in his black boiler suit, with his wild black hair and his cruel dark eyes. I shivered, remembering my dream.

Quite suddenly I realised that the elevator was ascending and warily enquired, 'Why are we going up? I want the ground floor.'

He strolled over to me and ran his finger down my cheek, smirking as I recoiled. 'Maintenance override twenty-one,' he stated. 'It takes us up to the top and down to the bottom without stopping. I figure that should give me enough time.'

'To do what?' I asked nervously.

He breathed in deeply. 'To bring you to orgasm.'

It was a struggle to find my voice, let alone inject confidence into it, but somehow I managed to say, 'How? By raping me? I'll scream the place down.'

He snorted laughter into my face. 'Is that what you want me to do? I was thinking of something else.' He flexed his fingers suggestively.

Grasping his meaning, I swallowed a gulp the size of an egg. 'You planned this,' I accused him.

He nodded slowly. 'From the minute I laid my "filthy

hands" on your lily-white arse,' he agreed, edging me into a corner with his body.

My heart started beating a panicky tattoo. 'I didn't invite that assault and I certainly didn't enjoy it,' I remonstrated hotly.

I could feel the hard muscles of his torso pressing against me. He dropped his voice to a husky purr. 'You wanted me to see you in your underwear. Why else would you send for me? Do you think I don't know a set-up when I see one?'

'I didn't send for you – Janice did!'

'You asked her to.'

'Is that what she said? It's a lie!' I exclaimed.

He grasped me under my chin, tilting my head back. 'What about your eyes; are they lying too? All those provocative looks and sexy glances. You've been inviting this for months. So, let's get on with it.'

I shook my head frantically. 'Don't even think about it, Flynn.'

His lips were nuzzling my ear and I could hardly make out his whispered reply. 'You've been thinking about it, you know you have.'

'That's not true.' I pressed my palms to his chest and pushed with all my strength.

He didn't budge an inch but slid his hands around my hips. 'I bet they're squeaking now, those skimpy panties of yours.'

His deep throaty voice and the heat of his hands were getting to me. I could feel the blood pounding in my veins and pulsing in my sex. But still, I said defiantly, 'Don't be ridiculous.'

'I think you're lying, Miss Roberts,' he said, clawing at my skirt with his fingers. 'Shall we check?'

'No, oh God, please no.' But, even to myself, my protest sounded weak. There was something about the savage roughness of his hands and the fierce ravishing of his lips and teeth, now sucking and biting on my neck, that was turning me on like crazy.

'You have to stop. Please stop.' But my plea, like the feeble fluttering of my hands on his chest, was but token resistance from the last bastion of my crumbling defences. And he knew it.

'Shut up,' he growled, hoicking my skirt up over my hips. 'Now, we start.'

As he lowered his eyes to my stocking-topped thighs, a groan of lust shuddered from his lips. Then his hand thrust deep into my panties like a spade.

All my breath was expelled at once in a shivery gasp of shock. I spurred my nails into his shoulder and stared, open-mouthed, into his eyes. For a cliff-hanging moment, he just stood there with his hand welded to my sex. Then one of his eyebrows lifted like a question mark.

Before I could stop myself, a judder of anticipation had bucked my hips and, encouraged, his scrabbling fingers burrowed into my sex, slipping and sliding and rolling around my clit, bringing wave after wave of steaming lust. I was panting so hard that I could hardly breathe.

'You love it, you dirty bitch,' he rasped. 'I knew you would. I could smell it in you.'

I tried to form words, but I couldn't speak and I couldn't stop my head from tossing and rolling as if my neck had snapped. I closed my eyes, trying to detach myself from who he was and where we were. The only thing that mattered was the exquisite thrill permeating through my loins.

'Come on, baby,' he droned in my ear. 'You're almost there. Only seven more floors to go. You can make it if you give me your leg.'

'Please, Flynn,' I begged. 'Don't make me help you.'

'Floor six,' he snarled, slapping my thigh. 'Give me your fucking leg.'

I lifted my knee and he hooked it around his butt,

spreading my crack so that every part of his hand could plunder it.

'Dear God,' I groaned, as his magical fingers rubbed harder and faster. Closing my eyes, I clenched my teeth and gripped him tightly.

'Floor five!'

I could feel my body quickening.

'Four!'

Hurrying.

'Three!'

Rushing.

'Two!'

Gushing.

My whimpering sigh went on and on as a searing backdraught of ecstasy blasted through my body, igniting all my senses. Then he stole the last of my breath with a melting kiss that made every hair on my body and on my head stand on end. Feeble with emotion, I sagged in his arms as if someone had sucked all the bones from my legs.

He lifted my chin. 'Look at me.'

I opened my eyes, expecting a smile. But instead he waggled his fingers, still slick with my juices, and languidly drew my scent into his nostrils. 'This is the ground floor and I smell an orgasm.'

Disgusted, I pulled from his arms and yanked my skirt in place. 'You're despicable.'

He laughed. 'No need to thank me.'

There was triumph in his eyes as he spoke into the VoiceCom. And, when the doors opened, there was an arrogant swagger to his walk as he stepped outside and beckoned me to follow like some randy bitch dog.

Something snapped inside me. 'Close doors!' I shouted, letting the cold steel blot out his face.

As I rode the lift back up the building, I didn't know where I was going or what I meant to do. I only knew that I needed to purge Flynn from my body and erase all the questions that were storming my brain: how could I have capitulated so easily? What had made me so hungry for this man that I despised? And why had his kiss touched my soul?

When the lift arrived at my office floor, I had only one purpose in mind: to fill the aching emptiness inside me, as quickly and cold-bloodedly as I could.

Tom peered at me from under the rim of his reading glasses. 'Did you forget something?'

'I forgot I was feeling horny,' I said, unzipping my skirt and letting it drop to my feet.

He took off his glasses and leaned back to consider me. 'I assume you'd like me to do something about it?'

I peeled off my jacket and sweater. 'Can you think of anything?'

He nodded. 'Oh, yes.'

I spent a fitful night, tossing and turning into the small hours before finally falling asleep. And, when I woke, still exhausted, only the prospect of Bethany's hen-night, planned for that evening, could drag me out of bed. I arrived at my office in no mood for confrontation and was pleased to find it empty.

I already knew that Tom was away – officially on business but, actually, on a fishing trip. But I wasn't expecting that Darren would still be off sick. And although I was glad of his absence because I wanted to be alone, part of me felt that, with Tom out of the way, it was a missed opportunity to set things straight between us.

I was pretty sure that Darren was still beating himself about the head for his presumptuousness and figured it might take him a few days to get over his embarrassment. I hoped he would spend the time reviewing his naïve interpretation of the signals I'd been sending. For it bothered me that he'd got it so wrong. I resolved to spend some time reconsidering my own strategy regarding the boy.

But Darren was the least of my worries. I still had the puzzle of Flynn to solve, and the enigma of Tom's jealousy. I was mulling over these matters while fixing myself a coffee, when the phone rang. Sidestepping to the VoiceCom, I instructed it to answer on audio and, when I heard a static crackle and the sound of breathing, I spoke my name. I sipped from my coffee cup as I waited for a response. But there was only heavier breathing.

'Pamela Roberts,' I repeated. 'Can I help you?'

This time, a slow, seductive exhalation.

'Who is this?'

Rapid panting, then a low groan that echoed eerily round the office.

Slamming down my cup, I stormed to my desk and snatched up the receiver. 'Flynn, you bastard, is that you?'

'Of course it's me,' he said.

'You scared the living daylights out of me,' I exclaimed furiously. 'What do you want?'

His voice dropped to a husky purr. 'Can you guess what I'm doing?'

'Probably something disgusting,' I said.

'I'm stroking my cock.'

I knew I should have put the phone down right away but, somehow, I couldn't. 'You're a sicko, Flynn,' I said scornfully.

'I'm running my hand along my thick shaft . . .'

'Sicko,' I repeated. 'If you don't get off this line, I'm going to report an obscene phone call.'

He groaned erotically. 'I'm rubbing myself hard; thinking of your hot little pussy.'

'Stop it!' My mouth was so dry that I could hardly speak. 'Look, yesterday was a big mistake.'

'I'm wanking . . .'

'Did you hear me?' I shouted. 'It won't happen again.'

'Wank . . . wank . . . wank.'

I could imagine him sitting there, lewdly caressing himself, his wicked black eyes smouldering with lust. 'That's enough.' I gulped. 'I'm putting the phone down.'

'I haven't finished,' he said. 'Are you a tease, Miss Roberts? A dirty little prick-tease? You should never leave a man with a hard-on.'

'Is that what this is about?' I snarled. 'You're angry because you didn't get to finish the job?'

'No – but I'm angry that Tom did. If he's the star turn, what does that make me – the warm-up man?'

'That's right,' I said. 'You were just an appetiser.'

He gave a humourless chuckle. 'Pigging out on a starter can ruin your appetite.'

'It didn't,' I declared. 'As a matter of fact, I was ravenous.'

'It's a pity you didn't stick around long enough to find out what I had on offer as a main course. If you had, we wouldn't be having this conversation,' he conjectured. 'You'd be too busy begging me for more.'

His arrogance inflamed me. 'If you think you're that good then you ought to try asking yourself why I didn't stick around.'

'I know that already,' he said. 'You're the one who should be asking yourself questions, Pam.'

'What do you mean by that?'

But the line had gone dead and I realised he'd hung up on me.

I spent an age staring at the phone. How did he know about Tom? And why was I feeling horny again? Damn the man. I'd only submitted to his abuse in a moment of weakness, and the cheap thrill he'd given me was something I could have gotten anywhere. He had no claim on my body and what I'd done with it afterwards was my own affair! And as for his egotistical conviction that he was the kind of man to whom women went 'begging for more' – it showed insufferable conceit.

OK, so he'd been good with his hand, but I'd known plenty of men just as good. And it wasn't as if he'd done anything unusual ... except ... I forced myself to confront the memory of his toe-curling kiss; but when it posed too great a riddle, I simply shook it from my head. He wasn't remotely my type and didn't warrant this much attention.

Nonetheless, I spent the rest of the day jumping every time the phone rang and, by five o'clock, I was a nervous wreck and more than ready for a drink.

Fearing that Flynn might be waiting to pounce on me, I hotfooted it to the ladies and had already changed my clothes by the time Bethany and the others arrived.

'Ooh, Pam, you look dreadful,' remarked Bethany.

'No change there then,' muttered Janice, walking past.

'I mean like you haven't had any sleep,' Bethany clarified apologetically. 'But, I must say, your outfit looks lovely.'

'I've got some Crystal-eyes in my handbag,' offered Asia, a petite, dusky-skinned brunette who worked with Bethany in Accounts.

Another of Bethany's friends, called Mel, who was studying herself in the mirror, asked dolefully, 'Have you got anything for crow's-feet? What about eye-bags and a double chin?'

Asia rummaged in her bag and withdrew a small pot. 'Refurbish anti-ageing cream?'

'It's too bloody late for that,' cackled Mel.

'It's never too late,' insisted Asia, who was a beauty-regime fanatic. 'You should moisturise every day and apply a face-mask at least twice a week.' She handed me the eyedrops.

Mel laughed. 'My old man thinks I need a face-mask made of latex these days.' She patted her large belly affectionately. 'But he's glad that I've kept my figure, although he's damned if he knows where I'm keeping it.' We all giggled as she waddled off to find an empty cubicle.

I was feeling much better now and if Asia's eyedrops hadn't already brought a sparkle to my eyes then the sight of Janice, trying to squeeze her bulky buttocks into a tiny white pelmet of a skirt, would have.

'Good God, Janice!' exclaimed Bethany. 'Is that a skirt?'

'I think it's a girdle,' I suggested. 'One of those "swaddle your arse" things our grandmas used to wear.'

'Bog off, Roberts,' grunted Janice. 'At least I'm not dressed like Batman's cock-sucking girlfriend.' She was referring to my black designer catsuit, which fitted me like I was naked but covered in oil.

Bethany sighed enviously. 'You should be a catwalk model with a figure like that, Pam.'

'I was a model once,' declared Janice, to no one in particular.

'You – a model?' I scoffed. 'What for – Balaclava helmets?'

'A photographic model actually,' she sniffed.

'Ah, that explains it,' I conjectured. 'A bunch of geriatric snappers with drippy hard-ons and no film in their cameras.'

'When was that?' Asia asked Janice.

Janice looked at me. 'When we were teenagers. But, of course, in those days Pam didn't have a figure to speak of. She was flat as a board and skinny as a rake. Whereas I had an hourglass figure, with a twenty-inch waist –'

'And a size twenty arse,' I chipped in. 'All her sand had run to the bottom.'

'Plus . . .' she continued, irrelevantly, 'I was captain of the netball team.'

She'd had to bring that up, hadn't she? She knew it still rankled with me. I shot her a blistering glance. 'You were shagging the PE teacher,' I reminded her.

'The PE teacher?' echoed Bethany, agape.

'He was a man,' Janice emphasised. Then she jiggled her head. 'No, actually, he was a pervy balding bastard who got his rocks off watching us girls in the shower.'

I chuckled. 'Do you remember when you smeared boot black on one of his spyholes and he came jogging into the gym looking like someone had socked him in the eye?'

She tittered. 'Oh yes, I'd forgotten. We called him "Panda Eyes" and everyone used to crack out laughing when he mentioned PE.'

In the middle of chuckling, I frowned. 'Hang on a minute – you blamed me for that boot black! I got fifty press-ups and a detention.'

She shrugged indifferently. 'I had to do press-ups with him underneath me! He was a rotten lay,' she reflected. 'I must have wanted that captaincy an awful lot.'

Bethany looked at us both. 'It's nice to see you two laughing together. I wish you'd do it more often.'

For a moment, Janice and I considered each other with our guards down and, for a brief second, I allowed myself to feel a flicker of warmth for her. But it was quickly extinguished when she said, 'Nah, we like things as they are.'

Her remark was punctuated by the loudest and most unladylike noise I'd ever heard, coming from the direction of Mel's cubicle. It was followed by her rapturous laughter from within. As she emerged, still giggling, Janice cast her a look of disapproval.

'I hope you're not planning on cramping our style tonight?' she uttered balefully.

'With these?' cackled Mel, opening her arms to reveal a pair of humongous breasts, either of which could have taken first prize at a pumpkin show. 'Someone had better remind me to pop my cardy back on before I go home tonight.'

'Do we have a route sorted out?' asked Asia, pulling

fish faces in the mirror as she applied make-up to her eyes.

'More or less,' reported Janice. 'We thought Matt's Place, the Frog and Slipper, and all stops in between. That sound OK to you, Asia . . . Asia?'

'Can't talk, I'm doing my eyeliner.'

'I'll take that as a yes then.'

'I won't be drinking any of those fancy cocktails,' Mel decided. 'I'm sticking to lager by the bucketload. I aim to get so drunk that I can look at my old man's face without thinking of Freddy Kruger for once.'

'She adores him really,' Bethany told me.

'Hmm?' I was looking at her critically. 'I hope you're not wearing your hair like that, Bethany. You look like a school marm.'

She patted the squashy doughnut of her bun. 'What's wrong with it? It's tidy.'

'Trust me,' said Janice, 'tidy is not the look that we're after tonight. Let's sort her out, girls!'

Cheering, we set about her reconstruction. And, after ten minutes of hairpin pulling, skirt raising, button opening and lip glossing, Bethany emerged a new and sexier woman.

She stared dubiously at her own reflection. 'Nigel would have a fit if he could see me like this.'

'Balls,' said Mel. 'Nigel would have a hard-on if he's any kind of a man. Is everyone ready? Let's go!'

Our first port of call was the local tube station, where we collected Bethany's friend from Wales. Her name was Megan and, at first glance, she looked exactly the sort of person one would deliberately exclude from anything as raucous as a hen-night. She was stick-thin with long straight hair, wore goofy spectacles and had a gummy smile. Her clothes were prim, her shoes sensible, and she laughed like a sheep. I saw Asia staring at her unplucked eyebrows in horror. But, when Bethany introduced her and she showed no sign of disdain for either Janice's bum-bandage of a skirt or Mel's immodest melons, I warmed to her. Particularly so when she produced from her rucksack a mock bridal headdress made of leeks and daffodils with a Welsh flag attached for a veil. Shrieking, we dressed Bethany up in it and, as we trooped to our first venue, Megan led us in a rowdy medley of Welsh rugby songs.

By the time we reached Matt's Place, we'd collected an entourage: a couple of Russian sailors, a drugged-up student and a bloke who'd been selling the Big Issue. Mel was given the job of dispersing them, which she effected in seconds by offering to snog them all.

'Bugger,' she moaned, as they fled. 'You'd have thought the Russian sailors at least would be used to big women.'

However, Mel's disappointment was nothing compared to Janice's gloom when she failed to find Lion at the bar.

'It's his night off,' Matt confirmed, without taking his eyes from Mel's cleavage. 'Did he not tell you?'

Janice grimaced as if someone had flung a netball into her face. 'Didn't he leave me a message?'

Matt scratched his ginger beard. 'Well now, that depends. Are you the blonde bird with the big knockers?'

Janice scowled. 'I should have thought that was obvious.'

Matt puckered his lips. 'Not to me, sweetheart. I mean, there are big knockers and there are those that should have "Dunlop" printed on the side.' He looked at Mel's chest again. 'I wouldn't want to make a mistake now, would I? Tell you what, if you all put your naked breasts on the bar, I could judge for myself who's got the biggest.'

'Stop teasing, Matt,' said Bethany.

But Matt was in playful mood. 'Those are my terms,' he insisted. 'While you're thinking it over, can I get you a drink? The house special tonight is a Donkey Jump. But, I warn you, it has quite a kick.'

'I'll try a Donkey Jump,' Bethany said sportingly.

Matt grinned. 'Trouble is, we're all out of donkeys – will you settle for a jump instead?'

Bethany was daft enough to think about it. 'Don't answer that,' I said. 'We'll have five pina coladas and a pint of lager.'

'Why isn't Lion here?' Janice wondered sulkily.

'Who's Lion?' asked Megan.

I was about to tell her when my gaze alighted on a figure crouched at the end of the bar. Though his back was to me, there was something about his menacing pose and the shaggy cut of his luxuriant black hair that reminded me of Flynn. My heart skipped a beat and I must have gone pale because Mel said, 'You look like you've seen a ghost.' Then, following the line of my gaze, she observed, 'Oh look, it's VoiceCom's devilishly handsome maintenance man.'

'Handsome?' I echoed. Flynn . . . handsome?

'I like them rugged and sexy,' drooled Mel. 'Pretty boys tend to be faggots.'

'Ooh, Mel!' scolded Bethany. 'You mustn't say that – you've to call them gay.'

Mel grunted. 'Oh, don't go all fucking PC on me, Bethany. Why isn't it politically correct to be fat, that's what I'd like to know?'

Bethany couldn't answer and peered down the bar. 'Flynn gives me the creeps,' she said.

'He looks a bit sinister,' Megan agreed. 'But I can't really see him from here. Why don't you introduce me?'

This was the last thing I wanted. 'Here come the drinks,' I said quickly in an attempt to deflect her attention. Then, as Matt took centre stage, seeking an answer to his ultimatum, I slipped away unnoticed.

Chapter Five

'What are you doing here?' I confronted Flynn.

His eyes strolled lazily from the glass he was holding. 'I often drink here.'

'I don't believe you.'

'I don't care.' His predatory gaze roamed stealthily over my body. 'You look good enough to ... eat.' He licked his lips suggestively and I shivered inside as I realised what he meant.

I had to admit that, taken out of his boiler suit and put into a cream designer jacket with a dark-red shirt, Flynn looked strikingly attractive, and it bothered me that I'd become conscious of it.

'You followed me,' I accused him.

'Relax,' he said, plucking up one of my blonde tresses and twining it around his finger. 'You're in a crowded bar with a group of friends. What are you trembling for?'

I hadn't realised I was trembling. 'You make me nervous,' I admitted. 'Keep away from me, Flynn. That's all I came over to say.'

He shook his head. 'No it isn't.' He yanked on the bell-rope of my hair, forcing my face close enough for his lips to caress my cheek as he murmured into my ear, 'You wanted me to see you in your slinky little outfit, with your hair all bouncing round your shoulders. And what you'd like me to do is hook my finger into this ring-pull thing and slide your zip down to your navel. Then, right here, in front of everyone, you'd have me plunge my hand inside and start kneading your breasts, for everyone to see.'

I gulped. 'You're crazy. You know that isn't true.'

'Oh, yes it is,' he continued huskily, running his fingernail down my zip. 'You want everyone to see me stroking your body. You want all the men in this room gaping and clutching their cocks as they watch me take your stiff swollen nipple into my mouth and suck on it.'

I was so mesmerised by his seductive voice that I barely noticed his finger trailing down beyond the end of my zip until, bang on target, he pressed my throbbing clit. Even through my clothes, his touch was electric.

Infuriated with my body's treacherous response, I snarled, 'Take your –'

'What?' he intercepted. 'Filthy hands off me? Why don't you make me?'

I clawed at his hand but he wouldn't move it until I'd drawn blood with my nails. I liked that it made him wince. 'Don't ever touch me like that again,' I warned him.

He didn't answer but delivered a devastating smile – slow, self-assured, and incredibly sexy. Then he swivelled on his bar-stool and picked up his drink.

Effectively dismissed, I stomped back to the others.

'There's no point in staying here without Lion,' said Janice, thrusting my drink at me. 'Get this down your neck. We're moving on.'

'So, is he coming to the wedding?' I asked her.

'Didn't you hear what Matt said?' She looked at me suspiciously. 'Where were you? Never mind. He can't make the wedding but he's coming to the reception and he'll be staying overnight at the hotel.'

'It cost her a boob flash for that information,' chuckled Mel. 'That Matt is such a swine! Did you know he slipped a Mickey into Bethany's drink? She's halfway out of her skull already.'

'Let's go then,' I said, knocking back my drink and slamming the empty glass down. 'The Duck and Feather?'

'I want to say goodbye to Flynn first,' insisted Mel.

To my horror, she plunged into the sea of bodies in her path and, catching Flynn unawares, threw her heavy arms around his neck. The next thing I knew, he was kissing her passionately.

I felt sick as I watched the sensual movement of his lips; saw his tongue weaving and his hands groping. All the ecstasy of his kiss came flooding back to me and I longed to be her at that moment; raking my hands through his hair and squirming in his arms as she was. When I caught his sly glance at me, I realised that he knew exactly what I was thinking.

Finally, Janice pulled Mel off him, muttering, 'Sorry, Flynn, she hasn't eaten since lunch.'

'Anyone else feeling peckish?' he enquired. 'How about you, Jan?'

Oh no, I begged silently, not Janice Becker. I balled my fingers into a fist, thinking, if you kiss that bloated bitch I'll punch you both. But she said, 'I'll take a rain check on that,' and winked at him.

I was racked with suspicion. What did she mean? And why was I getting myself into such a state? I could feel Flynn's eyes drawing my gaze like a magnet, and I couldn't resist a final look into their glittering black depths.

Asia rescued me from drowning in them with a tug on my sleeve. 'Let's go, Pam.'

Anxious to empty my mind of Flynn, I threw myself into the party spirit as we wove in and out of bars and pubs, getting more and more gloriously drunk as the night progressed. Man after man swam in and out of my vision as – talking, laughing, dancing, smooching – we flirted with them all. Even Bethany was kissing strangers in the street.

Having reached a plateau of intoxication well beyond the point of no return, we were ready to begin the final assault and, as a precaution against fallers, had taken to clinging to one other for support. So when Mel, leading us in a meandering conga, suddenly pulled up sharply, we all cannoned into the back of her like a collapsed concertina. 'Tarts up ahead!' she proclaimed.

A group of prostitutes was patrolling the pavement. One of them, a skinny blonde in a crop-top, hot pants and thigh-high crimson boots, was leaning on a lamppost watching us impassively as we picked ourselves up. She wagged her cigarette at Bethany. 'Lookee here sisters. It's a little Welsh bride!'

The hookers jeered and catcalled. Then a shadowy figure stepped out from a shop doorway into the lamplight. He, she or it was over six feet tall and I could see stubble beneath a layer of heavy make-up. 'Ooh get you,' the lady-boy said, plucking at Bethany's headdress. 'Is this some kind of fashion statement?' His overly made-up eyes panned across our faces to alight on Mel, who was gawping at him dumbly. Aggressively, he said, 'What are you staring at, Jumbo?'

'Are you a bloke?' she asked bluntly.

The transvestite squealed and threw up his hands. 'Do I look like a man!'

'I don't know what you are,' Mel said, 'but I wouldn't want to wake up in bed with you.'

He trilled with laughter. 'Are you kidding me, Jumbo? There's only one thing brave enough and small enough to get into bed with you and that's a bedbug.'

The skinny blonde tugged on his elbow. 'Leave the hens alone, Bambi. They're putting off the punters.'

'Bambi?' echoed Mel, spluttering with mirth. 'I haven't

heard such an unlikely name since my next-door neighbour called his Rottweiler "Trevor".'

Janice stepped up to the blonde to deliver a poke to her prominent ribcage. 'I object to what you said. I'll have you know that my friends and I are perfectly capable of pulling in punters.' To demonstrate her point, she hoisted up her skirt and mooned to a passing motorist.

'Ohmigod!' wailed Asia. 'She's going to get us all arrested.' Clucking like a mother hen, she gathered up a bewildered Bethany and bundled her into a doorway.

'Amateurs,' muttered a black girl in a purple wig, with a rueful shake of her head. 'Sister,' she advised Janice, 'you don't show them the merchandise until you've seen the colour of their money.'

'Rubbish,' said Mel, striking up a pose by the roadside. 'How do you expect to sell anything if you don't put your goods on display?' She slid up her hemline and stuck out a leg.

'Who's gonna wanna buy that?' wondered Bambi, peering at her thigh. 'Jumbo, if that ain't a bad tattoo of Elvis then you've got varicose veins!'

'Don't you listen to her . . . him . . . it, Mel.' I came to her defence. 'That car just tooted you.'

'Didn't stop though, did it?' said the black girl. 'Ain't none of you could stop a lorryload of lifers just broken out of jail!'

'I bet I could,' I said swankily.

'Go on, Pam,' cheered the others. 'Show her how it's done.'

Strutting boldly, but not too steadily, to the kerbside, I pulled down the zip of my catsuit, shivering as my bra-less breasts jumped out into the cool night air. Then I sashayed along the pavement, flaunting them at passing cars. A few went by merely honking their horns but then one pulled up with a screech.

'Yippee!' yelled Megan. 'Go get him, Pam!'

'But don't sting him,' snorted Janice. 'If he offers you a fiver, don't forget to give him change.'

As I tottered gamely up to the car, the tinted glass window on the passenger side slid down. 'How much?' rasped a voice from within.

I leaned in. 'Twenty pounds oral and fifty pounds a shag,' I replied. Then I banged my head on the roof as I recognised the man inside. 'Oh shit!' I exclaimed.

'They can't be paying you enough at VoiceCom,' Flynn said dryly.

It was too dark to see his expression but I could tell from his voice that he was trying to conceal his amusement and, if I hadn't been so tipsy, I would have been mortified. 'I'd say fifty quid is a fair price if that free sample I had yesterday is anything to go by,' he casually observed.

'Damn it, Flynn. Just forget about that!' I was wildly tugging on my zip, which had stuck halfway up.

'Need any help with that?' He had leaned right across to plunge his gaze into the gap. 'How much is a tit fuck, by the way?'

'No sale!'

'Then what about some hand relief? I think you owe me that.'

'The only thing I owe you is a slap,' I grumbled. 'But, if you're desperate, Flynn, I have a friend who might be interested.' I summoned Bambi, who clomped over to me with high heels wobbling beneath the weight of his hulking frame. I relinquished my place to him. 'He's a wanker,' I advised.

'Heavenly!' squealed Bambi.

I turned away and, nanoseconds later, heard Bambi's cuss being smothered by the sound of screaming wheels. Laughing, I joined the others.

'What was he like? What did he say?' demanded Janice.

'He asked me if my fat friend takes it up the arse. I said you did.'

'Oh cheers,' she muttered flatly.

I strolled over to the black girl, dusting off my hands. 'How's that for an amateur?'

'Not bad,' she conceded. 'Maybe you girls have a little of "all that" after all.'

'All what?' wondered Mel.

'All that,' I informed her. 'It's a compliment.'

The girl nodded her purple head. 'That's right, Jumbo. Tell your lover man that a lady of the night gave you praise.'

'Oh, I can just picture his face,' Mel said sceptically. 'And, assuming that I can drag his head out of the racing pages long enough for him to listen, I know exactly what he'd say: "All that – my arse! Get the bleedin' kettle on."'

The girl was laughing but stopped in mid-flow as if someone had clamped a hand over her mouth. Then, suddenly and without word, all the hookers scattered.

'Was it something I said?' grunted Mel.

'Listen!' shouted Asia, running from her hidey-hole. 'It's a police siren! We have to get Bethany out of here.'

Sobered by the threat of arrest, we hurried along to the last venue on our list and quaffed several stiff drinks for the road.

Eventually, but without Mel who'd had to go home, we ended up at my flat where we flopped into chairs for an impromptu game of pass-the-parcel with a wine box as our fuddled brains attempted the rocket science of releasing the tap. Presently, it fell to me to stab the bastard open with a bread knife and rescue the silver bladder within. We were cheering so loudly as I filled up the glasses that I almost didn't hear the doorbell ring.

I noticed that my knees seemed to be working at different speeds as I loped to the front door, and that my tongue had tied itself into a knot when I tried to speak to the young man standing there.

'My name's Paul,' he said. 'I'm the stripper.'

I looked him up and down, nodding in approval of his tall, athletic build and nice-looking features. He was dressed as a Celtic warrior with a wild wig and woad on his face. I found the prospect of seeing him naked a sobering thought.

'Follow me,' I said, grabbing his hand and leading him in.

At the lounge door, Paul switched on the ghetto-blaster he was carrying and handed it to me. Then, as music blared out and he went in dancing, I heard Bethany shriek, 'You rotten sods!'

Following him in, I saw her grab a cushion to cover her face. 'I can't look. It's too embarrassing!'

Janice whipped it away. 'You damn well will, girl. This could be the last naked man you ever see, apart from Nigel.'

Asia and I dragged Paul in front of her and she squealed as his undulating hips set his kilt swinging like a pendulum. We were all mesmerised by the motion except Megan, who was too drunk even to focus on him, and just lay on the floor kicking her legs and screeching, 'Get 'em off!' at the top of her voice.

But Paul took his time, teasing and tantalising with glimpses of golden flesh, before baring his chest to wow us with an impressive display of rippling muscles. Gulping wine as she watched him, Bethany declared him a good dancer and everyone pelted her with cushions.

'Off! Off! Off!' ranted Megan, lobbing a shoe that bounced off Janice's head. But Janice was too engrossed in Paul's flexing pecs to notice.

Taking a bottle of baby oil from his sporran, he ignored the forest of hands that went up to receive it, and gave it to Bethany who giggled, 'I hope this hasn't been tested on animals,' as she poured some into her hand.

Asia, meanwhile, had crawled under his kilt. 'You should see how smooth his arse is,' she slurred. 'I bet he uses face-cream on his butt.'

While Bethany was rubbing Paul's chest, Janice and I joined Asia under his kilt. 'It's like camping out,' I said.

'There's going to be a full moon tonight,' predicted Janice, tugging on his briefs.

Paul sashayed deftly out of our reach to whip away our erstwhile tent, which he flung with a flourish over Megan's drooping head.

'Who turned the arsing lights out?' she moaned. 'Has he got his kit off yet?' As I freed her head, she shook it in perplexity. 'Why the fuck has he still got his pants on?'

Since I couldn't think of a single good reason, I struck up a chorus of 'Paulie, Paulie, Paulie, get your fuckin' knob out!' And, when the others joined in, Paul obligingly whisked off his briefs with a crackle of Velcro. We cheered, and then booed at the thong underneath.

'You can take that off as well,' Bethany instructed him boldly. We all gaped at her. 'I've seen *The Full Monty* – we're entitled,' she said.

Paul pretended to look at us warily. 'Is it safe?'

'Of course it's safe,' hissed Janice, tiptoeing her fingers down the centre of his six pack to his firm flat belly. 'Let's see what you've got, big boy.'

He let her rummage inside his thong. 'Could I take this home in a party bag?' she wondered wistfully.

With her hand still attached to his crotch, Paul held up his arms and jiggled his hips. All eyes were glued to his pouch bulge as distressed Velcro fastenings strained and creaked. Then, suddenly, with a ripping sound, his thong split apart and the pieces dropped to his feet.

'Da dah,' trumpeted Janice, removing her hand to reveal his semi-erect penis, which continued to grow as we scrutinised it.

'Good God!' exclaimed Bethany. 'It's enormous!'

Surprised by her outburst, the rest of us swapped puzzled looks. 'Not particularly, Bethany,' I said.

'But it's huge!' she proclaimed.

Asia rubbed her cheek thoughtfully. 'Er . . . this doesn't bode well for Nigel,' she forecast, wiggling her little finger.

'Can you see how eagerly it's pointing at me?' Bethany babbled on. 'Nigel has a sulky one that only looks at his toes.'

'It's a nice cock,' Asia agreed diplomatically. 'But pretty much average. Sorry Paul,' she added with a smile.

He shrugged philosophically. 'I can live with average. It's stamina that counts.' He was as relaxed in his nudity as a naturist and carried on dancing till his tape ran out. 'That's your lot, girls,' he concluded with a bow.

'Oh, don't go,' Bethany pleaded. 'Stay and have a drink with us.' She prodded Megan. 'Tell him to stay.'

Megan opened one eye and resumed her mumbling chant of 'Get 'em off', until Janice rattled her shoulders. 'Wake up, Meg. He's bollock naked.'

Megan gazed at her blearily. 'Fuck off, fatty. You ate all the pies.' I loved her for that.

'She's delirious,' snorted Janice. 'We had bagels.'

'You lot are pissed off your heads,' Paul concluded.

Asia patted his thigh. 'Sit down and have a drink. There could be a job in it for you.'

Intrigued and still nude, he sat down. 'You were my last gig anyway.'

I poured drinks for everyone and then we all looked expectantly at Asia, who was sitting cross-legged like Buddha and wearing an expression of inner wisdom on her face. 'It seems to me,' she intoned, 'that our beloved Bethany is about to set sail on the sea of matrimony without a lifeboat on board.'

'Hang on,' said Janice. 'If you're going to talk bollocks, I'm getting a spliff.' She rooted around in her handbag and withdrew a joint like a fat cigar then, lighting it, inhaled so deeply that her eyes crossed. 'OK, carry on,' she wheezed, passing it to Paul.

'What I mean is,' continued Asia, 'when an iceberg strikes, sometimes a woman needs a memory to cling to.'

'Like in the film *Titanic*?' Janice offered obscurely. 'Kate wotsit clings to Leonardo da Vinci. But,' she added gloomily, 'he sinks as well.'

'Exactly,' said Asia, sucking on the spliff.

'Oh, give me that joint,' I moaned. 'I've lost the sodding plot. And, please, someone kick Megan, she's snoring.'

Megan stirred as Paul prodded her with his foot. 'Get 'em off,' she grunted irritably and went back to sleep.

'Icebergs,' stated Asia emphatically. 'Like when Beth's lying in bed with Nigel, counting cobwebs on the ceiling because their sex life has grown stale enough to grow penicillin. What can she cling to if not the memory of that shit-hot fuck she once had?'

'Ah right!' I wasn't sure if it was the grass but I was beginning to understand. 'So what you're saying is – Bethany needs to shag someone else before she sets sail?'

Bethany, who had been listening without comprehension, suddenly pricked up her ears. 'Do what?'

'But of course!' exclaimed Janice, sliding her arm around Paul. 'And here's the man to do it.'

He eyed Bethany speculatively. 'It'll cost extra,' he said.

'Come off it,' Janice told him. 'She's practically a virgin.'

'Now, hang on a minute,' cautioned Bethany.

'Just think about it,' Asia urged. 'A man with a man-sized cock. You could spend the rest of your life wondering what you missed.'

Janice pulled a condom from her purse. 'And Nigel need never know,' she said, wiggling it.

But Bethany was unconvinced and pleaded for a change of subject. However, half an hour later, after another spiked drink and a couple of dozen hits of marijuana, she suddenly lunged at Janice, who was nibbling Paul's neck, and warned her distortedly to, 'Get your man off my hands, bitch.'

Though thoroughly smashed and stoned by now, suddenly everyone popped wide awake.

'Game on,' giggled Asia. 'Way to go, Beth!'

Bethany staggered and then flopped onto the couch. 'I wanna make a lifeboat,' she tittered, flinging her arms out.

Janice tweaked Paul's butt. 'Come on, Braveheart, do your stuff.'

The rowdy cheer, as Paul manfully flung himself on top of Bethany, roused Megan. 'Wass going on?' she wanted to know.

'She's shaving a hag ... she's having a shag,' I explained.

'Oh, right.' Megan nodded like she was wearing a brick hat. 'Better use some baby oil up there – Nigel's no horse.'

'I don't want an oily baby!' wailed Bethany.

'S'OK Beffy, he's wearing a congdong,' I said.

'Congdong?' tittered Janice. 'Don't you mean congdong?'

'That's what I said.'

She scratched her head. 'Is it? I thought you said congdong.'

'What's he doing now, Beth?' Asia wanted to know.

'I dunno,' Bethany answered dumbly. 'I think he's looking for his car keys.'

'I'm trying to get her fucking knickers off,' Paul growled, 'but she won't stop fidgeting.'

Janice moved in for a closer look. 'For goodly sake, Bethany, where d'you get the passion killers? Hey, Pam, didn't we used to wear these knickers for school?'

I had to squint Beth's briefs into focus. 'Oh yeah. You used to wet yours.'

'I fucking didn't!'

'You fucking did!'

Suddenly we were five years old again.

'Did not!' she insisted, stamping her foot.

'Soggy boggy knicks,' I jeered, grinning like a frog.

'I'll fucking hit you in a minute,' she warned me.

I balled my fingers into a floppy fist and flapped it in front of her face. 'Want a fight do you? Come on then, you bastard lard-bucket!'

'Girls! Girls!' shouted Asia. 'Let's have some respect for this intimate moment of carnal knobbing.'

'Ooph!' grunted Bethany as Paul thrust himself into her. 'Oh, wow!' she cried, beating his head with her hands until his wig flopped over his eyes.

'For chrissake, will someone hold her hands please!' he yelled, snatching it off his head.

As Asia and Megan took her wrists and Janice and I held her feet, Bethany sucked in her breath and grew rigid with expectancy.

'Ohmigod!' cried Megan. 'She's turning blue. He's killing her!'

'That's woad,' tutted Asia. 'It'll wash off . . . I hope. If not, we'll just call it "something blue".'

'Full steam ahead,' we cued Paul. 'Give it some wellie!'

The pumping of Paul's glistening haunches was such a horny sight that I found my hips twitching in time to Bethany's 'Ooph, ooph, ooph'.

'Not fast enough!' moaned Janice. 'Smack the pony!'

Paul's smooth pert buttocks seemed to quiver invitingly. So I smacked them.

'Oh yeah,' he moaned. 'You can do that again.'

I looked at Janice. 'Go on,' she dared me. 'Do it.'

Then, all at once, I was beating his bare bum with the flat of my hand, spanking him like a schoolboy till his cheeks were glowing red.

'Let me have a go,' Janice said hotly, brandishing one of my bunny slippers. 'Faster, you bastard,' she commanded, thwacking his arse so hard that he whooped in surprise. But he begged her for more, clearly loving it. 'It'll cost you,' she cackled wickedly.

'Anything, anything,' he groaned.

Asia handed me my other slipper. 'Go to it, Pam. He's a very naughty boy.'

As Janice and I took a buttock apiece and lashed him with our bunnies, all manner of things went hurtling through my mind. And, before I knew it, I was yelling 'Take that Tom!' and 'Take that Flynn!' as I vented all my anger into his punishment.

Suddenly Bethany climaxed, baying like a wolf. Paul followed, whimpering softly. And when all was quiet, Janice turned to look at me quizzically.

'I knew about Tom,' she said. 'But Flynn? What was that all about?'

Because I was drunk, I told her.

Chapter Six

*I*n the morning, despite interference from the steel drum band banging inside my head, my brain hammered home a message of reproach. Not only had I given it one lulu of a hangover, but I'd also violated its most sacred taboo by confiding in Janice Becker. For, in the cold light of day, my telling her what Flynn had done to me in the lift seemed an act of sheer lunacy and I was sure that she'd use it against me. So sure, in fact, that I would cheerfully have kicked myself in my big fat mouth were it not for the unstable condition of my legs, which felt like columns of half-set jelly.

I had a pocket of memory loss as to what her response had been. But, knowing Janice, she would have held me responsible for the incident, branding me a reckless flirt who had no one to blame but myself.

It occurred to me that I must have been seriously smashed to choose Janice, of all people, to confide in. And I began to wonder what else I had done last night. It was then that I discovered the absence of a whole chunk of memory surrounding the interval between our departure from Matt's Place and our arrival at mine. I had only a hazy recollection of some people prancing around half-naked in the street and, although I couldn't remember precisely, I had a horrible gut-instinct that one of them might have been me.

Probing deeper merely threw up the word 'Bambi' but I couldn't attach any significance to it and gave up trying when my head started throbbing again. Someone else would have to enlighten me.

We'd spent the night like sardines, with Janice and Asia in the single spare bed and the rest of us squashed in the double. I remembered leaving Paul sprawled out on the sofa and half expected him to be gone. But, when I went in, holding my head as if it were a fragile glass bauble, he was still fast asleep and totally oblivious of Asia's ministrations to his black and blue butt.

She held up the ointment she was using. 'It's for chapped lips,' she chuckled.

I winced through my teeth as I looked at his bruises. 'Did we do that?'

'No way,' yawned Janice, walking in. 'As I recall, he was attacked by randy rabbits. We'd better get him out of here before Bethany wakes up. We don't want our bride-to-be blushing for all the wrong reasons.'

'The minibus is coming at eleven,' I advised. 'That doesn't give us much time.' Kneeling down, I shook Paul's shoulders. 'Wakey, wakey, lover boy.' And when he lifted his head, I saw that most of the blue woad from his face was now on my sofa.

'Where am I?' he wondered, easing himself upright. We all flinched as we watched him settle onto his bum. 'Ouch,' he confirmed. 'That hurts.'

'Um ... we're sorry about that,' I said. 'We don't usually beat up strangers. It must have been the grass.'

He waved his hands. 'Think nothing of it. The pleasure was all mine, I assure you. In fact, if you ever want to do it again –'

'Yes, we'll call you,' I hurried him, 'but could you please go now?'

Ten minutes later he was gone and I was making coffee in the kitchen when Bethany walked in.

'Ooh,' she groaned. 'Do you have an aspirin? There's something with clogs on dancing in my head.'

'Are you OK?' I asked her anxiously.

'You mean – apart from my head?'

'I mean about last night.' I handed her some aspirin from a drawer. 'Do you feel guilty at all?'

She thought about it. 'I suppose I feel cheated more than anything. Was he really just average?'

I stared at her. 'There's never been anyone else, Beth?'

'Just one,' she confided, lowering her voice. 'We didn't go all the way but it was far enough for me to say with confidence that he wasn't any bigger than Nigel.'

I patted her shoulder. 'You seem, literally, to have drawn the short straw when it comes to men. But you do love Nigel, don't you?'

'I've loved him longer than I can remember,' she said. 'But we've never talked about "saving" ourselves for each other. I'm pretty sure he's been with other women . . . maybe even Megan.'

'Why do you say that?'

Bethany swallowed the aspirin with the coffee I gave her. 'Don't you remember last night when she said, "Nigel's no horse"? How could she know that, Pam?'

'Because of the way you reacted to Paul?' I surmised.

'She didn't hear that. She was out of it.'

'She was in and out of it,' I asserted. 'Bethany, if you're feeling guilty, don't hang it on Megan. In fact, why don't you just forget about it? You're getting married tomorrow. Anything that happened before is history.'

'You're right,' she agreed, looking at her watch. 'We'd better make tracks. Uncle Jack will be here with the minibus any minute now.'

The vehicle duly arrived with Bethany's aunt, uncle and her cousin, Neil, who was driving. I found myself, unhappily, seated next to Janice, who started on at me at once: 'Tell me more about Flynn. Was that where you disappeared to when we were talking to Matt?'

'I don't want to talk about Flynn,' I stressed, sounding prickly.

Ignoring me, she speculated, 'But, if you were so angry with him, why speak to him at all?'

I knew that if I didn't respond, she'd start thinking the unthinkable. 'If you must know, I wanted to warn him off. I thought he might be stalking me.'

Her pupils shrank to pinpricks as she peered into my eyes. 'You're lying to yourself about Flynn. You want him. I can see it in your eyes.'

Oh God, I thought. Is this what Flynn could see? 'I don't even like him,' I said.

'When has liking ever had anything to do with lust?' she observed. 'I suppose you know that Flynn and I –' Suddenly, her mobile phone rang and she broke off mid-sentence to answer it.

Flynn and I . . . what? Flynn and I are friends? Flynn and I are lovers? What had she been about to say? I didn't want to think about it. I couldn't bear to think about it. To distract myself, I eavesdropped on her conversation.

'No, I haven't forgotten, Tom.' She was giggling. 'I promised you, didn't I? . . . Yes, me too.' She grew conscious of me breathing down her neck. 'I can't talk now. I'll see you Monday.'

'That was Tom?' It was an accusation.

She looked guilty, but I couldn't tell if it was genuine or contrived. 'He's still hassling me for that guest list,' she said.

'Why?' I queried sharply. 'Monsieur Planquet doesn't arrive for another week and a half.'

She shrugged. 'You know Tom, he likes things tidy. He just wanted to be sure that I had it in hand.'

And what else did he want her to have in hand – his cock? Or maybe the cunning cow just wanted me to think

62

that. Either way, it was typical of her, and I wasn't going to give her the satisfaction of knowing that it bothered me. I gave an exaggerated yawn and closed my eyes so that I wouldn't have to speak to her or look at her smug face a minute longer.

She reminded me of a spider – a voracious bloated spider, weaving her web around all the men in my life: Lion, Flynn, Tom. Just as she had in the past.

My mind floated back through the years, returning me to the arms of my first love, Steven Millway.

'Come on, Pam. Let's have a feel of your titty.'

It wasn't so much that I didn't want him to touch me, I was petrified of him discovering the sock ball inside my bra. And I couldn't let his hand creep any further up my skirt because I was sure that I'd wet myself when he was kissing me. I felt all squishy inside.

He was angry and his words were like a slap. 'Janice said you were frigid.'

'Janice Becker is a tart!'

He didn't care about that – none of them did. She was the big-breasted captain of the netball team whose popularity had soared when she'd started wearing on her arm the most coveted fashion accessory of the day: a black boyfriend. And Charlton wasn't just anyone. He was the school's star striker and he was Steve's best friend.

I wasn't surprised when Steve's mother told me, 'He's upstairs with Charlton.' They were always together, sharing everything. But I was disappointed. I'd taken my sock balls out. I was wearing clean panties. I'd made up my mind to show him how much I loved him.

I don't know why I didn't knock on the door. But they wouldn't have heard me anyway. And she wouldn't have heard me because she was moaning so much.

I couldn't see her face but there was no mistaking those huge billowing breasts of hers. She was always flaunting them in the shower, teasing old Panda Eyes.

It was so weird, what they were doing to her. One black face and one white, pressed against her squashy breasts, gorging on her nipples like greedy suckling twins, chewing, licking, flicking with their tongues while she threshed and quivered as if possessed by a demon.

One black hand and one white, crawling up her legs. I had to tilt my head to see where they were going. And I didn't know why but I could feel that squishy feeling inside me again as I watched those ill-matched hands wriggling into her knickers and fiddling around in her most private and intimate place.

And, oh, their pricks were so big: not like my little brother's but as big and hard as the object I'd once found in my mother's knicker drawer. One black, one white. And yet the hands around them did not match: the white was on the black and the black was on the white. They were jerking each other off as their fingers pumped inside Janice. I could feel my heartbeat racing to keep up with the speed of their rhythm.

They were panting like they'd been running. Pumping and panting. Pumping and panting.

Then, suddenly, it happened. First Steve, my Steve, and then Charlton. This horrible, thrilling, disgusting thing. These jets of creamy fluid squirting like sun lotion all over her breasts. How she moaned as they rubbed it in!

I must have fallen asleep because, the next thing I knew, someone was tapping me on my shoulder. 'Do you need any help with that?'

'What?' Bethany's cousin's face swam into focus. He was looking down at my hands, which were clasped around my breasts. 'Oh no, was I –?'

'Fondling yourself?' He nodded. 'That must have been quite a dream.'

I sprang upright. 'Where is everyone?'

'Pit stop,' Neil informed me. 'You were sleeping so

64

soundly that we didn't like to wake you. I just came back to check on you.'

I felt mortified. 'Did anyone . . . see anything?'

'Relax,' he told me. 'You were sleeping like a baby.' He sat down next to me. 'So – what was the dream all about?'

I considered him. There was something of Bethany in his face that I liked, but he wasn't my type at all. And he'd shown more interest in Janice than in me. The worm of an idea was gnawing in my brain.

'Actually, I was dreaming about Janice,' I said.

His eyes grew wide. 'Really? Are you and she –?'

'Oh no,' I said quickly. 'Nothing like that. Did you know that she likes you, Neil?'

'She does?' He looked pleased. 'What did she say?'

'Only what a drag it is that she's lumbered herself with this guy, Lionel, who's coming down tomorrow. Otherwise you'd have been in with a chance, I'm sure of it. She goes for –' I tried to think of something '– mousy hair,' I concluded lamely.

He rubbed his lips together. 'I must admit, I wouldn't mind a portion of Janice. She's really hot.'

'You've no idea how hot,' I said. 'Let me tell you about that dream . . .'

It was some time later that Janice sat down, frowning. 'I can't think what's got into that Neil. He gave me such a look just now, like I was boarding the bus in the nude.' She thrust a can of coke and a wrapped sandwich into my hands. 'Beth's idea,' she explained. 'I said we should let the lazy bitch starve, but the others outvoted me.'

I smiled sweetly. 'You're all heart, Janice Becker. No wonder Neil's so smitten with you. I suppose the poor sod will end up as another notch on your belt?'

'Are you kidding?' she said. 'With Lion on the menu tomorrow, I wouldn't even consider him as an hors-d'oeuvre.'

I pretended to look relieved. 'So you won't mind if I

help myself then?' I took a huge bite out of my sandwich so I wouldn't have to talk as she mulled my question over.

I was calculating on her being too mean-spirited even to allow me the crumbs from her table. She walked straight into my trap. 'On the other hand,' she said. 'Lion doesn't get here till tomorrow afternoon and a girl has to eat in the meantime.'

'Are you still hungry dear?' enquired Bethany's Aunt Peggy, turning round to face us. She'd caught the tail end of the conversation. 'You should have had the hotpot.'

'Oh, don't talk about food,' groaned Megan. 'I feel ill.' She was looking decidedly green around the gills. 'And it isn't helping that every time I close my eyes I keep seeing this grotesque man in drag. Was that the stripper?'

'No, that was Bambi,' Asia said.

I tried to fit Megan's description to the name that I'd remembered. But it was like peering into a void and nothing coming out of the darkness. 'Who's Bambi?' I enquired.

'One of the hookers,' Asia supplied. 'Don't you remember?'

'What hookers?'

'You can't have forgotten flashing your boobs?' Janice challenged me.

I looked at her blankly. 'Please tell me I didn't do that.'

Her expression became evil. 'So you won't remember giving that kerb-crawler a blow-job then?' My face must have mirrored the shock that had registered on Aunt Peggy's face. 'I'm joking,' Janice cackled.

I sagged in relief. I'd done crazier things before and I wouldn't have put it past me.

'You were mooning motorists,' Asia reminded Janice.

I puckered my face in distaste. 'They must have thought it was Hallowe'en.'

Uncle Jack, who'd been snoring, stirred from his slumber. 'Soft white buttocks,' he mumbled rapturously.

Peggy cuffed him round his ear. 'Shut up, you dirty bastard.'

There was a moment of awkward silence. 'Shall we have a singsong?' Bethany suggested brightly.

'Oh Bethany,' groaned Megan. 'Don't be such a pilchard. This isn't a trip to summer camp.'

'Ah, bless, she's happy,' said Janice. 'Go ahead and sing, Bethany.'

Bethany started singing and, after a while, we all joined in except Megan, who had her head in a paper bag.

When we arrived at the hotel it amused me to see Janice commandeering Neil; making sure that I didn't get a sniff at him. She was laying it on with a trowel: flirting, fondling and kissing, especially when she thought I was looking. What she couldn't know was that her predictable dog-in-the-manger behaviour was exactly what I'd been hoping for.

'Janice and Neil seem to be hitting it off,' Bethany commented.

'Hmm,' I agreed. 'It must be love at first sight. I know she's regretting inviting Lion now. I expect it will break Neil's heart to hand her over to him.'

It was all rubbish and I didn't truly believe that even a soppy romantic like Bethany would swallow such twaddle, but she said, 'If they really want to be together, don't you think that we should help them?'

'I suppose so,' I said, pretending to think it over. 'Of course, the only solution is for one of us to take Lion off her hands tomorrow.'

'You could do it,' Bethany said appealingly. 'He likes you.'

'Well, I wouldn't normally do Janice any favours,' I admitted. 'But since it's you that's asking ... Tell you what – why don't you make sure that we're seated next to each other at the wedding breakfast?'

'Good idea,' she said. 'And if I put Janice next to Neil, then everyone will be happy.'

I was congratulating her on the scheme when Asia came up to inform Bethany of her parents' arrival at the hotel. As she hurried away, Asia cautioned me, 'Watch out for Mr Edwards. He pinched my bum.'

Bethany's parents, who had flown in from their retirement home in Spain, were looking tired but very tanned. I was surprised how attractive her father was for his age.

'This is Janice and Pamela from work.' She introduced us. 'These are my parents, Bryan and Ria Edwards.'

Her father looked us over with hooded lecherous eyes. 'My workmates were never this pretty,' he commented.

'You worked down a mine,' muttered Megan, looking at him with loathing as Ria embraced her.

'Megan, my sweet,' she gushed. 'It's so lovely to see you again. But how sickly and pale you look.'

'She's hung over,' Bethany explained. 'Neil had to stop the bus three times to let her throw up. I wish you could have come to the hen-night, mum.'

I choked back a chuckle as Janice's face telegraphed her horror at the idea of Bethany's mother witnessing her daughter's drunken union with a masochistic stripper. 'I'd like to hear about it,' Mr Edwards said, observing our covert grins. 'Why don't you take your mother upstairs while I get to know your friends, Beth?'

As soon as they were gone, he slipped his arms around our waists. 'Let's go and have a drink and you can tell me the wicked details.'

I noticed that Megan dragged behind us reluctantly, and saw her look of relief when she spotted some friends of the bridegroom gathered at the bar.

At the first opportunity, I drew her aside. 'You can tell me to mind my own business, Meg, but I sense some animosity between you and Bryan Edwards.'

My observation disturbed her. 'Does it show that much? Please tell me Bethany doesn't suspect anything.'

I was intrigued. 'Bethany's so happy she's on another planet right now. I don't think she'd notice if we were all shedding tears. Do you want to talk about it?'

She looked doubtful. 'I've never told anyone.'

'Then don't, if you don't want to.'

'But I'd like to,' she admitted. 'I've kept it to myself for so long. Can I trust you, Pam?'

'I wouldn't do anything to hurt Bethany,' I assured her. 'I wouldn't even tell her if I suspected that her best friend had slept with her fiancé.'

She stared at me, mortified. 'How do you know about that?'

'You let something slip last night,' I revealed. 'Bethany picked up on it, but don't worry, she isn't quite as worldly-wise as I am.'

She wrung her hands. 'Oh, it's all such a mess. Let's go outside into the garden and I'll try to explain.'

We found a quiet bench in the hotel grounds and Megan spilled out her story.

'It was years ago. Not long after Bethany left Wales to work in England. We were all living in the same street: her parents, my family and Nigel's. I was lonely after she'd gone; she'd been like a sister to me, and then when Nigel went away as well, to university in Aberystwyth, I was desolate. I'd lost both my friends. I swear I never thought of him as more than a friend, Pam. He and Bethany were sweethearts. Everyone knew they'd get married one day.'

'So, what happened?' I prompted her.

'It was summer. Nigel was home for the holiday and I was looking forward to seeing him, so I left work early that day. When I got home, I caught my mother in bed with Bryan Edwards. I knew they'd finished doing whatever they'd been doing because the room stank of sex. She was fast asleep and he was just sitting there, smoking, with his hand on her bare backside. He smiled when he saw me; I'll never forget that lewd, dirty grin on his face. Then he opened up the bedclothes and stood up. He was butt-naked, with this great python of a cock hanging down between his legs. I'm not kidding, Pam. The last time I saw anything that big, it was snuffling for peanuts in the elephant house at the zoo.

'I couldn't take my eyes off it as he came towards me. Then he held it out to me and asked me to touch it. I felt sick, but in a funny kind of way it was turning me on.'

'What did you do?' I probed her.

'He kept urging me to touch it and, God help me, I wanted to, just to see if it was real. But, instead, I ran. I ran down the street to Nigel's house, and when I told him what I'd seen he –' She broke off.

'Comforted you with his cock?' I suggested.

'That's pretty much what happened,' she agreed. 'We both felt awful about it afterwards.'

There was something in her face that made me say, 'But you didn't stop there, did you?'

She shook her head shamefully. 'It went on for almost a year: every time he came home. There was nothing in it but sex and even that was no good. And then it just stopped.'

'And the affair between Bryan and your mother?' I queried.

'It just fizzled out. I think he dumped her. She never knew what I'd seen and I've kept it from my father. That's why I hate Bryan Edwards – for all the sordid secrets I've had to keep. Do you think Bethany would forgive me if she knew?'

I thought about it for a few moments before reaching my conclusion. 'I only know that Bethany screwed another man last night and barely gave it a second thought. She's not marrying "No-Horse Nigel" for sex, Meg. She's marrying for love and you didn't steal any of that.'

She rubbed her forehead. 'That doesn't make me feel less shitty about myself.'

70

'It wasn't meant to,' I said. 'It was meant to make you feel happier for her. She's going to have a great life. Take my advice, Meg: toss all that baggage you're carrying into Lost Property and forget about it.'

She squeezed my hand. 'Thanks, Pam.'

'Come on, let's get back to the bar,' I said, rising. 'It's full of men and I haven't met any of them yet.'

But, as we went back in, I had eyes only for one man, or rather for his crotch. The bulge in Bryan's trousers seemed to bear out Megan's testimony.

'Ah, there you are, beautiful girl,' he greeted me. 'Let me get you a drink.'

Chapter Seven

'*I*t's too fucking tight,' moaned Janice.

I had to elbow her to remind her that Bethany's mother was in the room.

'Sorry, Mrs Edwards,' she mumbled.

Ria Edwards had been flapping around like Mother Goose all morning: fixing our hair, helping us dress, and even loaning me her earrings after I'd dropped one of my pearl studs and Janice, like a clumsy wildebeest, had trampled it underfoot.

'Take care of them,' she entreated me. 'They were given to me by someone very special.' I sensed a story behind her remark but she rushed away without explanation.

Bethany's last minute idea of turning us into maids of honour to accompany her official bridesmaids was degenerating into a farce. The off-the-peg outfits she'd hired – all she could get at short notice – were hideous ensembles in violet satin, comprising straight skirt and matching camisole top, with a monstrous scoop-necked blouson thing, in purple chiffon, that floated over the top. They were all ill-fitting, but Janice's camisole was practically bursting at the seams.

'I can't breathe,' she complained.

'You'll have to take your bra off,' Ria advised her.

'That'll keep her belly warm,' I quipped.

'Put a sock in it, Roberts,' growled Janice. 'Oh, I forgot, you don't need them anymore, do you?'

'Take no notice of the kitty cats,' advocated Asia. 'They're always bickering.'

'Oh dear, I hope they'll call a truce for the ceremony,' muttered Ria, rearranging Janice's bosom for a third time. 'That's the best I can do, dear. Try not to breathe too often.' She picked up her hat. 'I must get back to the little ones. I'll see you all in church.'

'I don't know about you lot,' grumbled Megan, after she'd gone, 'but I feel like a right twat in this gear.'

We assembled in front of the mirror. 'At least no one can accuse us of stealing Beth's thunder,' Asia reasoned. 'We all look like shite.'

'Shite is right,' Janice concurred, flapping her floaty sleeves. 'I can see what's going to happen – the congregation will take one look at us and start humming the *Ride of the Valkyries*.'

'Dadum-dadada-dum,' boomed Megan, leading us out. We all took up the tune as we trooped downstairs.

At the church, however, our mood jumped swiftly from jocular to wistfully sentimental when Bethany arrived in her fairytale gown, with her two little Bo Peep bridesmaids. She looked so radiant and serene that we were instantly overcome by the romance and solemnity of the occasion and fell in behind her like nuns as she walked down the aisle.

It was a beautiful ceremony, and I was moved to tears, which I might have shed but for Janice ruining the moment with a honk of suppressed laughter on belatedly discovering that Bethany Edwards was to be joined in holy matrimony to Nigel Raymond *Littlewick*. After that, an infection of giggles afflicted us all and we had to spend the rest of the service restraining ourselves.

73

'Why were you all laughing?' Bethany wanted to know, as we were lining up for photographs.

'We're just so happy for you,' Janice declared. 'Aren't we, girls?' The rest of us nodded like puppets, echoing similar sentiments to throw her off the scent.

'Is it traditional for the bride's father to kiss the maids of honour?' wondered Bryan Edwards hopefully.

'Not unless he wants the bride's mother to handbag him over his head,' Bethany said. 'Behave yourself, dad – mum's watching.'

I was shiftily eyeing him up as they spoke, thinking how handsome and distinguished he looked in his wedding suit. Plus I couldn't help noticing that he appeared to be concealing something that resembled a rolled up umbrella inside his trouser leg.

'What are you looking at?' Janice rasped into my ear. 'Are you so desperate for a man that you'll settle for a wrinkly?'

'As a matter of fact, I was thinking how much he looks like Cousin Neil.' I said. 'I trust you'll be ready to hand over that particular baton when Lion arrives?'

'Forget it,' she said. 'I'm keeping them both.'

'Not if I get to sit next to Neil at the wedding breakfast,' I murmured softly, but loud enough for her to hear.

I could tell by her face that she'd go out of her way to make sure that didn't happen. And when I saw her talking to Bethany, and Bethany nodding, I knew that I'd tricked her.

Lion was waiting in the hotel lobby and it was all I could do to stop myself from laughing when I heard her explaining that they'd have to sit apart for the meal.

He didn't seem at all disappointed when I sat down beside him. 'This is an unexpected pleasure,' he said, sweeping a tawny curtain of hair behind his ear to get a better look at me.

'That's just what I was thinking,' I replied, making my eyes wide and flirtatious as I gazed into his. Close up, I

74

could see their extraordinary colour: golden brown with flecks of orange, which gave them an amber glow like flickering fire.

'I remember you,' he told me. 'You used to come into the Singapore Sling a couple of times a week. Your name's Pat, isn't it?'

'Pam,' I corrected, vaguely disappointed. 'We stopped going after you left. The place just wasn't the same any more.'

'I didn't realise I had a fan club,' he lied, flashing his gorgeous smile.

While the soup was being served, I studied his chiselled profile, which carried the hallmarks of aristocracy in his sweeping nose and high intelligent forehead. He even lifted his spoon like an aristocrat.

'Why do you work as a barman?' I asked. I'd always wanted to know.

'I get to meet pretty girls like you,' he answered evasively.

It occurred to me that he must have been asked the same question a hundred times before. 'Is that your bog standard answer?' I wondered.

'Actually, it's the one I use for pretty girls,' he said. 'So, how did the wedding go?'

But I wasn't quite ready to surrender the topic. 'Bored little rich boy?' I suggested. 'Rebel without a cause?'

He smiled at my persistence. 'Something like that.'

I looked down the table to see if Janice had noticed him smiling at me. But she and Neil were on the other side of the bride and out of my field of vision. I realised that I would have to work faster if I were to snatch Lion from her clutches.

'You probably know that I've always liked you,' I stated bluntly.

His spoon stopped at his lips. 'No, I didn't know that. You should have made it a little more obvious.'

I put my hand under the table and laid it on his knee. 'Am I making it obvious now?'

He gulped down his spoonful. 'I think I'm getting the picture.'

I massaged his thigh. 'Let me tune it in for you.'

'Won't that involve twiddling my knob?'

'Perhaps,' I purred. 'You'll have to wait and see.'

He looked at me curiously. 'Not that it matters, but I thought that Janice was your friend.'

I waved my hand dismissively. 'We work together but I hardly know the girl.'

'That's funny – she said you were at school together.'

'What else did she say?'

He slid his hand under the table and drew mine higher up his thigh. 'She said you're a man-eater. Is that true?'

I peered at him from under the fans of my eyelashes. 'Did you know that when a lion fucks a lioness it can go on for hours?'

He exhaled a deep breath. 'This is one hell of a conversation.'

We broke off to pick at our main course. He kept watching my lips as I ate. 'Tell me about yourself,' he said.

But I was racing against the clock. 'My name is Pamela Roberts. I have perky breasts and a penchant for men with double-barrelled names, Mr Lionel Piers-Vaughn.' My fingers fluttered at his groin. 'I can think of better ways of getting acquainted, can't you?'

He bowed his head as I started rubbing and, with his hands clasped together, looked like someone who'd forgotten to say grace.

After a minute or so, he growled, 'Fucking hell, darling, if you buff my crotch any harder you'll put a shine on these trousers. I believe I've got your message loud and clear.'

'Good. I wouldn't want to be ambiguous,' I said.

'You could have just asked me for a fuck.'

'I didn't want to embarrass you.'

His smile was ironic. 'I'm sitting at a wedding break-fast with a hard-on somewhat bigger than the cake, and you don't think that's embarrassing?'

I leaned close to him and whispered in his ear. 'I know a magic cure for hard-ons. I can make them disappear.'

'And what about Janice – can you make her disappear?'

I sighed. 'Unfortunately, I don't have a spell for casting out demons and bitches. But, if you're willing to skip dessert, we could slip away for what your mother might call some après-ski. It's room 203,' I said, rising. 'Give me a few minutes and then follow me.'

I wasn't sure if he would, but I wanted to be ready for him if he did. As soon as I'd closed the door to my room, I stripped off my clothes and reclined on the bed, practising sultry looks and seductive poses as I waited.

Presently, there was a knock on the door.

Fluffing up my hair, I called, 'It's open.'

He entered warily at first but when he saw my naked body on the bed, an eager smile sprang to his lips. 'Wow!' he exclaimed, sitting down beside me to ruffle the tight golden curls of my bush. 'A natural blonde,' he murmured appreciatively. 'You don't see many of those.'

My fingers flew to his buttons with an urgency that must have made him think that I was desperate. But actually I was nervous and, fearing that we could be discovered at any moment, I wanted to make it a quickie. But when I opened his shirt and my eyes fell upon the thick sprawling pelt of golden hair that covered his upper torso, I abandoned that plan in an instant.

I had a thing about man-fur. The feel of it on my skin was an aphrodisiac to me, and I simply couldn't resist the temptation to indulge my fetish. Peeling off his jacket and shirt, I caressed his chest with my hands, relishing the cashmere softness of his pelt and the hardness of the muscles underneath.

He could see how turned on I was and, yielding the initiative, allowed me to finish undressing him. When he was naked, I leapt tigerishly on top of him. Then, pressing my breasts to his chest, I drove my rigid nipples into his furry forest. My body writhed luxuriantly as I thrilled to the teasing touch of his manly fleece.

'You like that, don't you?' he said, gripping the cheeks of my arse and drawing me higher up his body so that my sex lips could brush against his pelt.

'It feels so good,' I moaned, nuzzling into him with my pussy as his hands sculpted my breasts. I leaned back, shaking my hair. 'I feel like I'm fucking a mink coat.'

I groaned lustfully as curls of hair surrounded my clit, rasping and tugging at my sensitive nub. My thighs began to quiver uncontrollably.

I was ready to let him take over and, as he slid from underneath me, I lay passively on my belly while his hands travelled up my legs to my buttocks, first kneading my flesh with his fingers, then brushing it with his fur. My spine tingled as he worked his way up my back, kneading and brushing. Then, as I felt his cock insinuating between my thighs, I grasped the pillow tightly, expecting to be taken from behind. But though his swollen cock prodded at my sex, he didn't enter me. Instead, he rolled me onto my back and, smothering my mouth with ravenous lips, drove his turgid prick into the creamy depths of my crack. His entry was slick and smooth.

What followed was a grunting feral fuck, with clawing and gnawing and fierce bestial thrusts. Through a haze of lust and the mane of tawny hair that was tumbling over my face, I saw his catlike eyes glowing with savage passion. I heard a sound like purring in his throat as I clasped him tightly, loving the animal feel of his body and the scrape of his fur at my breasts.

I half-expected him to roar as he raised his tempo but

he only groaned and gritted his teeth, holding himself back.

The savagery was thrilling but there was more to my excitement. Was it knowing that Janice could walk in at any moment and see me screwing her man, or was it that I was, as Flynn had surmised, a dirty bitch who liked it rough?

It was a mistake to think of Flynn. As his face flashed into my thoughts in a snapshot image of his wicked grin and glittering eyes, I launched into a flailing orgasm, which had me wailing so loudly that Lion was forced to clamp his hand over my mouth.

'Fucking hold it a minute,' he grunted, gripping my threshing hips so he could spend himself.

He wanted to snuggle up to me afterwards. But now that I'd had him I didn't want him any more. He was a used item and Janice could have him back. It pleased me to think of her flaunting her second-hand goods in front of our friends.

I dressed myself and, after a minute, he got the message and followed suit.

'I don't think I've ever been used like that before,' he said, without rancour. 'I'm usually the one who fucks and leaves.'

'Then I hope it's been a novelty for you,' I said, straightening the bed.

He caught me up in his arms. 'It was much more than that, you bewitching little wild cat. If I had the time, I'd tame you.'

'You forget, I'm the female of the species. We do all the hunting.'

Gripping me, he bruised my lips with a kiss. 'Didn't anyone tell you that the lion is king of the jungle?'

Suddenly, we heard a noise at the door.

'It's Janice,' I warned, breaking out of his arms.

'Shit!' he exclaimed. 'Get in the wardrobe – quick!'

Before I could tell him it was a ludicrous idea, he'd

dragged me with him into the closet and had his arm around my mouth to stifle my giggles. But my foot banged against the door and as Janice yanked it open I fell out, laughing.

Her look could have flattened Hiroshima. 'Don't tell me,' she said. 'Sardines?'

Thinking quickly, I replied, 'It's not as fishy as it looks. I told you it wouldn't work, Lion.' He stared at me blankly while Janice glared at me with daggers in her eyes. 'He had this stupid plan to make you jealous,' I informed her.

'Why would he want to do that?' she asked, cynically.

'Because I told him about you and Neil.'

This, she believed. 'You bitch!' she spat.

Lion cottoned on swiftly. 'I was angry. I wanted to get back at you.'

Unconvinced, she glanced about her. But the bed was straight and we were dressed. Despite this, she concluded, 'Something doesn't smell right.'

'Don't be ridiculous,' I said. 'We knew perfectly well that you'd follow us.'

'How long have you been here?' she queried suspiciously. 'I didn't notice you were missing until they cut the cake.'

'Exactly,' Lion said angrily. 'If you hadn't been so wrapped up in this Neil you would have noticed straight away.'

I added weight to his argument. 'What the hell took you so long? I was getting claustrophobia in there.'

It sounded so plausible that I almost believed it myself. But Janice didn't trust me one iota and was still snooping around for clues when Bethany and Nigel came in.

'Ah, here you are,' Bethany said. 'What's going on?'

Janice looked at her, scowling. 'I found Lion and the bitch in the wardrobe.'

Nigel cracked out laughing. 'Was the land of Narnia in there too?'

'It's quite simple,' I explained. 'Lion was pissed off with Janice about Neil and wanted to make her jealous. So we hid in the wardrobe, knowing that she'd find us and suspect the worst.'

'And did she?' asked Nigel.

'Oh yes,' I said. 'It worked a treat.'

'Well, I'm glad it was just a joke,' said Bethany. 'I'm looking for Mum. Have you seen her?' No one had. 'Well, if you do, will you tell her that I need some help getting out of this dress?'

'That's what husbands are for,' I reminded her.

'Not this one,' muttered Nigel. 'Apparently, I've got chimp's fingers when it comes to hooks and eyes.'

After they'd gone, Janice nailed me with a murderous look. 'If I thought you were lying . . .'

Lion flung up his arms in a convincing display of pique. 'Do you really think I'd come all this way to be with you and then shag someone else?'

'You might,' she retorted, huffily folding her arms. As she did this, her camisole cracked open at the seam. 'I'm going to fix this bastard thing once and for all,' she snapped, stomping off to the bathroom.

'You're almost as good a liar as I am,' Lion acknowledged to me softly. 'Cunning as well as predatory. I suspect that any man who takes you on will have his hands full.' His look suggested that he might be considering the proposition for himself.

But, a minute later, he was thinking of other things to fill his hands with, because Janice had come out of the bathroom minus her camisole and her voluptuous naked breasts were clearly visible through her purple chiffon blouson thing.

As Lion stared, dumbstruck, she looked at me triumphantly.

'You haven't changed since we were teenagers,' I levelled at her scornfully. 'When in doubt – tits out.'

'It never seemed to bother Steven Millway,' she

gloated, taking Lion by the hand and leading him across the room like a lamb to the slaughter.

I let her think that she'd had the last laugh. But I'd taken my revenge for Steven and the dish had been all the sweeter because I'd kept it on ice for so long. I savoured the taste in my mouth as I watched them go out. Then, as the door closed behind them, somewhere in my mind, another door closed on a painful memory.

Chapter Eight

Waking up the next morning, I wasn't surprised to discover that Janice's bed hadn't been slept in. I'd seen the way that Lion had been groping her on the dancefloor, grabbing handfuls of flesh like he was mauling the carcass of prey that he'd felled. There was no doubt in my mind that he'd spent the night devouring her.

I didn't feel any jealousy because I'd already had him and I was pretty sure, in any case, that she wouldn't have enjoyed him half as much as I had. For, whereas I adored hairy chests, Janice loathed them to an extent where I could imagine her insisting on his shaving it off before she'd agree to have sex with him.

To amuse myself at the reception, I'd flirted and danced with Neil for most of the evening. But I had shunned his half-hearted attempt to seduce me. For, having exacted my revenge on Janice, I wasn't remotely interested in helping him get his. Not that he was undeserving of my sympathy after the way she'd cold-bloodedly cast him aside in favour of Lion. But it was enough for me that it must have irked her to see me in his arms after all her endeavours to keep me out of them.

I was pleased to have the room to myself. For now I could wallow in the memory of my craftily executed plan, which had bloodied my enemy without her even knowing it. But my victory was not as satisfying as it might have been because of a self-inflicted hollowness inside. I had tainted my moment of triumph by allowing Flynn to infiltrate my thoughts and it gnawed in my mind that I had climaxed thinking of him. Why had I conjured his image at such a crucial point? And how much had it contributed to my exuberance?

I shook my head to get him out of it. He was an infestation, a morbid disease that was starting to consume me and I needed to flush him from my system. I went to the bathroom and showered vigorously. But somehow I knew that it would take more than this symbolic cleansing to purge myself of Flynn.

Later, as I was dressing, I noticed on the bedside table the antique earrings that Ria Edwards had loaned me and decided to return them.

Mr Edwards popped his head around the door when I knocked. He greeted me warmly.

'Pamela, my dear. Do come in.'

I hesitated. 'Is Mrs Edwards, I mean Ria –?'

He didn't let me finish. 'Come in, come in,' he urged me. 'Don't just stand at the door.'

As I entered and he closed the door briskly, I saw that he was wearing just his underpants. Discomfited by the sight, I reached behind me for the handle. 'Oh, look, I'm sorry, you're not even dressed yet. I'll come back later.'

He positioned himself between the door and me. 'Don't be silly, Pam. I'm not going to bite you. I'm sure you've seen more shocking things than a man in his underwear. What did you want, my dear?'

I looked towards the bathroom. 'I came to return Ria's earrings. Is she here?'

'She's gone into town,' he replied. 'She'll be a couple of hours yet. Why don't you give them to me?'

I thrust them into his hand. 'Will you thank her for me? I'll leave you to get dressed now.'

Still barring my way, he looked at the earrings. 'She must like you to loan you these,' he said bitterly. He moved away from the door. 'Did she tell you where she got them?'

I watched him walk to the bedside table, pick up a velvet-covered jewellery box and drop the earrings inside. 'Probably not,' he sighed, snapping it shut. 'She's unlikely to tell Bethany's friends about her sordid affair.'

He'd roused my curiosity. 'You mean, a lover gave her those, and you know about him?'

Still with his back to me, he laughed ironically. 'Would a man show such good taste in jewellery? Actually, her lover is a woman and, factually, I've known about it for years.'

I was gobsmacked. It seemed the Edwards family cupboard had more skeletons in it than a graveyard. I felt sympathy for him. 'But you've been married for so long. She can't always have been a –'

'Lesbian,' he finished for me. 'Well, it's not something you catch, is it? She never liked sex – I know that. She always said it hurt her too much.' He gave a wry chuckle. 'Sometimes Fate is a cynical bastard. It must have a bloody good sense of humour to bestow on me what I have, and then saddle me with a woman who prefers her own sex.'

He turned round to face me and I jolted as I saw that he'd pulled his cock through the opening in his Y-fronts. Even limp, it was enormous. 'Look at it,' he commanded me. 'Watch closely and I'll show you something amazing.'

I started backing towards the door but I couldn't take my eyes from his cock as he ran his hand up and down its impressive length. After a couple of passes, it was fully erect and everything Megan had said.

'All this,' he groaned, 'and no one to share it with. Don't you think that's a tragedy?'

I knew that I should have been disgusted by this dirty old man exposing himself to me – except it wasn't like that at all. Bryan was mature but still attractive and, although the hair on his head was grey, his pubic hair was thick and dark. His plums were firm and plump and his mighty cock was as ageless as a giant stone-carved phallus on a pagan fertility god. I had never seen anything so magnificent.

Perhaps he caught the admiration in my eyes, for he laid it across the palms of his hands and offered it like a pet. 'Won't you stroke it, Pam? It yearns for the gentle touch of a woman.'

'Any woman? Or just Bethany's friends?' I accused him.

He had the grace to hang his head. 'Megan told you about that unfortunate incident, did she? I suppose she accused me of being some kind of pervert? I'm not, Pam. It wasn't like that. She wasn't as innocent as she makes out. She used to flirt with me . . .'

'She was a kid, barely out of school,' I interjected.

He looked at me archly. 'It's not unheard of for teenage girls to screw older men you know.'

'You were screwing her mother,' I reminded him.

'Yes,' he admitted. 'That was greedy of me. Especially since I'd been nailing her for three hours straight that day.' He hefted his cock from one hand to the other. 'The beast was insatiable in those days.'

I stared in awe at the 'beast'. 'The size alone must have intimidated Megan,' I said.

'But not you,' he concluded. 'You're not frightened by it. You're fascinated. What are you thinking, Pam? Are you curious? You're a woman of the world but you've never seen anything like it, have you? Perhaps you're wondering if you could accommodate a thing like this inside you. Would it split you apart or would your hungry little pussy be able to swallow it all up?'

I found his lilting dialect strangely calming and, although I was conscious of him inching towards me, I didn't back away.

'Go on, touch it,' he urged me. 'You'll never know what it feels like if you don't.'

Incredibly, I half-extended my hand, but then I realised what I was doing and whipped it back. 'Jesus Christ, you're Bethany's father!' I exclaimed.

He shook his head. 'Don't think of me like that. I'm just the man on the other end of this cock.' He coiled his fingers around his shaft, just below the helmet, demonstrating an impressive two-inch gap between forefinger and thumb. 'Look at it, Pam. Imagine its fat swollen head nudging into your pussy lips. Parting your curtains of flesh and driving into your cunt.'

My sex clenched and I could feel myself lubricating. 'Come on,' he whispered. 'Touch it. Stroke it. Take it in your hand.' I had started to breathe heavily and he was watching the rise and fall of my breasts. 'You know you want to. You know you can't leave until you do.'

I reasoned with myself: what harm could it do just to touch it? Not fondle it, but slide my finger down its barrel just to feel its length.

He saw my hand rise. 'That's it,' he coaxed. 'Come on. Reach out.' As my index finger made contact with the bulbous tip, he inhaled through his teeth. 'Oh yeah,' he sighed, closing his eyes.

The minute I touched it, I knew that I shouldn't have, for it wasn't enough any more simply to run my finger over it. I needed to explore it, feel its warmth and its weight in my hands. Before I knew what I was doing, my fingers were circling and gliding over its vein-rippled surface.

It felt smooth and thick and wonderful and, once I'd started, I couldn't stop. Even when I felt him backing towards the bed, my hands kept up their worshipping caress.

'Oh God,' he groaned, dropping onto the mattress. 'Yes, my darling girl. You know what Daddy likes.'

I pumped his shaft slowly, enjoying the rolling ecstasy in his eyes and the croaking moans issuing from his throat. His excitement was turning me on and I didn't stop to think as he started rolling down my tights and panties. I even stepped out of my shoes to make it easier for him.

'I'm going to make you wetter than you've ever been,' he murmured, plunging his fingers inside me. I was soaking already but I knew that I needed to be wetter still and spread my legs wide, giving access to more of his fingers. Three, then four, were rammed into me, while his thumb rubbed skilfully at my clit.

'Wider,' he snarled, grasping my ankle and lifting my foot to the bed. I struggled to keep my balance, quaking with excitement as the frenzied driving and thrusting of his fingers stoked my feverish body into a rapturous spurting climax. But I was robbed of my pleasure when his hand became a fist, forcefully and brutally invading my sex. I cried out in agony, squeezing on his cock to hurt him back.

'You bastard, you filthy fucking bastard!'

He winced but carried on fisting me, stretching me with his knuckles, turning my pussy into a squelching, yawning cavern from whence my juices dripped like rain.

'You're ready for me now,' he rasped. 'This is going to feel so good. Come on, ease yourself onto me.'

Shunting eagerly onto his lap, I parted my sex lips with one hand and, grasping his huge helmet in the other, steered it towards my opening. But my muscles contracted rebelliously.

'You can do it,' he encouraged me, pushing my thighs apart.

I wriggled and twisted, nervously coaxing the tip of his cock into my ravenous hole. But when my slick sinews grabbed him, he suddenly clamped his hands on my hips and thrust me towards him, bringing tears to my eyes as his cock lunged halfway into me. It hurt like hell. 'I can't do this,' I bleated. 'You'll split me in two.'

'Ssh,' he hissed, rocking gently backwards and forwards. I could feel the blood surging in his prick, pulsing and vibrating against the walls of my vagina. Gradually, the pain subsided and I began to enjoy the feeling of fullness. Every added inch was a cocktail of pain and pleasure, but I was loving the sensation of having a man screwed into me so tightly that his cock felt like part of my own body.

Experimentally, I started jerking my own hips and, as my movements drew whimpering cries from his lips, I felt like I was fucking him with my own magnificent penis. The thought was exhilarating. I wanted to own more of his manhood and pushed even harder. Too hard: suddenly and without warning, he ejaculated.

I was exasperated with him. 'What did you do that for?'

'It's been so long,' he groaned, resting his head on my breasts. 'I'd forgotten how good it feels.'

I looked down at his head, noticing a bald spot and realising quite suddenly that I didn't like the spicy smell of his aftershave. 'I have to go now,' I said, extricating myself. It was a whole lot easier getting him out than getting him in had been.

He watched me regretfully as I hastily put on my underwear and, when I reached for my shoes, tried to kiss me. But I didn't want that. In truth, I'd never wanted Bryan Edwards at all. It was his mighty cock that I'd wanted and if I could have severed it from his body and taken it back to my room, I would have. I realised that I'd been hankering after it ever since Megan had told me her tale. But now that I'd examined the myth for myself and tried it on for size, my curiosity was sated. All I wanted to do was leave.

'Thank you so much,' he was saying. 'I only wish that I . . .' His voice trailed away.

'It doesn't matter,' I insisted. 'Have a good flight home, Bryan.'

As I left him and hurried down the hall, my only thought was to get back to my own room for another shower before the hotel cleaners started herding out the stragglers. It didn't cross my mind to knock as I rushed into the bathroom because I wasn't expecting anyone to be in there.

Luckily, Janice was squatting with her back to me, and all I could see were the great dimpled moons of her arse pressed against the shower door. At first, I thought she was giving him a blow-job. But when I saw her hands squashing her breasts together, I realised that he was fucking her tits.

Lion was leaning back with his face under the shower-head, pumping his slippery cock into her soapy cleavage with grunting thrusts that squelched and squished as the steamy water spilled over them.

Through the mist, I could make out the gleaming smoothness of his shaven chest and wondered if, like Samson, he'd been robbed of his leonine strength. Distracted by this, I didn't notice that he'd seen me until I grew suddenly conscious of his smouldering gaze. As soon as he'd caught my eye, he flexed his biceps and pecs for my benefit. I nodded in approval then, pretending to be aroused, caressed myself lewdly, knowing that the combination of my actions and my voyeuristic presence would stimulate his climax. When Janice wailed out in protest at his early ejaculation, I discreetly retreated.

I met Asia and Megan coming down the hall on their way to breakfast. 'Aren't you coming?' Asia asked me.

'I need to take a shower first,' I said, 'but Janice and Lion are in there.'

'Use ours,' offered Megan, handing me their key. 'But it's a bath, not a shower.'

It just so happened that a soak in a hot tub was precisely what my sore little pussy required. But there was a catch. 'Er . . . we ought to warn you that we've left someone behind. He's still in bed,' Megan confessed. They both giggled.

'What have you been up to?' I demanded.

But they wouldn't tell me. 'You'll find out soon enough,' cackled Asia.

When I entered their room, the lump under the duvet was still snoring, but I could tell who he was from the tuft of mousy hair on the pillow. I pulled back the cover and prodded him.

'Oh, no,' he groaned. 'Not again.'

'Well, well, Cousin Neil,' I declared. 'Who'd have thought you'd turn out to be a stud?'

He opened one eye. 'Pamela?'

I patted his butt. 'Don't let me disturb you. I only came in to use the bath.'

He yawned and stretched. 'You wouldn't believe the night I've had,' he told me. 'One minute we were playing strip poker at two o'clock in the morning and the next – I must have died and gone to heaven. These two naked angels were crawling all over me.'

'They were no angels,' I advised him.

'You should have been there,' he called after me as I went into the bathroom to turn on the taps.

I popped my head back into the room. 'You think you could have managed the three of us? Neil . . . what side of the family do you come from?'

He looked puzzled. 'Bethany's father is my blood uncle: my mother's brother. Why do you ask?'

I considered him thoughtfully. 'You don't look much

like Bryan. Do you know if you resemble him in other ways?'

He scratched his head. 'I don't think I know what you mean.'

'It doesn't matter,' I said, deciding that one giant prick a day was probably enough for any girl. 'I'm having my bath now.'

'There's no lock on that door,' he warned me.

He was right, but it didn't stop me from stripping off and stepping into the cappuccino froth of scented bubbles. I settled into the water and, as the foam snuggled around me like a baby's blanket, I closed my eyes, wallowing in the blissful sensation. I must have lain there, luxuriating, for a full ten minutes before my senses alerted me to a physical presence in the room. I could feel the intruder's eyes scanning my body. 'What do you want, Neil?' I asked, without opening my eyes.

'You've a fabulous body,' he responded frankly. 'You don't mind if I just sit here and admire it, do you?'

'You'd be better off admiring the ceramic soap dish,' I advised him. 'You'll find it a lot more receptive to flattery than I am right now.'

He was undeterred. 'You look like a water nymph with your hair cascading over the edge like that.'

I opened my eyes. 'That's quite romantic coming from someone who's sitting on a loo wearing boxer shorts.'

He smiled. 'At least I'm not having a dump.'

I liked him for that. 'Could you hand me that sponge?' I requested.

'Why don't you let me do it?' he suggested, dipping the sponge into the bath water and running it down my leg. 'I'm a dab hand at massage.'

I decided that his appreciation of my naked body was more aesthetic than lustful at that moment. And if he was as knackered as he looked then it was probably safe to let him do it. 'All right,' I said. 'But no funny stuff.'

He soaped the sponge and then, leaning me forward,

parted my hair so he could work a lather into my back and shoulders. It felt heavenly.

'Relax,' he said, easing my head back, and then lifting and soaping my arms.

Moving down, he cupped my foot in his hand and sucked on my toes as he massaged the soles of my feet. Gradually his hands moved up my legs and I felt deliciously pampered as he worked the balls of his fingers into my calves and thighs. With my eyes closed, they might have been anyone's hands and it was easy to imagine myself in a massage parlour with some oily-chested hillock-muscled hunk slavishly attending me.

The hands were turning me on and I made no protest as water trickled from the sponge onto my nipples or when his soapy palms rotated my breasts. They were disembodied hands: stroking, kneading and manipulating my flesh. I sighed as they slithered erotically down my body to the curve of my belly and then sank beneath the waterline. But when his thumb pressed my clit, an alarm bell rang.

'That's enough,' I said.

'But this is the best bit,' he told me, sliding his thumb up and down.

My clit started throbbing. 'Neil, I said no ... oh!' I gasped, as his fingers circled my nub. Without a pause in their motion, he lifted my leg over the side of the bath so that the warm water lapped and slapped at me as I twitched my hips to the rhythm of his hand. Wantonly aroused, I hardly noticed his other hand sliding underneath me until I felt a soapy finger twisting and wriggling into the tight hole of my anus.

'Ahhum.' An artificial cough cracked like a whip into my horny haze. 'I suppose,' declared Janice, glaring down at me, 'that Neil is only doing this to make me jealous? And that the only reason for the hard-on hanging from his boxers is to get back at me for Lion?'

'This has nothing to do with you,' I told her coldly.

93

'You made your choice last night. So why don't you piss off and let me get on with my bath?'

'I'm only here to let Neil know that Uncle Jack wants to go home and is looking for him. Megan said I'd find him here. But don't let me hurry you.' She paused at the door to deliver an evil grin. 'Oh and Neil, don't forget to wash her crabs behind their little ears.'

Neil and I looked at each other after she'd gone. 'She's joking,' I uttered flatly.

'All the same,' he said, leaping up. 'I'd better go and find Uncle Jack.'

Cursing, I submerged my boiling head beneath the water.

Chapter Nine

On Monday I was glad that I'd arranged to have the morning off work. I was drained after the weekend's events and slept all the way through to midday.

Rising at last, I realised that couched within my reluctance to leave the warm cocoon of my bed was a feeling of dread. And this, more than tiredness, was weighting my movements and making me listless. It didn't take me long to identify the cause of my anxiety. I was fearful of another encounter with Flynn. The weekend had revealed an absence of strategy in my defences against the sexual warfare that he was waging on me. And should I be exposed to another lethal dose of his abominable magnetism I could be in danger of becoming obsessed with him.

I was also concerned about Janice and Tom. Their phone conversation had troubled me and, having caught him last week with his hand up her skirt, I suspected her of plotting to capitalise on his influence with Michael Main, the managing director. A good word from Tom could put her neatly in the frame for Beryl's job. The cunning tart would know exactly what to do to get him singing her praises and I would have to think long and hard about how I was going to stop her in her tracks.

When I entered the office in the afternoon and saw movement behind the frosted glass of Tom's door, I decided to confront him with my suspicions while Darren was still at lunch. To give me an excuse to go in, I picked up some correspondence for France that needed his signature.

Fixing a smile on my face, I went in. 'We have a pile of French letters to get through, Tom,' I said cheerfully. But I dropped them all when I saw that it wasn't him.

'Oh really,' Flynn uttered sardonically. 'Making up for a dull weekend? You'd better hope he's in the mood.'

He was sitting in Tom's chair, wearing Tom's glasses, and playing with Tom's executive toy: a little bird with a magnetic beak that collected individual paperclips from a tray.

His unexpected presence triggered a spasm of jittery nerves in me. To cover my consternation, I bent to retrieve the letters. Making my voice sound irritable, I demanded, 'What are you doing here, Flynn?'

Leaning back, he ran a hand through his thick black hair as he swivelled in the chair. I felt a lump in my throat as I watched him. 'I'm getting on with my work,' he said.

I gave a cynical laugh. 'I wouldn't have thought that keeping Tom's chair warm was part of your job description.'

'I wouldn't have thought that keeping Tom's cock warm was part of yours,' he retorted glibly.

I felt my cheeks burning and turned away to pluck a leaf from an artificial plant. 'My relationship with Tom is none of your bloody business,' I stated firmly.

A waft of smoke reached my nostrils. Turning back, I saw that he'd lit a cigarette. 'Mr Carson doesn't allow smoking in his office,' I informed him.

He inhaled deeply and then squinted at me through a haze of smoke. 'Not even after a fuck?'

'You're disgusting,' I said. 'Don't you think of anything but sex?'

He gave a lazy smile. 'That depends who's in the room with me.'

'What's that supposed to mean?'

His sloe-black eyes travelled lewdly over my body. God, they were sexy. 'Meaning that if I fancied you as much as you think I do then I'd probably have a hard-on under this desk. Why don't you check it out if you're curious?'

'Get out from behind that desk,' I snapped. 'You don't belong there – you belong in the bowels of the building.'

He laughed. 'I told you, Miss Roberts, I'm working.'

'No you're not,' I insisted. 'You're sitting in Mr Carson's chair flicking ash into his executive paperclip tray.'

'But I'm also installing a prototype of VoiceCom's security/fire alarm system.' He nodded towards a CCTV camera in the corner of the ceiling, which I hadn't noticed before. 'Guess where he wants the VoiceCom module installed?'

'On his desk,' I uttered dully, feeling like a total idiot.

'So, if you don't mind, Miss Roberts,' he said, gloating, 'I'd like to get on with my work.'

Darren, who was hanging up his coat as I strode out, copped the flak of my irascible mood. 'Why didn't you tell me about the new installation?' I barked.

His stricken blue eyes were as innocent as a baby's. 'But ... I ... um ... you weren't here, Miss Roberts. I didn't know about it myself until this morning.'

'Why is our department always the last to know about VoiceCom's new products?' I fumed.

'I guess it doesn't come to Promo until they're ready to market it,' Darren said mildly. 'A lot of prototypes don't even make it out of R&D.'

97

I plonked myself down in my chair. 'I'm not surprised when we have people like Flynn working with Research and Development,' I snapped. 'The man is an arrogant pig!'

Flynn put his head round the door. 'You can tell Mr Carson that the arrogant pig has completed the installation. Are you ready for a demonstration?'

Not wanting to be alone with him again, I said, 'You can show my assistant how it works.'

He quirked a black eyebrow. 'I guess you already know what to do when your alarm bell starts ringing.'

His words were thick with meaning and I understood every one. 'I certainly wouldn't stick around long enough to get burnt,' I declared.

His long eyelashes swooped in a wink. 'You're wise to run. A fire can get out of control before you know it.'

'On the other hand,' I parried coolly, 'some can be extinguished merely by pissing on them.'

He laughed. 'Anyone pissing on a fire had better keep an eye out for sparks.'

'Would they expect us to save the files?' wondered Darren, totally unaware of the crossfire whizzing over his head. I was struck by the difference between the two men: one blond and angelic, the other fiendishly saturnine.

'No, boy,' chuckled Flynn. 'You save your own arse.'

Darren scratched his head, puzzled. 'Why link the security system to the fire alarm anyway?'

'So that we'll know where the fire is and who's in the area,' Flynn explained. 'The cameras have their own built-in ultra-sensitive smoke detectors. They'll activate automatically and pan towards the slightest whiff of smoke. That'll tell us how the fire started even if someone puts it out before the alarm goes off.' He looked at me squarely. 'But we're still working on desensitising them to tobacco smoke.'

It embarrassed me that I'd chastised him for smoking

when he'd probably been testing the equipment, and I was glad of Tom's arrival in time to spare my blushes.

'Afternoon, Pam,' he said, slapping my butt. 'How was the wedding?'

I was outraged that he'd abused me in front of Flynn and if he hadn't been my boss I would have bitten his hand off.

'Good afternoon, Carson,' Flynn said sharply. 'I've fitted the security system and I have that promotion sample with me if you'd care to take a look at it.'

'Ah yes.' Tom nodded curtly. 'I'll need your help with this, Pam.'

'With what?' I asked, following them both into Tom's office.

Flynn withdrew an item the size of a fountain pen from his pocket and handed it to Tom who held it up. 'The R&D boys have come up with a novelty gift for next year's exhibition. It's a voice-activated rape alarm.'

I looked at it dubiously. 'Does it work?'

'That's what we need to find out,' Tom stipulated. 'I hate to ask, Pam, but I'm going to need a victim to test it on.'

'You'll need a rapist as well,' Flynn advised with a sinister smile. 'Shall we flip for it?'

Tom shook his head. 'Regrettably, I'd better watch.'

Dark humour flashed in Flynn's eyes. 'Looks like you're stuck with me then,' he told me.

'Oh no.' I waved my hands emphatically. 'Call Darren – he'll do it.'

'I'm fucked if I'm raping him,' growled Flynn.

'Don't be juvenile, Pam,' scolded Tom. 'It's only a demonstration and we need a woman for it. Get the bloody thing on her, Flynn, and let's get on with it.'

Flynn was grinning like the devil as, stepping forward, he parted my jacket. But when he started unbuttoning my blouse, I exclaimed, 'What the hell do you think you're doing?'

'It clips to your bra,' he said casually. 'I'd let you do it yourself but it's only a flimsy prototype and requires delicate handling.'

'I don't need you to undo my buttons,' I snarled at him. Then both men watched lasciviously as I performed the task myself, their eyes feasting on the bulging globes of my cleavage.

'Excuse my fingers,' said Flynn, plunging his hand into the crevice between my breasts. I gasped, appalled by a sudden rush of heat to my loins.

He sucked in his cheeks, trying not to smile as his impudent fingers fiddled inside my bra. 'You're making a meal out of this,' I snapped at him.

He shrugged. 'It's tricky. There's not a lot of room in here. It'll be half the size when it goes into production.' He stepped back, declaring huskily, 'You're switched on, Miss Roberts.'

I hated to admit it, but I was.

'OK,' Tom said eagerly. 'You shout "help" three times to set the alarm off, Pam. I want to see exactly what happens when a woman is attacked. Try to be as realistic as you can, Flynn.'

'No problem,' Flynn said, and before I knew what was happening, he'd launched himself at me and grappled me to the floor.

I was too shocked and too winded to speak and could only stare at him despairingly as he commenced a running commentary: 'If I were a rapist, I'd pin her body down like this and cover her mouth to stop her from screaming.'

'Put up a fight, Pam,' Tom urged me hotly.

I struggled but he'd trapped me so well that I could hardly move. I was horribly conscious of his body pressing into mine.

'I'd lift up her skirt,' continued Flynn, his eyes burning into mine as his rough hand scuffed up my leg. My own were darting wildly as I threshed underneath him. 'I'd

100

tear her underwear off.' His expression was demonic and I sensed that he was perfectly capable of raping me right there in front of my boss. I was quaking with fear – I hoped it was fear, and directed a pleading look towards Tom, but he was away with the fantasy and totally engrossed in watching Flynn's hand wrenching my skirt up over my thighs.

I felt a finger hook into the waistband of my tights and, for a horrible moment, I truly believed that I was about to be stripped. But he only pretended to pull them down.

'What now?' croaked Tom excitedly.

'I'd open my fly.' He did. 'Then I'd pull down my trousers.' He didn't.

'What then?' rasped Tom.

'Then ... I'd fuck her hard and fast.' As he panto-mimed the act, grinding himself into me, I could feel myself being sucked once more into a murky swamp of desire and, so compelling was the urge to respond to him, that I found myself consciously anchoring my hips to the floor. He lowered his head and, pressing his cheek against mine, rasped his stubble against my skin. Then, as I felt the contrasting softness of his lips, I was suffused by an overwhelming desire to kiss him. 'She might resist at first,' he murmured softly, 'but she'll soon be begging for more.' Then his mouth crushed down on the hand still smothering my lips. I bit him out of sheer frustration.

He grimaced. 'But then again, she might bite me.'

As he lifted his hand to shake it, I yelled, 'Help, help, help!' at the top of my voice and the alarm between my breasts emitted a panicky scream that was loud enough to deafen.

As Flynn rolled off me, I kicked him. 'You didn't have to make it so damn realistic!' I yelled.

He grabbed me and thrust his face into my cleavage. 'Fuck me,' he said.

'How dare you!' I exploded.

Tom laughed. 'That's the voice command to turn it off, Pam.'

Red-faced, I realised that the alarm had stopped screaming. 'You expect a woman to say "fuck me" after she's just been raped?' I exclaimed.

'It's only temporary,' Flynn explained, adjusting his trousers to accommodate an erection, which he didn't attempt to hide. 'We're still trying to come up with a deactivation command that won't turn it off prematurely. Things like "be quiet" and "shut up" are what the rapist himself might say.'

'So is "fuck me",' I pointed out, ignoring his proffered hand as I rose to my feet.

He shrugged. 'Like I said – we're working on it. But you have to admit that it's a useful command if a woman should change her mind.' His sultry look told me that he knew how aroused I'd been. 'Women do change their minds,' he stated bluntly. 'Don't they, Pam.' It wasn't a question.

Flustered, I turned away from him. 'Are you finished with me, Tom?' I demanded.

'No, I need to speak to you. But you can go, Flynn. Personally I think we have a winner here and I'll pass it on to finance for costing. Give the boys a pat on the back for me.'

Flynn nodded and I averted my eyes as he headed for the door.

Tom waited for him to withdraw before telling me, 'Christ, I could do with a cock suck after that. But we don't have time.' He glanced at his watch. 'The meeting is in half an hour. That should give you just enough time to nip down to Fielding's office.'

'What for?'

'For a briefing about tomorrow. I'm loaning you to Roger for the day.'

'You have to be kidding,' I groaned. 'Is Janice off sick?'

'Janice has her hands full getting the invitations out for

the wine and cheese thing next week. Roger needs a PA for the Surrey sales conference so I volunteered you.'

'You might have asked me,' I grumbled. 'You know I can't stand Roger.'

'I owe the man a favour,' Tom said firmly. 'It's all settled, Pam. You're going.' He squeezed my arm. 'You should be back by five. That'll give us a couple of hours.'

'To do what?'

He winked at me. 'The usual.'

I hated it when he took me for granted. 'I have a date tomorrow. What's wrong with tonight?'

He shook his head. 'I can't make it tonight. I'm playing squash with Michael Main this evening. It'll have to be tomorrow.'

'I told you, I have a date,' I insisted.

'So, cancel it. This isn't a request, Pam. I won't take no for an answer.'

The clout of his power always had me reeling in rapture when he wielded it like this. I was still in thrall to his dominance and he knew perfectly well that I didn't have the will-power to refuse him. 'Run along now,' he said. 'I'll meet you in the boardroom in half an hour.'

In a way, I was pleased that Tom had chosen such an opportune moment to assert himself, for his power over me remained a greater weapon of seduction than Flynn's aggressive sexuality and therefore represented a formidable obstacle that I could throw in the path of Flynn's creeping advance. I made my way to Roger's department with a confident spring in my step. I'd use Tom to protect me from Flynn.

I caught Janice eating a doughnut with her coffee.

'Good afternoon, Lard Arse,' I said chirpily. 'This would be the new doughnut diet, would it?'

She scowled at me. 'Why don't you help yourself to the crumbs from my table like you did at the weekend?'

'Are you referring to Lion or Neil?' I asked spitefully.

Her eyes narrowed into hostile slits. 'Lion told me that nothing happened between you.'

'Well, he would, wouldn't he? I shouldn't pin too many hopes on him, Janice. He's fickle. You know the type – hair today, gone tomorrow.'

Spluttering doughnut, Janice leaped to her feet. 'What do you . . . shit!' She'd knocked her coffee cup flying.

'Oops,' said Roger, walking in. 'That was a close shave, it nearly went over the keyboard.'

'A very close shave,' I confirmed with a giggle. Janice glowered at me and I could sense her racking her brains, trying to figure out how I knew about her shaving Lion's chest hair. But she had no time to cross-examine me because Roger was ushering me into his office. She was waiting for me when I emerged.

'What did you mean?' she snarled at me.

'No time for chatting, girls,' Roger chided us. 'We all have a meeting to go to.'

During what turned out to be another dull debate on budgets and targets, I kept a close eye on Janice and Tom, watching for covert eye contact or any other kind of surreptitious signal that might indicate collusion. I saw his eyes straying towards her once or twice but no more than was normal for a red-blooded male; it would have been far more suspicious had he avoided looking at her altogether. Based on my observations, I was glad that I hadn't challenged him over their phone conversation after all.

After two hours of tedious talk, the meeting came to a close. I left Tom chatting to the finance director and returned to my office.

'You have voicemail,' Darren advised me as I entered. He sounded peevish. I'd been neglecting him since he'd stepped out of line and he'd been mooning around with his tail between his legs waiting for a pat on the head.

But I wasn't ready to give it to him yet. I wanted to be

sure that he'd learned his lesson and I'd make him whimper and whine a little longer before I threw him a crumb of hope. 'Why didn't you take the call?' I demanded.

'He wouldn't leave a message,' he answered sullenly. 'He said it was personal.'

I was intrigued. More so, after I'd listened to the three messages from a man calling himself Ray, which shed no further light on who he was. He merely insisted in a deep baritone that I rang his mobile phone number. I rang it.

'This is Pamela Roberts. Am I speaking to Ray?'

'Ah, Pam.' He sounded pleased. 'I'm so glad you called me back. I didn't think you'd remember me.'

'I don't,' I admitted. 'Who are you?'

'We met at the Frog and Slipper on Thursday night,' he advised me. 'You were out on a hen-night.'

'That would explain why I can't remember you,' I said. 'I'd had one or two drinks that night.'

'I'd say more like a couple of dozen.' He laughed. 'So, you don't remember sitting on my knee while your fat friend was dancing on the table?'

'That would be Mel. What else happened?'

'Search me,' he said. 'I went to the bar to get you a refill and when I came back the table was in two pieces and the whole lot of you had been thrown out. You might try asking your friend, the Asian-looking girl, if she remembers me. She was with my mate, Terry. We were hoping to make up a foursome tonight; go for a meal somewhere. What do you say?'

I said I'd get back to him once I'd spoken to Asia.

I was hoping that she'd be able to tell me whether Ray's dark handsome voice was in any way a match for his looks. But she couldn't remember him either.

'Heavens,' she declared. 'We were chatting up anything in trousers that night. I don't recall a Terry or a Ray.'

105

'I must have liked him to give him my number,' I suggested.

'But did you?' she countered. 'You could have given him your name and told him where you worked.' I hadn't thought of that. 'Consider this, Pam. How drunk do you have to be to chat up a total jerk?'

'About as drunk as I was,' I admitted.

'So there's a fair chance that you wouldn't have looked at Ray twice if you'd been sober,' she reasoned. 'How do you fancy the odds?'

I spun the question on her. 'Would you pass up a date with a man whose voice sounds like he gargles with Baileys?'

'I didn't say that we shouldn't go,' she said. 'After all, it's a free meal they're offering. I don't know about you, but my gourmet supper tonight was going to be a pork pie past its sell-by date.'

I grew conscious of Tom hovering behind me. 'In that case, I'll tell them to pick us up at eight.'

'Rearranging your date?' he grunted, as I put the phone down.

'It's what you wanted isn't it?'

He held back his response waiting for Darren, who was leaving, to put on his coat.

To irritate him, I blew the boy a kiss. 'Goodnight, sweetie.'

As soon as he'd gone, Tom's fingers dug into my shoulders. 'You know I hate it when you go out with other men. God, I wish I didn't have this game tonight. I keep thinking about that demonstration. What did you make of it, by the way?'

'It's certainly an unusual novelty gift,' I said. 'It should guarantee that VoiceCom gets plenty of media attention at the exhibition.'

He clutched the tops of my arms. 'I wasn't talking about the rape alarm; I meant the role-play. What did

106

you think of Flynn's performance as a rapist? Were you turned on by it? You looked like you were.'

I laid a hand on top of his. 'You know perfectly well that what turned me on was knowing you were watching.' I stood up. 'I'd wish you good luck for your game but I know you won't beat Michael Main.'

Smiling, he stepped aside. 'Are you kidding? I like this job.' He caught up my hand and drew it to his lips. 'And, besides, I'm going to need all my strength for tomorrow. You ought to conserve yours as well. Why don't you stay home tonight?'

'Maybe I will,' I said, gently withdrawing my hand from his grasp.

But, on my way home, I telephoned Ray on my mobile.

Chapter Ten

*O*n reflection, my decision to date a man that I knew nothing about aside from the sound of his voice seemed downright foolhardy when I considered that all my previous experiences of blind dates had been disastrous. But Asia made light of my doubts.

'It's too late for second thoughts now. They'll be here any minute.'

I thrust a yellowing scrap of paper into her hand. 'Read this,' I instructed her. 'I kept it for a reason.'

With a shrug of perplexity, she unravelled the paper and read from it aloud:

'Valentino Johnson – age 33
This handsome Italian stallion is suave, debonair and romantic, the kind who will shower you with roses and give you a night to remember. At the end of your date you will arrive home breathless and exhilarated, still clutching the cork from the champagne bottle. Give him a go girls!

What's this, Pam?'

'It's from the register of a dating agency that I once joined during a famine in my love life,' I explained.

'He sounds yummy,' she said. 'Did you give him a go?'

'They all sound yummy until you learn to read between the lines,' I informed her. 'Intellectual, for example, means a geek in glasses who'll turn up at your door wearing an anorak, probably orange, and then whisk you away to a cyber café to spend the evening surfing the Internet.'

'I get the idea,' she laughed. 'So, what about Valentino?'

'His real name was Norman and he came from Southend. But I can't deny that he was a stallion of sorts. He looked like a horse, chomped his food like a horse, and whinnied whenever he laughed.'

She tittered. 'I take it you didn't come home clutching the champagne cork then?'

'No,' I answered grimly. 'I came home clutching my head in despair, swearing that I'd sooner be buggered by Beelzebub than go on another blind date.'

'You should have thought of that before,' she chided me. 'I think I hear a car.' She ran over to the window to peer through a gap in the curtains. I saw her shoulders slump. 'Oh no,' she groaned. 'If mine's the Spamhead, you're dead!'

I slunk to the front door and, when I opened it, the dim light of the porch deceived me for an instant into a false sense of relief. For the man standing there was surprisingly good looking. But when he stepped into the bright light of the hall and his head combusted into a fierce fireball of carroty red, my spirit dived into my shoes. He was ginger in the most vermilion sense of the word.

'I'm Ray,' he said. 'Do you remember me now?'

With such hair, he should have been infinitely unforgettable and it was a sad testimony to the number of brain cells I must have destroyed that night in order to overcome my usual abhorrence of redheaded men. Either that or the dark lighting in the Frog and Slipper had loaned him a brunette wig.

But at least mine had hair! Asia's, on the other hand, sported a bald pate the size of a tea-plate. And, what's more, he was a foot and a half shorter than her and well into his forties. She was practically shaking her head with disbelief as she looked from him to me. But there was no way out for either of us.

To make up for our disappointment, I suggested that we went to the most expensive restaurant that I knew and then Asia brightened when she saw Terry's Mercedes parked outside.

It seemed that money was no object to the balding little man who ordered champagne and lobster thermidor without even checking the price. But as we were cracking our claws, Asia spotted something. 'Isn't that Tom over there?'

I craned my neck and, sure enough, seated in a romantic alcove in a corner of the room, was my boss having dinner with his wife. I was furious.

'Looks like they're celebrating,' Asia observed.

My eyes flicked over the roses on their table and the champagne cooling in ice to alight upon the face of Sheila Carson. I did not consider her my enemy. She was an inconvenience; an innocuous obstacle standing stupidly in the path of my relationship with Tom but posing less of a threat than Janice Becker.

Her face was mildly pretty but want of a chin made it hamster-like and, in my opinion, her figure had ventured beyond the petite to cross the border into cadaverous. Her waifishness was hardly surprising given the way she was picking at her food without appetite, worrying and chasing it around her plate with cutlery too big for her dainty white hands, which looked like mice trying to joust with heavy weapons. Tom watched their contest with a look of concern on his face. I saw him tempting her with morsels from his own plate and feeding forkfuls of food into her birdlike mouth.

I balked at the intimacy of the act and, turning away, discovered Asia regarding me with critical eyes beneath a furrowed brow. Meeting her gaze squarely, I steered it towards the indentation of a wedding band on the third finger of Terry's left hand. She wiped the look of disapproval from her face.

Sometime during dessert, Tom noticed me and, thereafter, kept an eye on our table. I made sure that he witnessed how attentive I was to my date. We must have confused the poor buggers no end as, later, we gave them the cold shoulder and went home unmolested.

I was thinking about Tom and how to handle his deception as I bundled into the lift with the morning rush of bodies. But when it stopped on the second floor and Flynn stepped in, a sudden surge of adrenaline flushed my thoughts away.

I watched him like a frightened rabbit as he pushed his way through to me. The tension in my muscles coiled them like springs, ready to launch me into the air should he touch me.

He seemed hatefully aware of my condition and mischievously suggested, 'Maintenance override twenty-one?'

'Shut up, Flynn,' I croaked, stepping forward to distance my body from his as he insinuated himself behind me.

'Maybe you're right,' he purred into my ear. 'It's a little crowded in here today.'

Although he wasn't touching me, his breath was in my hair and his deliciously masculine aroma was permeating my senses. Deep inside me, something stirred and groaned with longing.

What if his hands should slide around my hips? Would I freeze with shock, unable to speak or move a muscle as he dragged my skirt up to my waist in front of everyone? What if his hands began slipping and sliding in and out of my underwear, lifting my top, grasping my breasts? Would I stand there like a statue, submitting to his touch while everyone's eyes looked on? What if his hand should curl around my throat, clutching my jaw, twisting my head, forcing my lips to meet his? What if he should kiss me?

I snapped out of my erotic daydream just in time to smother an escaping sigh with a cough. Bringing my hand up to my mouth, I bit hard into my knuckle to punish myself for my thoughts.

I couldn't get out of the lift fast enough when it stopped on my floor and I didn't dare look back in case Flynn's eyes revealed that he knew what I'd been thinking.

It was unfortunate for Tom that my encounter with Flynn had put me in the mood for confrontation. I strode into his office, slamming my hands down on his desk as I fired an accusation. 'You bastard! You lied to me!'

'Shut the door,' he commanded. And, out of habit, I obeyed. 'That's better,' he said. 'You never know who's listening out there.'

'I couldn't give a monkey's shit who's listening,' I stormed.

'That's because you don't have a marriage to worry about,' he reminded me. 'I don't know what you're getting yourself into such a state for, Pam. It's not like you caught me with another woman last night.'

'Oh, I get it,' I said. 'That was no lady, that was my wife? Is that the best you can do, Tom?'

He put his hands behind his head. 'She *is* my wife,' he stated blandly.

'The same wife who refuses to sleep with you, who kisses you like a wet fish?'

He brought his hands down and folded his arms. 'You've no right to be jealous of her.'

112

'Don't flatter yourself,' I insisted. 'I'm not jealous of her, I'm just angry with you. Why couldn't you tell me that you were taking her to dinner instead of making up some cock-and-bull story about a squash game?'

He looked at me calmly and then played his ace. 'Because I did play squash until seven.'

'Oh.' I sat down, deflated.

'And, as a matter of fact,' he continued, 'I didn't even know she'd booked the restaurant.' He lifted his hands in an uncharacteristic gesture of helplessness. 'You know how hopeless I am at remembering anniversaries.'

Realising that I'd run out of ammunition, I lobbed the equivalent of an empty gun. 'Your anniversary was three months ago. You sent me shopping for a present.'

'I didn't say it was our wedding anniversary. Apparently, we were celebrating the day we first met – not that I'd remember.'

I shook my head in defeat. 'If she knew what you were doing behind her back, she'd curse the day she ever met you.'

Darren's voice crackled over the intercom. 'Mr Carson, Mr Fielding is here to pick up Miss Roberts.'

Tom stood up and then, drawing me from my chair, gathered me into his arms. 'I'll make it up to you tonight. I promise,' he told me. Then his kiss carried away the last of my doubts.

He handed me over to Roger with a caution. 'Don't work her too hard. She's doing overtime tonight.'

Roger gave him a knowing look. 'I'll try not to wear her out.'

I decided that I didn't like the way he was looking at me as he held open the door of his executive company car. In fact, I didn't like Roger Fielding at all. He was pugnacious, oily-skinned and fat, with a sweaty upper lip and wet spaniel eyes. It was one of the things I despised about Janice – that she'd had sex with someone so physically repulsive merely to advance her career.

'I was talking to Michael Main the other day,' said Roger, lighting up a cigar as he drove. 'I told him that I envied Tom his PA as much as I envied his golfing handicap.'

'What did he say?' I asked eagerly.

He glanced at me sideways. 'He agreed.'

I was so delighted to have been mentioned to the big boss that I hardly noticed his hand scraping against my leg as he changed gear.

He puffed on his cigar. 'You know, Pam, a spell in the sales department could broaden your experience. You and Janice might consider swapping jobs.'

I knew that I must be careful how I answered. He was sales director, after all. 'I can't speak for Janice, but I'm too ambitious to move sideways, Roger.'

'You might enjoy being under a different boss,' he said, smirking at his double entendre.

'I'm sure I would,' I lied. 'But my eyes are firmly focused on the main chance, Roger.'

'You mean the Michael Main chance,' he surmised. 'I can put in a good word for you, Pam. You know that I like you.' He patted my knee to show me how much.

I was thinking quickly. How could I remove his loath-some sweaty palm from my knee without offending him? I yawned hugely and then apologised. 'I'm sorry about that. I was up till all hours last night.'

He moved his hand back to the steering-wheel. 'Take a nap if you want. It's a long enough journey.'

I wasn't really feeling sleepy at all but I pretended to nod off and as I lay back faking sleep, my mind wandered into the past to an occasion when I'd done the same thing but for an entirely different reason. I'd been nineteen years old and on my way to London for a job interview.

*　*　*

Bippety-bob bippety-bob bippety-bob.

The sound doesn't belong in my dream but seems to permeate in and out of it: intrusive, persistent and irritating. Like a wasp at a picnic. I keep swatting the sound away but each time it comes back more insistent than before: Bippety-bob bippety-bob bippety-bob.

I know it's trying to wake me, but I don't want to wake because I'm dreaming about my new boyfriend, Luke. I haven't stopped thinking about him since we met a couple of weeks ago: thinking about his body, thinking about his cock, thinking about sex because I want him so much and I'm longing for us to do it.

I'm sure I've dreamed this dream before . . . Luke and I in the cinema, his arm around my shoulder. It's so dark that I can't see his face. But I know it's him. I can see his signet ring catching the light from the cinema screen. I can see his signet ring moving down and down to the swell of my breast.

Bippety-bob bippety-bob bippety-bob.

Bugger off, you bastard noise. Get out of my dream. You're spoiling it.

But the sound has jumped the dream forward and now I've missed the part where he fondles my tits. But it doesn't matter because his hand is squeezing between my thighs and I can feel his fingers probing the lacy leg-hole of my panties.

They seem so real, these fingers. My pussy is dribbling as it waits for their touch. My juices seem so real. Am I having a wet dream?

Bippety-bob bippety-bob bippety-bob.

It's a train! What the fuck is a train doing at the cinema? Make it a film. Yes. We're watching a film about a train. I try so hard to hang onto the dream because the fingers are so real, slithering and sliding inside my wet cunt.

But reality is seeping in now: the rocking motion of the

train, the bippety-bob of its wheels on the track. I'm on a train to London.

But I can still feel Luke's phantom fingers frigging my pussy. Or can I? My God – this isn't a dream any more. I'm in a railway compartment. I'm not alone. I dare not open my eyes. Something is warning me not to reveal that I've woken. All my instincts demand that I keep still and quiet.

There's a man. I can smell it's a man. He's sitting next to me. He's drawn my skirt up to the top of my legs and his hand is moving inside my panties. If I open my eyes a tiny fraction and peer through the blur of my eyelashes, I can see the shape of his hand through the filmy fabric. I can hear him grunting like a pig. Is he wanking? I think he's wanking.

What shall I do? I try to think but it isn't easy to think with his fingers worrying my clit. What would he do to me if he thought I was awake? Would he rape me? Would he hurt me? Was I safer if I appeared to be asleep?

Oh, I wish he'd stop doing that. It feels so good. I wonder what he looks like? Maybe he looks like Luke. I'm finding it so hard not pant. He'll know that I'm awake if he hears me panting. But a moan ... people moan in their sleep all the time. I'm moaning because I can't help myself. I love what he's doing. I love it. Don't stop, stranger. Fuck me with your fingers. Oh, I'm coming! I'm coming like a river all over the bastard's hand.

The train is slowing down and so is he. Gently, gently stroking my bush as my climax subsides. The train stops and then suddenly his hand is gone and he is gone. But I don't open my eyes until I'm sure, quite sure, that I'm alone.

The compartment is empty. I pull my skirt down over my soaking panties and stare out of the window.

The train starts up again: bippety-bob bippety-bob bippety-bob.

* * *

'Wake up, Pam, we're here.'

'Already?' I couldn't believe that I'd been drifting around in the twilight zone between daydreaming and sleep for so long, or that I'd managed to survive the journey virtually unmolested. 'I'm sorry I haven't been much company for you.'

Roger shrugged and said ominously, 'You can make it up to me later.'

His words kept niggling me all day, but I didn't let it interfere with my efficiency. I was determined to prove myself a better secretary than Janice in the narrow hope that he might commend me to Michael Main for my skills rather than my willingness to let him paw me.

Roger's own performance at the conference stand was impressive. He was a riveting speaker: upbeat and humorous to begin with and then dynamic and commanding as he drove his message home to the company representatives.

It was my job to record the questions and comments from the floor, so I faithfully jotted everything down, from the voice that shouted, "None of our fucking products work!", to the discontent delegate who grumbled, 'Roger Fielding is a wanker.'

As the day wore on, I began to think seriously about what I should do if Roger made another pass at me. An outright rejection was out of the question but I was damned if I was going to let the sweaty little pig take advantage of his position. I decided to pre-empt the situation by using a tried and tested ploy to dampen his ardour before it even had a chance to materialise.

As we were getting into the car to go home, I said, 'I'm sorry if I've been a bit tetchy today.'

'Tetchy?' He looked puzzled. 'You've been marvellous, Pam.'

'Oh good,' I said. 'Only ... at certain times of the month I get tetchy without even knowing it.'

'Oh, right, yes.' His hangdog look revealed that I'd

guessed his intentions correctly. I just hoped that he didn't confer with Tom, who knew my cycle better than I did. But I was banking on the notion that men tended to be squeamish about certain topics.

Roger was quick to change the subject to the day's events and I made sure that the conversation remained impersonal. It was after six when he dropped me at the office.

On the fifth floor, the only light burning was Tom's.

Chapter Eleven

A lover once told me that my eyes darken to a velvety midnight blue when I'm aroused and that my lips blush redder than a wild strawberry. Then, with hands even gentler than his words, he'd caressed me as a blind man touches an alabaster statue: slowly, tenderly, softly.

What would you know of tenderness, Tom? You can't even see my face when I'm sprawled across your desk with my arse in the air. But you don't want to see my face. You don't want to focus on anything but the creamy smooth flesh of my buttocks. You don't care if my eyes are darkening to midnight as you maul and fondle and grasp and pummel and pinch. You don't care if I like what you're doing or not, you arse-worshipping arsehole! You brute! You pig!

It's not your clumsy brutal hands that turn me on – it's the way that you do what you like with me. It's the way that you don't give a shit about anyone else. You're the ultimate challenge, Tom. Your heart is as hard as your hard-on.

'Ouch! Don't bite me, Tom.'

'Shut up. You know you love it.'

He wouldn't have stopped if I'd begged him. I gripped

the edge of his desk and winced as he sank his teeth into my flank.

'Your arse is so lush I could eat it. I'm going to fuck you so hard. I'm going to fuck you like a dog. I'm going to fuck you till you scream.'

I could feel his erection pushing into my thighs, bludgeoning between my labia. He stroked back and forth without entering me. 'Can you feel it? Can you feel how hard it is?'

When I didn't answer, he grabbed a clump of my hair and pulled my head back. 'Tell me you want it.'

'I want it.'

He tugged harder. 'Tell me again'

'I want it.' You bastard, I thought. I'll make you pay for this when I've got your cock in my mouth again. I'll make you whimper and plead like a baby.

But, for the moment, the power was all his. And as he drove himself into me like a battering-ram, I thrilled to his might.

'Ooph!' The force of his second delivery smashed my belly into the desk, winding me. His balls smacked against my arse.

He thrust again, digging his nails into my haunches like needles. 'Oh Tom, you're hurting me.'

'Fuck you,' he snarled, ramming his cock in to the hilt. 'Who's the boss? Are you the boss?'

'No,' I squealed.

He rammed again. 'Tell me you love it.'

'I love it,' I whimpered.

His hand thwacked on my buttock. 'Who's fucking you, bitch?'

'You are,' I gasped. 'You're the best. You're the boss.'

'That's right,' he said, pumping harder and faster. 'I'm the boss and don't you forget it.'

But the boss was losing control. I could feel him quivering and shuddering. And then, as the momentum of his climax took primeval possession of his body, he growled and grunted like a rabid animal.

My own gratification, or lack of it, was irrelevant. It didn't matter to him whether I came or not. The sole purpose of my being there was to satisfy his needs. But, in surrendering my body so completely, I'd discovered a sense of freedom more euphoric than any orgasm I'd ever known. And its effect on me was addictive. I'd come away from our sessions feeling drugged up and high like a junkie after a fix.

I was still buzzing when the telephone started ringing. 'Shit,' snarled Tom, tearing off his condom. 'That'll be Sheila, checking up on me.'

'Don't answer it,' I said. 'Let her think that you're on your way home.'

'No,' he decided. 'It'll be good for her to know that I'm still here and not in some sleazy motel fucking the arse off my secretary.' He picked up the phone. 'Tom Carson.' Then, immediately, his expression changed from smug to paranoid. 'You fucking *what*? You're fucking kidding me ... I want to see your arse in here first thing in the morning.' He slammed the phone down forcefully. 'I don't fucking believe it!' There was panic and fury in his face.

'What is it?' I asked, hurriedly putting on my underwear.

'That was Flynn,' he uttered woodenly, 'calling to inform me that the new surveillance camera has switched itself on. It was so kind of him to wait until we'd finished, don't you think? It's been recording for the past fifteen minutes.'

I felt sick. 'Oh my God. This has to be a joke.' But when I looked up and saw the red light above the CCTV camera flashing furiously, my heart sank like a stone. 'Turn it off!' I shrieked.

'I can't,' he said. 'It's hooked up to the mainframe.'

'There must be an override. Surely Flynn can turn it off?'

He shook his head. 'He said there's a fault in the override program.'

'I don't believe it.' I spoke directly into the camera lens. 'The sicko wanking pervert must have rigged it.'

Tom looked at me strangely. 'Why would he do that? No one knows about us, Pam.'

I snorted a laugh. 'Are you kidding? The whole ruddy building knows about us.'

He stared at me. 'Jesus Christ! If this gets back to Sheila . . .'

I was surprised at how distraught he looked. 'Would it be the end of the world, Tom?' Part of me yearned to hear him say that it wouldn't really matter because he'd been meaning to tell her anyway.

He flicked his head towards the camera. 'For the record, Pam, I love my wife. You and I are just sex. We should go home now. I'll sort this out in the morning.'

'You have a meeting with Michael Main in the morning,' I reminded him coldly.

'Damn it,' he cussed. 'Then you'll have to deal with it. Get Darren out of the way and talk to Flynn. I want to know exactly what he saw and how much is on film.'

As he went out to fetch his coat, I pointed my finger at the camera lens. 'You bastard, Flynn. If you've done this on purpose, God help me, I'll make you pay for it!'

Anger was all I could summon at that moment to conceal my embarrassment and shame. For it devastated me to think of Flynn's brooding black eyes watching my submissive performance. He wouldn't know that this was just one of many sex games that Tom and I played and I hated the idea of him thinking of me as some kind of passive sex slave to my boss. I knew that it shouldn't have mattered what he thought – but it did, and I had to set him straight.

I could barely sleep at all that night and, when I did, it

was only to dream that I was running like crazy to escape from a hungry black panther, which remained just a leap away no matter how fast I ran.

There were dark circles under my eyes in the morning. Darren noticed them straight away. 'You look tired, Miss Roberts. Didn't you sleep well?'

'Maybe she works too hard.' Flynn's voice, as he came up behind me, made me jump like a rabbit. With my heart pounding, I turned to face him and, once again, was struck by a lightning bolt of physical attraction. I couldn't seem to look at him now without feeling a shivery yearning inside me. But, somehow, I kept it from my voice. 'I take it you're here to check out the security system?'

He nodded. 'Sure. Any chance of a coffee?'

'Two coffees please,' I instructed Darren. 'In Mr Carson's office.' I handed him a pile of papers. 'Then you can photocopy these for me. Why aren't the computers switched on?'

'I was just about to do it,' Darren said meekly.

'Then do it,' I snapped, determined to show Flynn that I could be dominant as well as submissive. Unimpressed, Flynn strode, whistling, into Tom's office and sat down in his chair.

I was quaking as I seated myself opposite him. 'Mr Carson wants a full report.'

He leaned forward, grinning mischievously. 'And do you always give Mr Carson exactly what he wants?'

I felt my cheeks blushing vermilion. 'I don't know what you mean, Flynn.'

'Don't you?' He spun off his chair and, rounding the desk, took my chin in his hand. 'You're the boss, Tom,' he mimicked. Then he laughed in my face. 'It would have been funny if it hadn't been so horny.' I tried to wrench my chin from his grip but he held on. 'It was better than a blue movie, Pam. I was wanking so hard, my dick was giving off sparks.' I was watching his mouth as he spoke, wondering if it was the cruelty of his smile that made his lips seem so sensual. 'The only thing that spoilt it was you,' he told me. 'I've seen inflatable dolls more responsive. Didn't you like it when he –'

'Stop!' I halted his words with fingers that trembled as I pressed them to his mouth. He caught hold of my wrist then, peering deeply into my eyes and without breaking his gaze for a moment, he moved his lips to my fluttering pulse and sensationally French-kissed it, reminding me once again of how he'd kissed me in the lift. 'If I'd been Tom, there would have been a lot more kissing and a lot less talking,' he murmured.

I caught my breath, imagining the scenario of Flynn in Tom's place: a picture that conjured extraordinary excitement and a heart-stopping emotion that I didn't care to analyse. 'But you're not Tom,' I managed to say, pulling my hand away.

He rubbed his cheek as if I'd slapped him. 'You prefer to be treated like a sex slave – is that it?' He hooked me round my waist and dragged me fiercely to his body. 'I can do that too.'

I let him mould his hands to the curve of my hips, quivering as he touched me. He lifted his eyebrow. 'No protest, Pam?' he asked thickly. 'Don't you want me to take my filthy hands off you?'

I couldn't answer. All I wanted him to do was kiss me and let me go. But the bastard knew what I was thinking and tormented me by brushing his lips across my mouth in a teasing taste of what his kiss might have been. 'If you think that I'd settle for a kiss then you don't know anything at all,' he said, pushing me away from him. 'Believe me, baby, you wouldn't settle for it either.'

Choking back a sob of frustration, I turned to answer Darren's knock at the door.

'You might ask Flynn to take a look at your screen saver,' Darren advised me, placing the coffee cups on the desk. 'I think someone's tampered with it. I'll do that photocopying now, if you don't need me for anything else.'

After he'd gone, Flynn moved back into Tom's seat and lifted his feet onto the desk. 'Hadn't you better check the system?' I asked him frostily.

'There's no point,' he said. 'There's nothing wrong with it.'

'But it switched itself on.'

He smirked. 'Someone must have said 'fuck' a few times.'

I frowned. 'Like the bidet flush? Of all the stupid schoolboy pranks . . .'

'Actually,' he interrupted, 'it's just a test word. We didn't plan on people going round the building shouting "fuck" into every VoiceCom.'

'What happens to the security footage?' I wanted to know.

'It's stored in an archive,' he told me, 'entitled "Tom's pornographic adventures". He's quite a stud, isn't he? I have to admire his temerity with women. He just takes what he wants when he wants it.'

'What do you mean?' I demanded.

He raised his eyebrows. 'Didn't you know you had competition?'

'You're lying,' I snarled.

'Am I?'

I could see that he wasn't. 'Don't fuck with me, Flynn. Tell me what you know.'

'I can do better than that,' he declared. 'I can show you. Come over here.'

Reluctantly, I went over and stood behind him as he booted up Tom's computer. 'Give me his password,' he said.

'I can't do that.'

He swore in a foreign tongue, but then shrugged. 'It doesn't matter. I can get in without it.'

125

'Was that Spanish?'

'Portuguese.' As if sensing my unasked question, he added the briefest of explanations. 'My mother's Brazilian.'

I didn't need to know more. It made perfect sense – with his swarthy dark looks and olive-toned skin – that he should possess Latin American blood, which, together with the Irish sparkle in his eyes, was proving such a lethal combination. Looking at him now, it seemed impossible that I could ever have questioned my attraction to him, let alone tried to fight it.

How could I ever have thought him not handsome? He was incredibly handsome. Everything about him was handsome: from the very masculine line of his jaw with its shadowy designer stubble, to the wayward dark waves of his hair, which I longed to run my fingers through. And I was hopelessly hooked on his wicked black eyes with their luxuriant lashes and sleek black brows.

But I still didn't like him. I hadn't altered my opinion of his loathsome cocksure manner one iota. And it made no sense to me at all that I could be so irresistibly drawn to a man that I despised.

As I watched his nimble fingers working deftly at the keyboard, I remembered how skilfully he'd manipulated my clit. And it was all I could do to keep my breathing steady as I stood there with my hands twitching, longing to grasp a hank of his hair so that I could pull back his head and milk the honey that I craved from his lips. Standing so close without touching him was more than I could bear. With my heart thumping, I casually placed my hand on his shoulder. 'Have you found what you're looking for?'

He stiffened and glared at my hand. 'If you can't keep that to yourself then slip it around my cock,' he said. 'Wanking helps my concentration if you do it fast enough.'

I snatched my hand away. 'I wouldn't touch your cock with a bargepole,' I uttered disdainfully.

He grinned. 'You'd probably get them mixed up anyway. I hope you've got your popcorn handy, the film's downloading. It's a recording from yesterday morning.'

Seconds later, the black and white interior of Roger's office appeared on the screen. He was sitting at his desk smoking a cigar.

'That's what kicked it off,' Flynn told me. 'I'll fast forward to the interesting bit.' He speeded up the film so that Roger, Janice, and her assistant, Kirsty, were whizzing in and out of the room. Then, suddenly, Roger and Kirsty disappeared and there was Janice alone, making up her face at break-neck speed. Then Tom came in and what followed seemed like a demented farce: kiss, kiss, kiss; Tom's hands all over her breasts in a frenzy; Janice whipping down his trousers: gobble, gobble, gobble on his cock.

'Stop the film!' I shouted.

He froze the frame and then let the film play on in slow motion. I watched the lewd bobbing of her head in disbelief. 'The fucking bitch. She can't do that. It's –'

'Your job?' suggested Flynn.

'Fuck you!' I screamed at him, with tears of anger in my eyes.

'I wouldn't have thought a shit like that was worth crying over,' he said, turning off the computer.

'You don't understand,' I raged. 'That cow is trying to steal my promotion.'

He looked at me, puzzled. 'That's the only thing that concerns you? I thought that you and Tom were having an affair.'

'Oh, come off it, Flynn,' I snapped. 'You watched it. Did it look like an affair to you?' I slid my arms around his neck. 'We just have sex. Dirty, filthy sex, right here on this desk.' I put my lips to his ear. 'He likes it doggy fashion. He likes to pummel my arse with his balls. Did it turn you on, watching him do that to me?' I licked his ear lobe. 'You should see me sucking him off. I'm so much better than she is.'

He gripped my hands. 'Stop it, Pam.'

'You liked watching, didn't you, Flynn? You saw him slamming his prick into me and it turned you on like crazy.'

'Shut up,' he said, jumping out of the chair. I hadn't realised how furious he was. His face was steaming with anger. 'You sick little slut. You don't even know what a tramp you are.'

'How dare you!' I cried, lunging at him with my hands flailing and slapping.

'OK, OK, I take it back,' he said, pinning my arms as he gathered me into a bear hug. 'Ssh.' He stroked my hair until my anger subsided. But, as he held me close, I was gut-wrenchingly aware of his body and, lifting my face, made my eyes and my mouth soft and inviting. It was a silent plea for his kiss and, for a heart-stopping moment, I could see that he was tempted. Then his eyebrows converged in a frown and he shoved me away from him. 'I'd better take a look at your computer.'

Confused by his rejection, I followed him sullenly into my office where he laughed as he sat down at my computer. Peering over his shoulder, I saw the words 'FUCK ME' in red, growing large and small as they undulated on the screen. 'If I didn't know better, I'd think you'd set this up for me,' he said. 'It's what you want, isn't it?'

'You arrogant pig,' I retorted. 'It's not what I want at all.' And it was true. All I'd wanted was his kiss, but he'd refused me. 'Could Darren have done this?'

He'd hacked into the program and was looking at a jumble of symbols. 'Maybe. But it's a tricky little worm. It's eaten up all your screen savers. I'll delete it and put in a fresh one.'

When he'd finished, he stood up. 'It seems like some-one was trying to tell you something.'

'Was it you?' I wondered.

He shook his head. 'Baby, when I'm ready to fuck you, I'll tell you.'

I gave an incredulous laugh. 'You'll just tell me? And what will I do – step out of my knickers and giggle?'

He smiled. 'If you like.'

'In your dreams, you egotistical arsehole,' I told him. 'Get out of here – if you can squash your head through the doorframe, that is.'

I could hear him laughing as he went down the hall. Annoyed, I turned back to my computer and then a smile broke on my face as I read my new screen saver: 'FLYNN SUCKS'.

Chapter Twelve

'*H*mm,' murmured Darren, peering at the words on my screen. 'It's not much of an improvement, is it?' He handed me the pile of photocopying that I'd given him to keep him out of the office. I threw it into the bin.

'I spent ages doing that,' he moaned.

'Stop whining, Darren,' I snapped. 'Get on with some work. I need to be alone.'

He slunk out like a scolded puppy. But I was too angry to feel remorse. I was rattled by Flynn's abrupt change of tactic and infuriated by Tom's betrayal.

I didn't want to think about Flynn – so much the better if he was playing hard-to-get. But Tom was a horse of a different colour. He'd been an integral part of my life for almost a year now and, whilst I didn't expect fidelity from him, it seemed morally wrong that he'd cheated on me with my arch-enemy.

I wanted revenge for his callousness in palming me off on Roger in order to set himself up with Janice, and for fucking me with the same cock that she'd had her lips round hours before. He must have flown to her office, with his flies undone, the minute my back was turned! No wonder the greedy pig had come so quickly later on

– he must still have been thinking of her whilst shoving his prick into me!

I planned to dump him, of course, but in a way that would hit him squarely in his ego. Ideally, I'd like him to think that I was ditching him for someone else: someone inferior, someone subordinate, a man who was young enough to make him feel old.

Calculating that he would be out of his meeting by lunchtime, I waited till one o'clock before summoning Darren and sending him into the stock room for some paper. After a few seconds, I followed him in. When the door clicked behind me, he glanced up and saw something in my face that made him return the ream of paper he was holding to its box.

'Come here, Darren,' I uttered softly. 'There's something I need you to do for me.'

His eyes flicked nervously towards the door. 'Mr Carson?'

'He won't be back for hours,' I lied.

He wiped a trickle of perspiration from his brow. 'I don't want to get into trouble. I like this job.'

I took my jacket off. 'My interim report on your progress is due at the end of the week,' I reminded him. 'I'd like to say that I'm happy with you. Do you know how to make me happier? '

His eyes were transfixed as he watched my fingers unfastening my blouse. I saw him gulp as it slithered from my shoulders. When I unclasped my bra and let it fall to the floor, his breathing grew frantic.

'Oh my God,' he gasped. 'You're so beautiful.'

I moved in on him. 'Touch me,' I urged, taking his hands and placing them on my breasts. He was trembling like a kitten. 'You like me, don't you?'

'Yes,' he croaked. His inexperienced hands felt heavy on my breasts and when his unsure fingers jiggled at my nipples like a schoolboy's, I had a flashback of Steven Millway and it crossed my mind to wonder what he would think of the voluptuous bosom that had grown in place of those sock-balls. Had I tits like these in those days he might never have touched Janice Becker's.

'Lick them, Darren. Suck them.'

'Yes, Miss Roberts.' I held his head as his wet lips slobbered at my flesh. 'That feels good,' I encouraged him. 'Do you like doing that?'

He nodded enthusiastically.

I reached down and rubbed his swollen cock bulge. 'And you like this, don't you?'

'Yes,' he rasped.

'Yes what?'

'Yes, Miss Roberts, I like it.'

As my practised fingers deftly unzipped his trousers, his breath caught in his throat and he grasped my breasts tightly, clinging onto them like a drowning man to a lifebelt as I slipped my hand inside his pants. Then he froze as I touched his cock. 'It's OK, Darren, you're allowed to breathe,' I said, sliding my fingers up and down.

He moaned and tossed his head. 'Oh, fucking hell, we shouldn't be doing this.'

'We can stop if you want,' I told him. 'But if you want that glowing report then you'd better start showing some initiative.' I pouted my lips invitingly.

Moving his hands to my shoulders to steady himself, he kissed me awkwardly and wetly. But I seized control of the kiss, gripping his arse tightly as I thrust my tongue into his mouth, my lurid snaking movements making him groan with lust until he pulled back, gasping for breath.

'Miss Roberts ... I ... I don't know what to do next,' he whispered timidly.

'You're a virgin?'

He nodded. 'I've never gone this far before.'

At any other time, I might have enjoyed breaking him in, but this was hardly the place to do it. 'I don't have time to teach you properly,' I said, pulling his trousers and pants down. 'Sit on that box.'

He sat with his eyes bulging as I stepped out of my underwear and rolled my skirt up to my waist. Then, spreading my legs, I slipped my fingers between them and masturbated. He rubbed himself excitedly as he watched me. When I was wet enough, I pushed him back. 'Relax,' I said, squatting on top of him and expertly guiding his cock into me. He moaned so loudly that I had to shove his face between my breasts to stifle his groans. 'Shut up, you idiot.'

'Oh God, oh God, oh God,' he babbled frantically.

'Keep quiet,' I grunted. 'I think I hear something.'

'No, no,' he grizzled. 'Not now.'

But I had popped him from me like a cork from a bottle and was reaching for my clothes. 'Quick! Get dressed! It's Tom!'

My timing was perfect. I rushed out of the stock room and blundered straight into my boss. He looked at the open buttons of my blouse and then past me through the door that I'd left open to where Darren was still struggling to pull his zip up over his erection. 'What the fuck is going on here?' he stormed.

I feigned guilt and surprise. 'We weren't expecting you back yet.'

'Evidently,' he uttered. 'In my office – now!' Despite myself, I still loved his autocratic manner and felt a thump of regret as I watched him turn on his heel and stride into his office.

'Take the afternoon off,' I instructed Darren. 'Don't worry. I'll handle this.'

Flushed and fearful, he smiled at me gratefully.

I strutted brazenly into Tom's office, buffing my fingernails on my sleeve. 'What's your problem?' I asked him indifferently.

He marched over to me and gripped my arm. 'What's my fucking problem?' He looked angry but there was something else in his eyes that I couldn't make out. 'What do you think you're playing at? I told you to leave that kid alone but you wouldn't fucking listen, would you?'

I pulled out of his grip. 'I wouldn't fucking listen because it's none of your fucking business,' I told him firmly.

He clenched his hands and for a minute I thought he was going to hit me. 'What do you mean? Everything you do is my business.'

'Not any more,' I told him firmly. 'I'm ending it, Tom.'

His face drained of colour. 'You can't be serious,' he said. 'You can't prefer that little runt over me.'

'Why not?' I countered. 'He's young. He's good looking. He knows how to please a woman.'

'And I don't?'

'No, Tom, you only know how to please yourself.'

He flinched at my words. 'You seem angry. Have I done something to upset you?' He came up behind me and put his arms around my waist. 'Are you trying to make me jealous?' He kissed my neck. 'You've succeeded, Pam; I'm livid.' I could feel the powerful muscles of his chest against my back and for a second I let my head lean back against his broad shoulder. 'You don't want to end it,' he said, squeezing my butt.

I wrestled out of his arms. 'Oh, yes I do,' I snapped. 'Go and find yourself another piece of arse. Maybe a big fat lard-arse for a change!'

He smacked an exasperated hand to his forehead. 'What's got into you today?' he exclaimed. 'You were fine last night. You were lapping it up. Is it Flynn? Did he say something to upset you?'

'No, he didn't say anything but he showed me something interesting. I've been meaning to ask, Tom, how did you cope without me yesterday?'

'I see.' He sat down in his chair, suddenly looking grey and tired. 'You know about Janice, don't you?'

'That's right,' I spat. 'You and Janice cock-sucking Becker. How long has it been going on?'

'It was just a couple of times, I swear it,' he said, lifting his hands in a gesture of innocence. 'Christ, what's a man supposed to do when a woman literally throws her mouth around his cock – tell her to stop because he's hating it?'

'You're saying it's her fault?'

'I'm saying I'm only human.' He thumped his fist on the table. 'Damn it, I shouldn't need to explain myself to you. It's my wife that I'm cheating on.'

'Don't even bother trying to explain. Like I said – it's all over.' I turned to leave.

'Pam!' The cry in his voice arrested me. 'She means nothing to me.'

I stiffened but didn't look back. 'Neither do I. All I've ever been to you is a convenient place to park your prick for an hour or so without fear of a incurring a penalty.'

'I won't let you finish it,' he told me.

'It's already over.'

'Did you hear me?' he shouted, as I went through the door. 'I won't let you finish it!'

I was fighting back tears as I sat down at my desk but I didn't know why. Perhaps something that I'd seen in his eyes or heard in his voice had resurrected a dream that I'd once nurtured and then suppressed; a dream that, someday, he would realise he loved me. But it was too late for dreams, and I wasn't even sure if I wanted that dream to come true anymore.

I was worried about my job. Would I be vulnerable to dismissal now that I'd withdrawn those sexual services that he'd come to expect and even demand of me? I didn't think so. I was good at my job, and he could hardly cite my refusal to copulate as reasonable grounds for terminating my employment. Nevertheless, it was bound to sour our business relationship and it seemed even more of an imperative now that I win my promotion.

The intercom crackled and Tom barked a terse command: 'Get me Roger Fielding.'

'Certainly, Mr Carson,' I answered formally. Was this how it was going to be?

Stabbing the buttons on my phone as if they were Janice's eyes, I assembled a collection of adjectives in my mind, ready to hurl them at her when she answered. But it was her assistant, Kirsty, who picked up the phone and then connected me to Roger.

'I'm putting you through to Mr Carson,' I told him.

'Hold on a minute. I want to talk to you, Pam.'

Reminding myself of his influence with Michael Main, I elected to be sweet. 'What can I do for you, Roger?'

'Did you get my message?' he asked, cackling snidely into the phone.

'Message?' My mind went blank.

'On your computer. I had one of the techs send you a love bug.'

'Oh, yes,' I answered dully, far from overjoyed by his revelation. 'I got the message, Roger.'

'I asked for something tasteful,' he said, 'but they can be a bit cheeky, the lads.'

I could hardly tell him what it had actually said. 'It was a very nice compliment,' I lied. 'Shall I put you through now?'

'Wait,' he requested. 'I've a favour to ask you. A client of mine is throwing a pool party on Monday. He likes to mix business with pleasure, so I'll be pitching and paddling at the same time. I need someone to take his eyes off the figures now and then, but, unfortunately, Janice has a funeral. What do you say, Pam, can I persuade you to take her place?'

The very last thing I needed was to get myself into a situation where I'd be fending off another of his passes. I dithered. 'Well, I don't know. I have a lot to do. Monsieur

Planquet is arriving next week and I don't think Tom can spare me.'

'I can square it with Tom,' he insisted. 'He owes me a favour.'

Another one? I was beginning to wonder if these favours had anything to do with Janice. Were Tom and Roger playing 'pass the PA'?

'There's a very big contract at stake,' he continued. 'That's why Michael wants me on it personally. If I can swing it, he's going to be a very grateful man.'

Put like that, I couldn't see that I had any choice. 'I'd be happy to help,' I consented, 'if you can make it OK with Tom.'

'Then, that's settled,' he chirped. I could imagine him rubbing his hands together with glee. 'I'll pick you up at your place at around eleven a.m. I'll have Kirsty ring you for the address. Wear your skimpiest bikini.'

I pressed the intercom. 'Tom, I have Roger on the line.'

'About fucking time,' he snarled.

As soon as I'd connected them, my phone rang. It was Asia, calling to remind me about her birthday bash on Friday. 'I've decided to hold it at Matt's Place. Everyone's coming.'

'Everyone?' I queried. 'What – even the boys from the basement?'

'Everyone,' she emphasised. 'I've even sent invitations to the other companies in the building.'

'I'm looking forward to it,' I said, secretly hoping that by overcrowding the venue, she'd reduced the odds of my bumping into Flynn. Damn it! I'd promised myself that I wouldn't give that wretched man another thought! Quickly changing the subject, I said, 'I've just heard that Janice is going to a funeral on Monday. Who died?'

'Oh, no one,' she answered. 'It was just an excuse to get her out of going to some party or other with Roger. She says the client's a total lech who keeps feeling her up whenever Roger's out of the room.'

'Guess who's going in her place?' I said miserably.

'Maybe he's not that bad,' she said reasonably. 'You know what Janice is like – she probably encouraged him.'

'I have to go now,' I told her as Tom stomped into my office and brandished a letter in front of my face. When I heard the phone click, I added wickedly, 'I'm looking forward to seeing you too, darling.'

'Who was that?' he demanded. 'Your little cherub-arsed toy boy?' He threw the letter at me. 'This is full of mistakes.'

There was one, which he'd underlined in red. 'Can't we be civilised about this?' I suggested calmly. 'We've had some good times and some great sex. I'll always be fond of you, Tom.'

'For Chrissake, Pam, it was a blow-job, not a steamy affair.' He sat on the edge of my desk. 'You got even. You've done your thing with Darren. Can't we call it quits?'

I heaved a sigh. 'We were never going anywhere, Tom. We were just using each other. I don't blame you for wanting someone else. It was getting stale, monotonous. We were doing it out of habit.'

Although it wasn't my intention, I could see that my words were wounding him. 'You don't mean that,' he said. 'I could never tire of you, Pam.' He cupped my face in his hands. 'I want you all the time. Damn it, I want you right now.' He leaned forward to kiss me but I drew back.

'You can't have me any more.'

He moved his hands to my shoulders. 'Do you remember the first time we made love? You were working in the general office. I noticed your arse first because that's what you wanted me to notice. You bent right down in front of me, picking something up or pretending to, and I thought to myself "that's the sexiest arse I've ever seen".

'I remember looking into those flirtatious blue eyes of yours and seeing a "come-on" that made my cock stiff.

And then you did this thing with a pencil, moving it around your lips so that I'd notice how soft and full they were. I did – and I wanted to kiss you.

'When you came for the interview, you didn't sod about. You made it clear that you wanted sex. You even sat on my lap when I gave you dictation and, when my hands crept under your skirt, you just carried on taking shorthand like nothing was happening. You were wearing stockings and nothing else underneath. It was such a surprise when I felt your naked pussy . . .' He broke off to emit a groan. 'You knew what I wanted right from the start.'

Had I really done all that? Was I as bad as Janice Becker? I didn't think so. 'I was crazy about you, Tom,' I confessed. 'I used to volunteer for the mail round just to catch a glimpse of you. You were so big, so broad, so powerful. You walked like a king. And you're right – I used every trick in the book to make you notice me and want me. I was so ready for that first fuck, I was almost too scared to sit on your knee in case I wet your trousers.'

He looked probingly at me. 'Then you didn't do it just to get the promotion?'

'Oh no.' I shook my head emphatically. 'I was happy to get it, of course. But I would have screwed you anyway.'

'Were you ever . . . in love with me, Pam?' It was the first time I'd seen him hesitant.

'I don't know,' I answered honestly. 'Maybe I thought I was.'

He rubbed his forehead. 'It's never even crossed my mind to wonder if I have feelings for you that go beyond passion. It was all about sex because sex is so important to me. It's what I think about when I get home at night and I'm lying in bed with Sheila. It's what I daydream about when I'm stuck in a boring meeting or having a bastard day. I need you, Pam. You've no idea how much I need you.'

'I'm sorry, Tom, but I can't be your sex slave any more. I've resigned from that job.'

'I know what you're doing,' he said, wagging his finger at me. 'You're still punishing me. You're hurt and angry, I can understand that. But you'll get over it.'

I rolled my eyes heavenward. 'You're not listening to me, Tom.'

'You'll get over it,' he repeated. 'And then I'll make love to you in the sweetest way – like I've never done before. I'll give you an orgasm that will keep you smiling for weeks. I'll make it up to you, Pam, you'll see.'

I didn't know what else to say to convince him that I meant what I said. For I had begun to realise that I was only using Janice as an excuse to rid myself of an obsession that had possessed me for far too long. This was my chance to break free of Tom's powerful grip over me. But he wasn't going to make it easy.

'There are still so many things we haven't done,' he said. 'Things I've never dared to suggest.' He dropped his voice to a whisper. 'But I've thought about them often; these wild fantastic things I want to do to you.' He raised his voice again. 'I'm not giving you up, Pam.' He slid off my desk. 'I want to see you in my office tonight after work. Do you understand me?'

I nodded obediently. 'Yes, Tom, I understand you.'

But at the stroke of five o'clock, I went home.

Chapter Thirteen

'**M**r Carson's in a filthy mood,' Darren warned me the next morning. 'I thought he was going to sack me.'

'He can't do that,' I said, hanging up my coat. Suddenly, the boy was standing behind me and his hands were all over my hips. 'It would have been worth it,' he purred, squeezing my thighs possessively.

'What the bloody hell do you think you're doing?' I exclaimed.

Stung, he leapt back. 'But I thought –'

'Whatever you thought, you thought wrong,' I interjected, pushing him aside as I picked up the mail. He stared at me dumbstruck. 'Get on with your work,' I commanded him frostily.

'But you can't . . . you just can't treat a man that way.'

'You're not a man, Darren, you're a boy,' I said scathingly.

'Is it because I didn't know what to do?'

I shook my head. 'It was a mistake. I acted on an impulse and now I regret it. Just forget it ever happened.'

I was surprised when he swung me round to face him. 'But I love you.'

I patted his cheek. 'You loved the feel of my pussy, that's all. Listen to me, Darren, you need to be grown-up about this. Women change their minds as often as they change their underwear. It's a fact of life.'

'Don't patronise me,' he protested. 'I've put up with all kinds of abuse from you since I started working here. But this is the limit. You're nothing but a . . . prick teaser!'

I laughed. 'Don't be childish.'

Outrage flushed in his cheeks. 'Don't laugh at me,' he warned. 'I won't be made a fool of.'

'Then stop acting the idiot,' I said. 'Go and make some coffee.'

'You don't have time for coffee,' he told me stiffly. 'You've had an urgent e-mail from Beryl Parker. She wants to see you in her office.'

'When?'

'Right away. It said as soon as you came in.'

'Then why the hell didn't you tell me at once?' I ranted. 'You dumb little arsehole, you've let me keep Mr Main's PA waiting with all this sulky schoolboy crap. I ought to kick your half-descended balls up your spotty little backside!'

He glowered at me and I thought I saw real menace in his eyes. But his voice was calm as he said, 'I'll tell Mr Carson where you've gone.'

As I raced up to Michael Main's executive suite on the seventh floor, I was racking my brains trying to think of a reason for the summons. Surely it was too early to expect an interview for Beryl's job?

But when I knocked on her door and she beamed at me as I entered, a tiny moth of hope fluttered in my heart. Perhaps someone had put me forward for appraisal?

But she swatted the moth with her opening words and then went on to trample it. 'Miss Roberts, I'm afraid that I have to speak to you on a very delicate matter of so personal a nature that Mr Main expressly requested that

I deal with it myself. He felt that the feminine approach would be more appropriate under the circumstances. Take a seat, my dear.'

I sat nervously as she scrutinised me with beady bird eyes through the granny specs perched on the end of her narrow, pinched nose. 'There's been a complaint against a company employee over an incident of sexual harassment,' she told me. 'Have you any idea what I'm talking about?'

I shook my head. 'I haven't a clue, Miss Parker.' Her question had fazed me completely. I knew that sexual flirtation was rife in the building and it didn't surprise me that someone had been caught overreaching the mark. But I couldn't figure out why she should think me involved. I looked at her blankly.

She smiled in a vague attempt to appear matronly. 'Anything you say will remain strictly confidential,' she assured me. 'You need have no fear of ramifications.'

'I'm sorry, I don't understand you,' I said.

'Then I'll come to the point,' she said briskly. 'It's been brought to our attention that you, Miss Roberts, were the victim of a sexual assault on these premises.'

I immediately thought of the security footage. Could it have found its way to Michael Main already? Caught on film, Tom's dominant and abusive behaviour towards me could easily be misconstrued as sexual harassment. 'If I'm the victim, as you say, then surely it would be up to me to bring a complaint?' I suggested evasively.

'Not necessarily,' Beryl replied. 'Quite often, in these cases, the victim is either too embarrassed or too frightened to come forward herself. And it's not unusual for a third party to intervene if they consider it to be in the best interests of their friend or colleague. But, of course, it's easier for us to determine the truth if we hear actual rather than hearsay evidence. I know this is hard for you, Pamela, but it would be very helpful indeed if you could give me your own account of last Wednesday's events.'

Last Wednesday? But this would be well ahead of the camera's installation. What was she talking about? 'I'm sorry, Miss Parker,' I said. 'There seems to have been a mistake.'

She looked at me sternly. 'Are you denying that you were physically abused by Mr Faraday?'

'Mr Faraday?' I echoed vacuously.

'Flynn Faraday, our chief product installer and technical maintenance engineer. According to our information, he's alleged to have assaulted you in the lift when you were going home that night.'

Flynn Faraday – how strange it sounded. I'd always known him just as Flynn, and if I'd ever thought about it, which I hadn't, I would have expected Flynn to be his surname. Now, suddenly, here he was – no longer Flynn the maintenance man, but Mr Faraday of the fancy job title whose length befitted his ego.

'Well?' she prompted me twitchingly. 'Are you able to recall the incident?'

'I can't think why this has come to your attention,' I said. 'I really don't want to make an issue out of it.' I was thinking hard as I spoke: why had Janice – it had to be Janice – opened up this can of worms? What did she hope to gain by it? I grabbed the chance to put the boot in. 'I've only told one person about this in absolute confidence – that person has betrayed me and proved themselves untrustworthy.' I wanted to add that these were not the best credentials for a managing director's PA but felt that she was probably astute enough to have figured that out for herself.

Beryl sniffed into a handkerchief. 'That person may have been motivated by a sense of this company's values. At VoiceCom plc we do not tolerate either sexual promiscuity or sexual harassment on the premises.'

I failed to choke back a snort of laughter. Clearly, the dried-up old dragon had no idea of the sexual shenanigans that went on daily.

She frowned at me. 'This is no laughing matter, Miss Roberts. The way I see it, either you took part in a complicit sexual act or you were subjected to one against your will. I would remind you that the former is also a sackable offence.' I could tell how much she'd enjoyed seeing my jaw drop to my knees from the smug expression on her face. 'Shall we continue?'

I sat up primly. 'What can I tell you?'

'You can begin by telling me whether you and Mr Faraday are having a relationship?'

'Certainly not,' I said. I could hardly tell her that just the mention of his name was making my knees go weak.

'Do you like him?' she asked.

'No,' I answered truthfully. 'I can't say that I do.' What she'd really meant to ask was whether I fancied him or not, but she was too stiff-knickered to put it that way.

'Then would it be fair to say that the sexual advance Mr Faraday is alleged to have made was unwelcome?'

I had to think about that. It was the crunch question. Both my head and Flynn's were on the chopping block and my answer was about to determine whose head rolled. I could see no reason to save his, for I was sure that I'd resisted his seduction right up to the point where he'd thrust his hand into my panties. And even though I'd enjoyed every minute thereafter, it had certainly begun without my consent. I did the best that I could for him.

'I believe Mr Faraday misread the situation. He thought I'd encouraged him.'

'And had you?'

Had I? 'Now you know what I know,' he'd said when he'd forced my hand to touch his crotch earlier that day. He'd been certain of my attraction to him long before I'd realised it myself. What subliminal messages had I been sending that had made him so sure?

'I'm not aware of doing or saying anything that could

145

be interpreted as encouragement.' It was as near to the truth as I could make it.

She skewered me with her eyes. 'Did you use the word "no", Miss Roberts?'

I nodded slowly, reluctantly. 'Yes. Yes I did. Several times.'

She was suddenly sympathetic again. 'That will be all for now, my dear. Mr Main will deal with Mr Faraday himself on Monday. I'm sorry if this interview has been painful for you.'

'You've been wonderful,' I told her smarmily. What the heck – I might as well come away with a Brownie point.

Walking back to the lift, it hit me what I'd done to Flynn: I'd thrown him to the wolves simply to save my own neck. Damn Janice Becker and her big fat gob. I had no wish to see him dismissed. I'd miss him. What did you say? I asked myself. I said I'd miss the black-eyed bastard – do you want to make something of it? I replied.

'No!' I exclaimed emphatically out loud.

'Are you talking to me?' It was one of the juniors from general office. I didn't know her name.

I shook my head. 'I was just thinking out loud.'

'It's this place,' she observed chattily. 'It gets you talking to yourself. I often go home at night and find myself telling the walls to turn on the lights. Floor five, isn't it?'

I nodded and, as we stepped into the lift, she spoke the number into the VoiceCom. 'The most embarrassing thing I ever did was commanding the toilet to flush in a public loo. You should have seen their faces when I came out! They must have thought I was stoned or something . . .' Blah, blah, blah. She went on and on, and it was a relief to escape from her babble.

My head was spinning and the last thing I needed was a confrontation with Tom. But, as soon as he knew I was back, he summoned me into his office.

'I'm taking you to lunch,' he informed me.

'Tom, I have a splitting headache ...' I started to protest.

'Then I suggest you take an aspirin,' he advised me coolly, 'because what I have to tell you is going to make your head explode.'

I sighed. 'If this is about last night – I didn't stay to have sex with you because I meant every word I said. You just wouldn't listen.'

'Save it, Pam,' he said. 'We'll have lunch at twelve thirty. I'll be doing the talking and you'll be doing the listening. Get me France on the phone. I want to speak to their personnel manager.'

I was baffled by his manner and intrigued by his request. Something had happened. I could tell by the way that Darren kept looking at me shiftily, like he was in on a secret.

The clock ticked slowly round to midday. Promptly at half past, Tom collected me. He took me to the tiny Italian restaurant where we had lunched in better days.

'It's a long time since I brought you here,' he said. 'Perhaps I shouldn't have stopped wining and dining you. Would the occasional meal or bouquet of flowers have made any difference?'

'It wasn't a romance, Tom. It didn't get that far. Like you said, it was all about sex.'

He placed his hand over mine. 'I was wrong. It wasn't just about sex; it was about great sex. I love the way you respond to me. I love the ecstasy on your face and the noises that you make. I've never met a woman who wants it and loves it and needs it as much as you do. That's what makes us so good together.' He broke off to let the waiter serve. After we'd ordered, I changed the subject.

'That call to France – I was wondering what it was about.'

'All in good time,' he said ominously. 'I've been meaning to tell you about the security footage. You'll be pleased to know that the file's been erased.' I assumed he meant both files. 'We'll just have to be more careful in future.'

'We don't have a future,' I reminded him.

'Oh, but we do.'

I had to wait until after we'd eaten for him to enlarge on his declaration. 'I have your future in my hands, Pam. You see, there's been a complaint about sexual harassment,' he told me.

I was livid. 'It was meant to be confidential,' I fumed.

'But you don't even know what it is.'

I looked at him quizzically. 'What are you talking about?'

'I'm talking about Darren.'

'Darren?' I couldn't believe my ears. 'What the fuck has Darren got to do with it?'

'I must admit I was a little surprised when he came to me this morning,' Tom reflected. 'But I warned you, didn't I?'

'What are you saying, Tom?'

Tom sipped his wine in an ill-conceived attempt to hide a smirk. 'He's made a complaint against you. He says you forced him to have sex with you.'

I laughed out loud. It was incredible: one minute I was a victim of sexual harassment, and the next I was a perpetrator. 'But that's ridiculous,' I said. 'I didn't force him to do anything.'

Tom nodded. 'I find it hard to believe myself. But he's quite insistent about it. He maintains that you threatened him with a bad report if he didn't comply.'

I stared at him incredulously. 'I didn't mean that. I only said it because he was being timid and needed a shove. Tom, you know how it was, how he wanted me. All this – it's just sour grapes. He tried it on with me this morning but I didn't want to know. I must have hurt his pride more than I realised for him to come running to you with this ludicrous story.'

Tom's steel-grey eyes were inscrutable. 'You've admitted to coercing him with a threat. So, it really doesn't matter if you meant it or not. Any court would find that since the boy isn't psychic, he couldn't possibly have known that you weren't serious.'

I put my head in my hands. 'The shitty little prick. How could he do something like this? You've seen the way he looks at me. He was gagging for it, Tom, I swear it.' It struck me as I spoke that these could be the very words that Flynn might use in his own defence: I could tell from the way she looked at me that she was gagging for it. He'd been surer of me than even I was of Darren. *Oh Flynn, what have I done to you? You don't deserve this crap any more than I do.*

Tom lifted my chin. 'It doesn't have to go any further,' he told me. 'I'm the only witness and I've told the little wanker that I can testify either way. He knows he can't win but he can kick up a stink that'll follow you around like a methane cloud. One more hint of a scandal and you'll be out on your ear with your career in tatters.'

One more hint of a scandal? It was almost funny. What would Tom say if he knew that I was already involved in one? 'You said it needn't go any further?' I prompted him.

'It seems that Darren has a hankering to go to France,' Tom revealed. 'He'll agree to drop the complaint in exchange for a transfer.'

'The phone call,' I realised. 'Can you swing it?'

A sinister smile crept over his features. 'It's more a question of whether I want to.'

'What do you mean?' I had a sinking feeling that I knew his answer already.

He quirked his chin. 'I can bury this, Pam, but there's a condition attached. I think you know what it is.'

'You want us to carry on,' I said woodenly.

'I want more than that,' he proclaimed. 'I want us to do some of those things that I talked about.' He slipped his hand under the table and fondled my knee. 'Imagine you're sitting here with no panties on and I'm stroking your pussy under the tablecloth. I wouldn't stop when the waiter came up. I'd carry on frigging you as I ordered the wine and he'd be so turned on that he'd have to stick his prick in an ice bucket to cool himself down.'

His eyes were shining because he knew that his power over me was even greater than before. I was cornered but I couldn't see any way out. If Darren pursued his complaint, not only would I lose my job but I'd also obtain a stain on my record that would stick to me like superglue. Even if I resigned, the rumours were sure to follow and I would find myself being passed over for promotion for no apparent reason.

My thoughts grew more devious. 'How quickly can you dispose of Darren?' I wanted to know.

'I've instructed him to take a week's sick leave and then I'll send him over on a three-month trial. You won't have to face him again.'

I was pretty sure that, once Darren was in France, he'd drop the whole thing. This gave Tom little more than a week in which to wield his new power. From my point of view, another week as his sex slave was a small price to pay for my redemption.

'It seems that I'm compelled to agree to your terms,' I admitted. 'But I have a condition of my own.'

'You're not actually in a position to bargain,' he reminded me. 'But I'll hear your terms out of politeness.'

'There has to be a limit, Tom. You can suggest whatever fetish or fantasy you like, but there are some things I simply won't do. I'm drawing a line in the sand. Do you understand me?'

'I hear what you're saying,' he acknowledged. 'And I'll make it easy for you, Pam. I'll give you a choice. There are a lot of things that I'm eager to try. I've always loved the idea of tying you up and having you totally at my mercy. Or there's "three in a bed" – two men or two women, I don't much care. I'll let you think about it. Tell me tomorrow and we'll do it at the weekend. Sheila's away at her mother's so I can stay with you Saturday night.' He rubbed his hands together. 'Whatever you choose, I know that we're going to love it, you and I, because we're two of a kind, Pam, two of a kind.'

Chapter Fourteen

'*T*wo of a kind . . .'
  The reason Tom's words kept echoing in my brain was because they'd evoked an old memory that I couldn't help linking to one of the fantasies he'd proposed. And, as I travelled home on the tube, sandwiched between two men who were hanging from the straps on either side of me, my mind drifted back to the past.

They were so alike. They were peas in a pod, Luke and his twin brother Jason. I never could tell them apart.

Because I'd met Luke first, he was my boyfriend, but it was only natural that I'd be equally attracted to his identical twin. And Jason was always there, sniffing around me like a dog whenever Luke was out of the room.

Foolishly flattered by their dual attention, I'd played a dangerous game of flirtation until one night I'd paid the price.

I remember thinking how aggressive Luke was that night, how hungrily he'd torn off my clothes. But I didn't suspect a thing. Not even when he sat down in the armchair and thrust my head between his legs, demanding a blow-job. I simply assumed that he was feeling hornier than usual and couldn't be bothered with preliminaries.

I remember how ecstatic he was, how his eyes had rolled in their sockets, as I'd run my lips up and down his shaft. I hadn't seen him so excited since the first time I'd fellated him in the back seat of his car. Looking back, I must have been so naïve not to guess, not to wonder at his rapture, when it seemed so obvious to me now.

I'd been concentrating so hard that I hadn't realised anything was wrong until his cock went limp in my mouth. Glancing up, I saw that he was staring, ashen-faced, across the room, with such a strange expression of guilt and anguish on his face that I thought his parents had come home early.

When I twisted my head and saw that it was only Jason standing there, I sagged in relief. I didn't even mind him seeing me in the nude. But Luke – Luke seemed so ashamed and I couldn't understand it. Then Jason spoke and, suddenly, everything became crystal clear.

'Does she know it's you?'

'No,' said the other one. 'She thinks it's you. I'm sorry, Luke, I just couldn't help myself.'

I gaped at the man who'd had his cock in my mouth just a minute ago. 'You're Jason?' I looked from one twin to the other but there was no way of telling them apart, except . . . 'Luke has a birthmark,' I remembered.

The one standing took off his trousers and pants to show me the tiny blemish on his otherwise perfect rear. 'That's why he's sitting down, so you wouldn't notice.' He turned back to face me and I saw that his cock had grown stiff. 'I want to see it again,' he said. 'I want to see you sucking him off. It's like watching myself from a distance. You can't imagine how horny that is.'

'But Luke, he's deceived us both!' I exclaimed.

'It's not my brother's fault,' he decided. 'You've been

153

flirting with him ever since we started going out. You've been asking for this and now you're going to get it.'

'Asking for what? I don't know what you mean.'

'The two of us,' he said. 'The two of us together.' He looked at Jason and Jason nodded eagerly.

'Oh, now, hang on a minute . . .' I started to protest. But as my gaze was drawn from their identical faces to their identically tumescent cocks, I went shivery with excitement. I was only nineteen but I could recognise a once-in-a-lifetime opportunity. Turning back to Jason, I lifted his dick and let my lips slide over it.

Just knowing that Luke was watching every movement made me tease and tickle and lick and suck with all the skill I could muster. And, after a while, he reached for me ravenously.

As he shoved me from my kneeling position onto all fours and then drove his fingers into my well-oiled sex, I carried on giving head to Jason. But it was hard to keep moving my mouth when all I wanted was to gasp as Luke's frigging fingers squished inside me. Then, suddenly, he withdrew them and plunged his cock into my hole with such force that I gagged on Jason's. But Jason wouldn't let me stop and, pressing his hands on my head, kept nodding it up and down as Luke rutted me from behind like a stag.

Afterwards, I couldn't remember which of us had climaxed first but it was Jason who recovered while Luke and I were still dozing. He roused me and fucked me with my legs over his shoulders. Then Luke woke up and took over. After that, I was passed from one to the other, positioned and repositioned like a rag doll and then fucked until my cunt was raw. But they didn't care: they kept on going. Even when I cried and begged them to stop. Even when I fought and struggled to get away. They just laughed and fucked me even harder, one pinning me down while the other raped me.

I was sore for days afterwards – my pussy, my anus, my breasts. They'd left no part of me unravished.

I never saw them again, but I'd often recall that night, reliving it in my mind and relishing every dirty detail of an experience I would never forget. But would I do it again?

Sorry, Tom, once in a lifetime's enough!

'Penny for them?' offered the stranger standing next to me.

I didn't usually converse with commuters but he seemed pleasant enough to deserve a reply. 'I was just thinking about something my boss said.'

'I wish my boss inspired thoughts like that,' the stranger said knowingly. 'But he's sixty years old and built like a sumo wrestler.' I smiled. 'That's the first time I've seen you smile,' he said.

I looked at him archly. 'Do you know me?'

'I've noticed you several times,' he replied. 'But you've never noticed me.'

'I'm sorry. I seldom notice anyone when I'm travelling,' I said.

He shrugged off my apology. 'One doesn't expect a pretty young girl to notice a nondescript man in his fifties.'

'Well, I promise I'll notice you now,' I assured him politely.

He looked at me speculatively. 'Since I have your attention at this moment in time, I may as well be presumptuous and invite you to a party on Saturday night.'

'I'm sorry,' I told him gently, 'but I'll be tied up this weekend.' Then I burst out laughing as I realised what I'd said.

It wasn't quite so easy to let Tom know my decision.

Friday began as a hectic day with our department

being given over to a team of copywriters from the advertising agency. And I was so busy servicing their needs that I hardly saw Tom at all. But as the afternoon drew to a close, he hooked my arm as I was passing and dragged me into the stock room.

'What's it to be?' he rasped excitedly. He must have been thinking about it all day.

'Do I have to provide my own silk scarves?' I asked coyly.

He smiled. 'I was hoping you'd pick that one. I'll be round at eight o'clock tomorrow night.'

He tried to kiss me but I jerked my head away. 'Just remember, I'm doing this against my will,' I reminded him.

'That'll make it so much more interesting,' he said, patting my butt as he followed me out.

I had to stay with the copywriters until after six and so was late getting changed for Asia's party. All the others had gone on ahead, which meant that the ladies was deserted when I got there. But I was glad of the solitude because it gave me a chance to work on a plan for getting my own back on Janice. I'd use her boyfriend, Lion, to exact my revenge. I'd seduced him once before and I was sure that I could do it again. But, this time, I'd make sure that she caught us red-handed. I wanted to see her pugnacious face crumple as I stole her man from under the very snout that she'd had the nerve to stick in my trough.

To make sure of success, I poured myself into my sexiest silk dress, which was the same sapphire blue as my eyes. It was slit to the thigh, and so clingy that I couldn't wear a stitch underneath. I spent an age tonging my hair into rivulets of curls.

When I arrived at Matt's Place I could practically hear the clicking of neck bones as heads turned to look at me.

'Bloody hell!' squawked Mel, nearly falling off her

stool. 'Is that a nightdress, Pam?' She rubbed her large belly dejectedly. 'I'd give anything for a figure like that.'

'Try giving up a few fry-ups,' Asia suggested.

'I suppose I could do that,' agreed Mel, 'but then my life would be meaningless.' She poured a handful of peanuts into her mouth. 'If someone offered me the choice between sizzling hot bacon and sizzling hot sex,' she chomped, 'I'd choose the pork over the pork sword any day of the week.'

'Speaking of porkers – where's Janice?' I asked.

'She's around somewhere,' answered Mel, waving her hand in a vague direction. 'Probably still trying to shake off Plug.'

'Plug?' I queried.

'Phil Bingley from bought ledger,' she clarified. 'He's the ugliest bloke in the building. You must have seen him, Pam. He looks like this . . .' She pulled a retching face. 'In fact, when he was born, he was so ugly the midwife threw him away and kept the placenta.'

'Are you talking about Plug?' guessed Asia, catching the tail end of Mel's joke.

I giggled. 'Is he really as ugly as all that?'

Asia nodded. 'Go and take a look if you don't believe us.'

'You'll need a well-polished shield or a mirror,' warned Mel, 'and don't stroke his hair, whatever you do.' The pair of them fell about laughing. Then Mel said, 'I'll come with you.'

I let Mel pioneer a path into the crowd and in the midst of the human jungle we came upon Janice talking to a pop-eyed man with a face like a warty toad. He was hanging from her shoulder pleading drunkenly, 'Aw, go on, princess, give us a kiss.'

'It's Friday,' she uttered sarcastically. 'I never snog frogs on a Friday.'

'Then give me your phone number and I'll give you a ring,' he persisted.

'Try ringing the bells of Notre Dame,' she snorted, plucking his hand from her shoulder. 'I have a suggestion to make – bugger off.'

Without her support, he staggered and fell to the floor.

Turning to escape, she bumped into Mel and me. 'Cute boyfriend,' I said.

She looked disdainfully at my dress. 'You're supposed to wear a Femidom on the *inside*, Pam.'

'I thought she'd come in her nightie,' chuckled Mel. Then, realising what she'd said, added ruefully, 'I haven't come in my nightie for years.'

'I can remedy that,' slurred Plug, climbing to his knees via her calves.

'I'm not that desperate,' she said, kicking him back to the floor. 'You'll know I've had enough to drink if I start fancying him later on, ' she advised us.

'Who invited him anyway?' grumbled Janice as we rejoined the others.

'No one,' said Mel. 'He's a gatecrasher.'

'He must have crashed into an awful lot of gates to end up with a face like that,' I commented. 'You must be slipping, Becker. You've been here an hour and all you've managed to pull is a "plug".'

'That's a good one,' tittered Mel.

But my own laughter gurgled in my throat like water in a blocked drain as I suddenly spotted Flynn. He was wearing black jeans and a crisp white shirt under a black leather jacket and, as my eyes travelled over him, a fist of desire punched me in the stomach. This was getting ridiculous. I was behaving like a schoolgirl with a crush and, if I didn't get him out of my system soon, I'd end up putting myself into therapy.

He hadn't noticed me and when he continued not noticing me, I was infuriated. I felt like going up to him and smacking him in the mouth: notice me now, you bastard!

At last, he looked my way and, when his slow smile

materialised, I knew that it was for me and not for the redhead standing next to him who quickly prodded him in the side to draw his attention to herself. I gulped in a lump of air that I couldn't seem to swallow as he hooked his arm around her waist and then lowered his head to kiss her. Pivoting swiftly, I bit into my knuckle as a wave of pure jealousy washed over me.

'What's up, Pam? You look nauseous,' Mel observed.

'I'm fine,' I said tightly. 'I just need a drink.'

I wasn't standing long at the bar when I felt the pressure of a body behind me. 'Hello, baby.'

Even his voice made me quiver. I struggled to sound indifferent. 'Hello, Flynn. Having a good time?'

'It's a little crowded in here,' he remarked, pressing himself into my silk-covered rear.

'It's not quite so crowded further down,' I said pointedly.

'Maybe not, but it smells better here.' He buried his nose in my hair. 'Your scent makes my head spin.'

His nearness was churning my insides and I couldn't trust myself to look at him. 'I think I'll try further down,' I gulped, starting to move away.

He stopped me with his hand. 'Running away again, Pam?'

'Don't flatter yourself,' I snapped. 'I just want a drink.'

He turned me round to face him and his dark devil eyes seemed to peer into my soul. 'Are you sure that's all you want?' He slipped his finger under the narrow strap of my dress and followed its line to the edge of my breast. 'Shall I tell you what I think? I think your head wants you to run away but your body wants to stay. Why is that, Pam?'

I flicked his hand from my strap. 'Why don't you tell me? You're the one with all the answers.'

'You don't deny it then?'

I lifted my chin haughtily. 'As a matter of fact, I do. As

159

far as I'm concerned, there's no conflict at all. I don't want to be with you in any sense of the word.'

He pulled a wry face. 'I wasn't offering myself. I'm here with someone else, in case you hadn't noticed.'

He was insufferable! Now he was telling me that I couldn't have him even if I wanted him. 'Just leave me alone,' I growled.

He put his head to one side. 'I wish I could.'

Fuming, I moved down the bar to where Lion was serving. I was in the perfect mood now to carry out my plan of revenge.

Lion's amber eyes glowed as he looked at me. 'Hello, darling,' he said. 'You're looking very silky tonight. I would hazard a guess that you're not wearing anything under that dress.'

I leaned across the bar. 'Not a thing,' I purred.

'Interesting.' He rubbed his chin as he looked into the cleavage I was displaying. 'That's a very provocative pose.'

'If you cast your mind back, you may recall that I'm a very provocative woman,' I reminded him.

'Ah yes – the lioness who likes to do the hunting,' he reflected. 'Can I get you a drink?'

I ran my fingers across my pouting lips. 'I'll have one of those cocktails with the sexy names,' I decided. 'I don't suppose you've got one called "Let's fuck and then hide in the wardrobe"?'

He smiled. 'No, but I'm thinking of inventing one called "Let's meet in the passage outside the cloakroom".'

'I'd like to try that,' I said. 'What's in it?'

'Just vodka with a cherry and a twist – the twist being that if you don't drink it in one go, the barman gets to eat your cherry.'

'Pour it,' I said.

He hit the optic three times, then plopped a cherry on a stick into the glass. We locked eyes as I lifted the drink to my lips, swallowed a mouthful, and then set it down.

'You weren't even trying,' he said.

'I guess I'll have to surrender my cherry then, won't I?'

He picked up the cocktail stick and rolled the glacé fruit around his tongue. 'Fifteen minutes?' he suggested, flicking his head towards the door.

I nodded. 'You're on.'

Picking up my drink, I wandered back to the others, half expecting Flynn to pounce on me again. When he didn't, I found myself actively searching for him in the crowd, but I couldn't see him anywhere. I felt a pang of disappointment but I pushed it aside as I strolled up to Janice.

'Hi, Pam. Look what Matt's just given me.' It was a swizzle stick in the shape of a penis.

'I want to talk to you,' I told her firmly.

'Naturally Mel's convinced that it's a life-size model of her husband's prick,' she giggled.

I was disarmed by her cheerfulness. 'This is serious, Janice. I need to speak to you.'

'So talk,' she said. 'What's stopping you?'

'Not now. I want to see you outside the cloakroom in twenty minutes.'

She frowned. 'Why can't we talk here?'

'It's about Tom,' I answered sternly, 'and you.'

Her expression became defensive. 'I see. Do you want to go outside now?'

'No. I want to make sure the coast is clear. I don't want anyone from the office eavesdropping. Meet me in twenty minutes.'

I moved away before she could answer and started chatting to one of the engineers. I asked him if he'd seen Flynn.

'Mr Faraday? I think I saw him going into the snooker room with a stunning redhead on his arm. Did you want him for something?'

Did I want him for something? Good question – what

exactly did I want from Flynn? Certainly not anything that I could speak to one of his minions about.

'It doesn't matter,' I said and moved the subject to a safer topic. When the time came for my liaison with Lion, I disengaged myself and headed for the cloakroom.

Lion was coming out of the gents as I entered the passage. He wasted no time in scooping me into his arms. 'I think we should say hello properly, don't you?'

When he kissed me full on the lips, I dug my fingers into his hair. 'I've missed you,' I told him huskily.

He lifted the curls from my neck and chewed at my skin. 'You should have called me.'

I needed to get him hotter than this. Clutching his bum, I pulled him close and, when our groins were touching, I ground my pubis into his crotch. 'I'm so hot for you,' I gasped.

Groaning, he pushed me up against the wall. Then, kissing me hungrily, he whooshed my dress up my thighs, filling his hands with my naked flesh. He was so carried away that he didn't hear the sound of the swing-door. But I did. And, for Janice's benefit, I threw every-thing into that final scene: a scene that was supposed to end with her shrieking in anger on discovering us. But no sound came.

And yet I knew that someone was watching. Twisting in Lion's arms, I pulled back from his ravishing lips to look over his shoulder. And when I saw who was stand-ing there, my heart flipped and then sank like a stone.

It was Flynn.

Chapter Fifteen

*H*is stance was pure Flynn. No one else could have stood there with arms folded, casually tapping a foot, as if waiting for me to me finish a conversation. No one else seeing me splayed against a wall with my skirt up round my waist and a man's groin pressed to my naked pussy, simulating sex, could have portrayed such perfect nonchalance.

Wriggling out of Lion's embrace, I detached his hands from my body and did a shimmy to bring my dress back down. 'We have an audience,' I warned him.

The two men exchanged affable nods. Then Lion said, 'Perhaps this isn't the right place or the right time. I'll call you.'

'Mmm.' I murmured, grinning stupidly as he pecked me on the cheek. But, as soon as he'd gone, the grin grew sickly and slid off my face.

Flynn rubbed his jaw. 'Well, what do you know – Pamela Roberts caught once again in a compromising situation. You just can't get enough, can you?'

'You needn't have stood there watching,' I reproached him. 'What are you, some kind of voyeur? You seem to have nothing better to do than observe my moments of passion.'

He arced an eyebrow. 'You call that passion? From where I was standing it looked more like adolescent groping. But, you're right – I do enjoy watching you. You're quite a performer. I must have viewed that tape of you and Tom a dozen times.'

'Then I'm glad it's been erased,' I retorted. 'I guess you'll have to find something else to amuse you.'

He laughed. 'Did you really think I wouldn't keep a copy for myself?'

Infuriated, I lashed out at him, but he caught hold of my wrists. 'Now, that's what I call passion,' he said.

'It's anger,' I stressed, stamping my foot.

He grabbed my arms and rattled me. 'Why don't you stop being angry and listen to your body for once? You don't want to fight me, Pam, you want to fuck me.'

Shocked by the baldness of his statement, I stared at him in confusion. 'What makes you so damn sure of yourself?'

His eyes bored into mine. 'I can read your body language,' he told me. 'I've no idea why you were letting that guy paw you like that, but I can tell you this – as soon as you saw me, you wanted his hands to be mine.'

It was true, so true. I covered my face with my hands. 'Why do you keep tormenting me? Why can't you leave me alone?'

His laugh sounded bitter. 'I guess you bring out the devil in me.' He lifted my hands from my face. 'Look at me, Pam. If you tell me one more time to leave you alone, then I will.'

I tried to say it but my free will had fallen into the bottomless black depths of his eyes. And I was so mesmerised that I scarcely noticed him taking my hands and placing them on his shoulders. 'Let me show you what I know,' he murmured softly. 'Let me show you what a difference it makes when it's my hands.'

Already, my nipples were hardening like bullets and, as my heart started racing, I stiffened and bit my lip, suddenly afraid of losing myself in my own desire.

'Relax,' he whispered, sliding his arms around my waist. I took a deep breath, closed my eyes, and gave myself up to the awesome sensation of being held by him, and then touched by him, as his incredibly sensual hands stroked over my silk-covered hips, creating a tingle of static electricity, which moulded the slippery fabric into every curve and crevice of my body. I felt naked under his gliding hands as they travelled slowly and erotically up to my shoulders before sweeping back down to my thighs. On the reverse journey, as his palms sculpted the outline of my figure, I could hear his laboured breathing above the tiny breathless gasps issuing from my own lips. And when his thumbs rolled over my breasts, my shivering excitement drew a shudder of response in him. I opened my eyes to see a tortured look of restraint in his.

'Do you want me to stop?' he uttered hoarsely, gripping my haunches with an urgency that revealed the extent of his own arousal.

'No!' All my pent-up breath expelled in the negative as I coiled my arms around his neck and pressed my breasts to his chest, welding my body to his.

With a grunting moan, he crushed me to him then, clutching a fistful of my hair, pulled my head back. My breath caught in my throat as I saw his eyes soften and his lips part. Then my heart stopped beating as I waited for his kiss.

But it never came.

Janice Becker, the bane of my life, had burst in on us to catch me red-handed – but with the wrong man!

'What's going on here?' She looked at me cynically. 'I see you've got yourself a warm-up man to get you in the mood for your night of passion with Tom tomorrow.'

Flynn's hands dropped to his sides and a muscle

quirked in his cheek. 'A warm-up man?' he echoed sardonically. 'Well, you can tell Tom from me that his bitch is smoking.' He gave me a withering look. 'If his cock melts in your cunt, don't ask me for a refund.'

'Flynn!' I called, as he walked away.

He paused at the door and, flicking two fingers off his brow in a mock salute, muttered something in Portuguese. When the door closed behind him, Janice sneered, 'I think that was Spanish for slapper.'

'Actually it was Portuguese for Janice is a big-mouthed fat-arse!' I snarled.

She pouted. 'What's the matter – did I spoil your little tête-à-tête?'

'How did you know about tomorrow night?' I confronted her.

'I saw Tom today,' she answered coolly. 'He told me that you'd found out about us and, can you believe it, he had this ridiculous notion that it was a good enough reason to give me the brush off. I wonder what he'd think if he'd seen what I just saw.'

'I don't care what Tom thinks,' I asserted. 'But I'd like to know what you're up to, Janice. I'd have thought you could find your way into Michael Main's trousers without having to go through Tom's first. Or is this some kind of contingency plan, in case you don't get the promotion?'

She lifted her head indignantly. 'It may surprise you to know that I've always liked Tom. But you've been in my way, Pam. You've always been in my way, dogging my footsteps, treading on my toes. You've been the bug in my salad for as long as I can remember.'

It was strange hearing her voice the very same things that comprised my own reasons for hating her. It had never occurred to me to view our relationship from her perspective before. 'Are you trying to blame me for Tom's decision to dump you?'

'If you'd told him it was over, he wouldn't have,' she

insisted. 'You're only hanging on to him because I want him.'

I shook my head. 'You've got it all wrong. But what about Lion? Where does he figure in all this?'

'Lion?' she echoed. 'Lion is just someone I fuck now and then. Don't even bother trying to get at me through him. I can guess what happened at the wedding – I'm not stupid. It didn't concern me then and it doesn't concern me now. But, in view of what you did, I'm surprised that you have the gall to confront me over Tom. At least I didn't go after him purely out of spite. I made my move on Tom because I want him.'

'That's not all you want,' I asserted. 'You're not fooling me, Janice. I know what you're planning. You're sick of Roger mauling you and, if you don't get Beryl's job, then you'd sooner have mine. Screwing Tom gives you access to both opportunities. Well, guess what, you're not getting him and you're not pushing me out of my job. You've lost this battle, Becker, and if you want to make a war of it, you'll lose that as well.'

'I'm amazed by your devious thinking,' she said. 'But you're getting me mixed up with yourself. I want Tom therefore I shall have him, one way or another. Why don't you sit on Flynn's face while you're watching this space? You seem to like him well enough.'

Before I could answer, the swing-door bashed open to admit a worried-looking Asia. 'Have you seen Mel anywhere?' she asked anxiously.

'She's not been through here,' I said.

Asia threw up her hands. 'Damn it! She's going to kill me.'

'What's wrong?' asked Janice.

Asia sagged forlornly. 'I was told she'd gone off with a man. But she's so rat-arsed, she won't know what she's doing. I was supposed to be keeping an eye on her.'

Janice lifted her shoulders indifferently. 'I wouldn't

worry about it. Mel's a very big girl – she can take care of herself.'

'But you don't understand,' wailed Asia. 'This man – the one she's gone off with – it's Plug!'

'If she's as drunk as all that, we'd better call an ambulance,' I suggested.

'Come on,' rallied Janice. 'We'll all go and look for her.'

As we were searching, I passed Flynn, reunited with his redhead. When he tried to ignore me, I tapped him on the shoulder. 'You think you have me all figured out, don't you, Flynn?'

The redhead looked at me frostily. 'Who's this?'

'Butt out, ginger,' I snarled at her. Then, pulling him to one side, I told him, 'What we did out there – it doesn't make me hate you any the less. I just wanted you to know that.'

He gave a clipped laugh. 'Do you think I care if Tom's little cock-slave likes me or not? I was just proving a point, baby.'

'You arrogant bastard. You're heading for a fall,' I warned him. 'And when you're lying flat on your arse, wondering what hit you, just look up and you'll see me laughing.' Then I returned his two-fingered salute with my own variation and strutted away.

Later that night, after I'd gone home, I thought about what I'd said to him. Was it physically possible to hate someone who could thrill me so much? Wasn't the very arrogance that I claimed to loathe a part of his attraction?

I knew that when it came to sex, my body was perfectly capable of detaching itself from my brain, enabling me to enjoy the pleasures of the flesh without any kind of emotional attachment. I actually preferred it that way – uncomplicated – because it suited my lifestyle.

But I hadn't always been so unromantic. Once, I'd 'made love' to a man: a man who'd owned my heart as well as my body; a man who'd once told me that my eyes darken to midnight blue when I'm aroused.

His name was Laurence Adams, and I'd fallen madly in love with him one long hot summer several years ago.

I'd met him at a party.

He was a student reading English Literature at university who looked every inch the romantic poet he aspired to be – gaunt and pale, with long black cavalier curls spilling over his shoulders, a clipped goatee beard and smoky green eyes. He was the most beautiful man I'd ever seen. It was love at first sight. But it was love like a butterfly – too perfect, too lovely to last.

We were lying in bed and I was teasing his nipple with a silky strand of my (then) waist-length hair.

'I love your hair' he said. 'I want to bathe in your river of golden hair.' Then he pressed my face to his beating heart and, drawing my hair over my head, splayed it across his chest.

My lips blazed a trail down his body. I kissed his belly, his cock, the inside of his leg, always dragging my hair behind me as I worked my way slowly down. I heard him sigh as my heavy tresses trickled over his manhood.

'What does it feel like?' I asked him.

'Like an angel's caress,' he answered rapturously. 'I'll show you.'

Rolling me onto my belly, he straddled me. 'Your milky white flesh tempts my tongue,' he purred, making me quiver as I felt the wetness of it flicking between my shoulder blades and then sliding down my spine, followed by the gentle sweep of his long hair. It was the most erotic caress I had ever known and, as the languid lapping of his tongue traversed the cheeks of my bottom, covering them with moisture, I whimpered with sheer delight. Drying me with his hair, he murmured huskily, 'Let's make love,' and flipped me over. But I had something to confess.

'Laurence,' I uttered softly. 'My darling Laurence. There is something I have to tell you.'

169

He kissed my forehead tenderly. 'What is it, my precious angel?'

'I think I might be pregnant.'

He sat bolt upright and stared at me in horror. 'But you can't be – you're on the pill.'

I looked at him helplessly. This wasn't the blissful reaction I'd been anticipating. 'I don't know how it happened. I'm not even sure that it has. I'm just a few days late, that's all.'

'You're never late.' He made it sound like an accusation.

I looked at him appealingly. 'Don't you think it would be beautiful to have a child of our love?'

He shook his head. 'I'm not ready to be a father. You'll have to get rid of it.' I'd never seen him so cold.

'But I love you, Laurence.' I pressed my hand to his cheek. 'I couldn't kill your baby, it's part of you.'

He snatched my hand away. 'It isn't part of me. It's one of several million sperm that I'll produce in my lifetime. If you've been stupid enough to let your egg get in its way then it's your own fucking fault. You should have been more careful.'

I stared at him in disbelief. Where was his poetry? Where was his bleeding soul? 'A minute ago, I was your precious angel,' I reminded him. 'I thought you loved me.'

'I thought so too,' he agreed. 'But I love my freedom more. I don't want to be trapped or tied down. How could you think of tricking me like this?'

'But I haven't,' I cried, with tears welling in my eyes. 'If I'm pregnant, it was an accident.'

He looked at me in disgust. 'I should never have trusted you. All women are devious. I should have stuck with men. Men understand my needs and never ask for more than I can give.'

I gaped at him in despair. 'What are you talking about?'

In an overtly feminine gesture, he flicked his hair behind his shoulder. 'I'm bisexual. Didn't you know?'

* * *

Looking back, I should have guessed: Laurence had been far too liberal and much too beautiful to be conventionally heterosexual. And I had been ludicrously naïve to think that someone so ethereal could give up his bohemian lifestyle for the drudgery of fatherhood.

In the event, it had been a false alarm and I'd emerged from the affair with no greater damage than a heart smashed to pieces and some cynical misgivings about romantic love.

But I'd forgiven Laurence, although perhaps not completely. Hadn't Flynn's hair been the first thing that I'd noticed about him? How richly black it was, like Laurence's. And if this one small thing had reminded me for a second of the man who'd crushed me emotionally, then no wonder I was scared of Flynn and disliked him more than he deserved.

What the hell was I thinking? Don't go there, I warned myself sharply. Keep away. Keep away from those thoughts. I shook my head to clear them from my mind as I poured out two cups of coffee and carried them through to the lounge.

'Wake up, Mel,' I called, nudging her with my foot.

She was sprawled on my sofa where the taxi driver had unceremoniously deposited her. She'd been sleeping for over an hour. I put the cups down and poked her. 'Wake up, Mel,' I repeated. 'I've made you some coffee.'

Stirring, she opened an eye. 'What time is it?' she asked blearily.

'Coming up to midnight.'

The information roused her into a sitting position. 'Midnight? Bloody hell, the old man will go spare.'

'Don't worry,' I reassured her. 'I phoned him to say you'd be late.'

She rubbed her face with her hands. 'He must have thought it was strange – you phoning and not me.'

'I told him we'd kidnapped you to take you clubbing and that you were tied up and gagged in the car,' I revealed. 'I don't think he'd be surprised if you didn't go home tonight. You're welcome to stay, Mel.'

She shook her head. 'I have to go home. We're taking the kids to the seaside tomorrow. I'll be OK when I've drunk this.' I noticed that her hand was swaying as she reached for her cup.

'You're still pretty pissed,' I pointed out.

She squinted at me. 'My head's still swimming. I think it's trying to cross the Channel. I guess I must have had a few too many "slammers" tonight.'

'What happened?' I asked her. 'We found you in the alley, sitting on a dustbin, fast asleep. Can you remember what you were doing out there?'

'Oh yes,' she nodded dreamily. 'I was having it off with Plug.'

'With Plug?' I scrunched up my face. 'Feel free to throw up, Mel – I know I would.'

'He was fucking ace,' she declared wondrously. 'Who'd have thought it? Admittedly, I'd probably have enjoyed it more if he'd worn a bag over his head. But he was amazingly good with his hands. Do you know, he must have finger-fucked me for forty-five minutes. What good-looking man would do that?'

'But Plug?' I repeated. 'God, Mel, if he entered a beauty contest for bloodhounds, he'd come last.'

'But that's the thing about ugly blokes,' she insisted. 'Who cares if they're enjoying themselves or not? You can just let yourself go and be totally selfish.'

I gave her a sceptical look. 'Personally, I think I'd sooner be selfish with a dildo made out of a pig's trotter. Surely you're not intending to do it again, are you?'

She thought about it. 'I'd need to be just as drunk,' she admitted. 'If he wanted to shag me sober, he'd have to tie me up and blindfold me first!'

Chapter Sixteen

'What are you laughing at?' Tom uttered irritably. 'This isn't supposed to be funny.'

'I was just thinking about something a friend said,' I giggled.

In truth, I was a bundle of nerves. I felt vulnerable and exposed, lying spread-eagled on the bed without a stitch on my body while Tom secured my wrists to the headboard and my feet to a couple of chairs that he'd placed at the end of my divan.

'You're not planning on doing anything unpleasant, are you?' I asked anxiously.

'On the contrary,' he said, tying a final knot in the silk scarf around my ankle. 'You're going to like this a lot.' He stood back to admire his handiwork. 'You look delectable,' he murmured, rubbing his naked cock lewdly. Somehow he seemed even bigger and broader than usual.

I tested my bonds. 'Did you have to tie them so tightly?'

He straddled me. 'I can't have you escaping,' he said, disregarding the fact that the weight of his body alone was enough to restrain me.

As he scooped up my breasts in his hands and suckled

them in turn, I began to relax. Perhaps this wouldn't be too much of an ordeal after all. Being highly sensitive, my breasts had their own hotline to my libido and within seconds I was making little whimpering sounds of pleasure. Hearing them incited the beast in Tom as, with increasing roughness, he nibbled and gnawed at my nipples until I was forced to utter a protest. 'You're hurting me.'

'I know,' he said, looking up to reveal a frenzied flicker of lust in his eyes. Then, taking my nipples between his forefingers and thumbs, he pinched them painfully. 'I can do anything I like with you.'

Wide-eyed and fearful, I tensed as he bared his teeth and clamped them to my breast. But when his bite was no more than a squeeze, I shivered in relief, swearing, 'You fucker, you bastard.'

'Don't get complacent,' he said, pinching my nipples again. 'And don't call me names.' Then he lowered his head and trailed his tongue across my bosom, blissfully soothing my tortured teats.

'Pig,' I tested him, this time enjoying the wincing pain as he twisted my nipples spitefully.

It became a game of alternate pain and pleasure, which made my hot swollen breasts so excruciatingly sensitised, that every touch added more kindling to the spluttering fire in my loins.

Tom probed my throbbing sex with his finger. 'That's nice – you're getting wet. But let's not rush things,' he said, glancing at his watch. He slid off my body to collect another scarf from the chair: a black one.

'What's that for?' I asked, surprised by own eagerness.

'To make it even more interesting,' he replied, lifting my head. I didn't object as he tied the blindfold around my eyes. Curiously, I felt less naked with it on.

He laid my head back down and spread my hair over the pillows as if he was preparing me for some kind of ritual.

'What are you doing now?' I asked as he moved away. When he answered, I realised that he'd gone to the foot of the bed.

'I'm going to give you a little hairdo,' he said, stroking my pubic hair with something that felt like a baby's brush.

I wriggled as the soft pliant fibres tickled my bush. 'That feels nice.'

He teased the brush hairs into the tight little curls of my thatch and, as he started brushing, they scraped across the delicate skin underneath, making my sex clench.

Then, stroking the feathery bristles back and forth across my vulva, he parted my lips with his fingers to expose my distended clitoris. I gasped in excitement, shuddering as my bud experienced the gentle scratching of the brush. It was a wild new sensation but I was soon bucking my hips in frustration, craving something more substantial.

'Are you ready for a fuck now?' Tom asked hoarsely.

'Yes, yes, I'm ready.' I struggled with my bonds, desperate to pull him on top of me.

'I can feel that you are,' he said, pushing his finger inside my vagina. I tried to grind myself onto it, but he snatched it out. Then he probed me with something that wasn't his finger. It felt cool and rigid and I guessed it was the blunt end of the brush. As he wriggled it inside me, I wasn't sure if I liked it. But, before I could protest, he'd withdrawn it and replaced it with two fingers, which he thrust in and out of me until I was squirming and panting and pleading for sex.

'Don't be so impatient,' I heard him say. 'The best is yet to come.'

I wailed as his fingers sucked out of me. 'What are you doing?' And when I heard the door click: 'Where are you going?'

'I'm going to get another toy,' he answered casually.

'Tom!' I exclaimed, twisting towards his voice. 'You can't leave me like this!'

He gave a throaty chuckle. 'I can do anything I like with you.'

He was only gone for a couple of minutes, but it seemed much longer as I lay there, helpless and alone, plaintively calling his name.

When, at last, he came back, I sensed him standing over me. I could hear his breathing, hot and heavy. 'What are you going to do, Tom?' There was a tremble in my voice.

He didn't answer but moved down to the end of the bed. Then I felt his hand, hot and clammy, turning my leg to one side so that his tongue could slide up my calf. As it slithered, wet and sensual, into my knee-pit and then out along my inner thigh, a tremor of anticipation shivered through my body as I realised where he was going.

Lapping and licking, it crawled slowly towards my quivering sex, inch by agonising inch. I was so breathless with tension, I thought my lungs would burst. And when, at last, the muscled meat of his tongue thrust between my labia, I arced my back, driving my sex into his face.

An uncontrollable moan gurgled from my lips as he flicked and lashed at my clit, sensationally alternating between chewing and sucking on my nub and delving deep inside me with dog-like slurps. The sizzling excitement searing through my loins had me jerking and threshing so violently that he was forced to anchor my hips to the bed with his hands. My womb was churning like it was being rotated on a spit. Then, suddenly, and with a huge cry, I went into an orgasmic spasm, squirting hot juice into his face as my body convulsed. A long sigh accompanied a rumbling aftershock of ecstasy, which, as it faded away, drained all my strength. As I flopped, exhausted, Tom pulled away from me.

I was only dimly aware of him moving about. I thought I heard the door open and close, but I wasn't sure. It was followed by another sound, a scuffling sound from outside the room. 'Tom?' I craned my head. 'Are you still here?'

'I'm still here.' He must have been standing by the door. 'Did you like that?'

I sighed contentedly. 'It was incredible. You've never done anything like that before. You always said it wasn't your thing.'

'It still isn't my thing,' he admitted.

'But you're so good at it.'

'Am I?' He laughed and came over to me. 'Well, I'm glad you enjoyed my little surprise.' He clambered on top of me and as he eased the blindfold from my eyes, I saw a strange look of triumph on his face. 'But I'm not as good as you think I am.'

I frowned at him in puzzlement. 'It's not like you to be modest, Tom. You were great, and I think it's wonderful that you did that for me, especially if you don't like it.'

'I don't like doing it,' he agreed. 'But I like watching it. You should have seen your face, Pam. You were so enraptured. You're a joy to observe, do you know that?'

'What do you mean, "observe"? How could you even see my face with your head in my crack?'

He smiled slowly, wickedly. 'It wasn't me.'

'What!' I exploded, yanking furiously on the scarves. 'What are you saying?'

'It wasn't me,' he repeated, enjoying my fury. 'It was someone else. But you were so high on lust, you didn't even notice. I was banking on that.'

'You bastard!' I spat at him. 'Who the fuck was it? A man, a woman, some tramp off the street? For God's sake tell me, Tom.'

'I'm never going to tell you,' he said, smoothing my hair from my face. 'I'm going to keep it a secret.'

I threshed underneath him. 'Get off me!' I yelled. 'Untie me!'

I felt his cock, warm and rigid, against my pubis. My anger was exciting him. 'I haven't finished yet,' he murmured softly, nosing his helmet into my bush.

'Don't you dare – I'll scream the place down,' I warned him, thrashing wildly.

He clamped his hand over my mouth. 'Do you know what I love about you, Pam? You're too sexy to fight me for long. I wonder how many inches it will take to break down your resistance. One?' He shunted his cock into the neck of my vagina. 'Two?'

Fighting the urge to contract my internal muscles, I speared him with my eyes and spat a torrent of muffled abuse into the gag of his palm.

'Three?' he grunted, pushing his cock deeper. 'Four?' In spite of myself, I gripped it. He seemed so omnipotent and my awareness of his power was flooding into my senses like an aphrodisiac. I could see the corded muscles in his arms as he held himself above me. I could smell his male musk permeating through his aftershave. I could feel his hot pulsing cock inside my sex. And, as he rammed it in all the way, my eyes rolled to the top of my head and I was lost.

I didn't care that he was laughing and mocking me with his eyes as I groaned and lifted my haunches to meet every dominant downward thrust. I didn't care that his fingers were digging into me or that his teeth were gnawing my neck. I wanted him to feast on me, to hurt me, to bludgeon me with his cock. To tear me to pieces, to rip me apart. To maul me, crush me, choke me with his tongue.

I loved that he was grunting like a pig. I loved the reek of our sweat, steaming and squelching, as the heat of our bodies pumped oily wetness through our pores. I relished the wantonness, the abandonment, the euphoria of absolute surrender. I held nothing back. I let it all go, crying with relief as I came.

Seconds later, Tom's climax ploughed into me like a train. His face contorted as he bellowed. Then he slumped on my body as if someone had shot him.

For a long time, neither of us moved. Then, slowly, he lifted his head to reveal a look in his eyes far softer than I'd ever seen before. 'I love you,' he told me, cradling my face in his hands with more tenderness than he'd ever shown. 'I love you.' He kissed my cheeks, my eyes, my lips. 'I love you, I love you, I love you.'

'Untie me,' I asked him gently.

When he'd released my wrists and ankles, he tried to gather me into his arms but I pulled back. He looked puzzled. 'Didn't you hear what I said?'

'Oh, but you said it too late, Tom,' I advised him coldly. 'Much too late.' Then I drew my arm back and struck him across his face with all the force I could muster. 'Get out!' I commanded. 'Get out of my house!'

Visibly shocked, he clutched his cheek. 'What the hell's got into you?'

I picked up the nearest thing – an alarm clock – and hurled it at him. 'Fuck off, you son of a bitch!' I shrieked. 'How dare you bring some stranger in here to do that to me? How dare you sit and watch, knowing full well that I thought it was you? What do you take me for? I'm not some goddamn whore to be passed around.'

'But you loved it,' he insisted. 'You loved every bit of it.'

'You don't understand me at all,' I raged. 'The only thing you know is what my body loves. I'm not my sex drive, Tom. I'm not as liberated as my libido would like me to be. You've gone too far. Can't you see that?'

He was putting on his clothes. 'I thought you'd enjoy it. I thought we were the same.'

I pulled the duvet around me to cover myself. 'We're not the same.'

'You've made your point,' he said, buttoning his shirt. 'I won't invite anyone else next time.'

'There isn't going to be a next time,' I told him firmly. 'I've done what you wanted and now it's over.'

'No it isn't,' he said, sitting on the edge of the bed to pull on his socks. 'Do you think, after tonight, that I could ever let you go?' He reached out to touch me but, shrinking back, I drew my knees up to my chest. 'You make me feel like no other woman can,' he murmured softly. 'When I'm fucking you, I'm a giant. I'm Samson. I'm Hercules. You're a drug to me, Pam. I need you.'

'You've been a drug to me too,' I admitted. 'You inject me with your big fat cock and I get a buzz that lifts me higher than a kite. But I won't have you treating me like some junkie who'd do anything for a fix. I mean to kick this dirty habit once and for all.'

'Why give up something you enjoy?' he wondered. 'Is there someone else?'

I thought briefly of Flynn. 'No, there's no one else. I'm just sick of being an addict.'

He pulled on his jacket. 'Just remember, Pam. This business with Darren has put you in the palm of my hand.' He splayed his fingers and then slowly closed them into a tight fist. 'Do you get the picture?'

When I shook my head defiantly, he yanked the duvet from my fingers and, brutally grabbing my breast, squeezed until his nails were almost biting into my skin. 'Who's the boss?'

'You are,' I whimpered.

He stroked a finger down my face. 'Next time I tie you up, you'll be face down, chewing your pillow as I fuck you up the arse.'

After he'd gone, I rushed to the bathroom and retched into the toilet but, when I couldn't make myself physically sick, I ran a scalding hot bath and scrubbed every trace of Tom and his unknown accomplice from my body. Then I sat up all night thinking of how I could break his hold over me.

On Sunday morning, I woke up in the chair with a crick in my neck and with soreness around my breast where fingermark bruises had formed. I still hadn't thought of a solution to my problem but, later that day, one presented itself unexpectedly.

I was doing some ironing when the doorbell rang. Since I wasn't expecting anyone, it occurred to me that it might be Tom. I looked at the hot iron speculatively. Perhaps I could just smash it across his face? I answered the door, armed with the iron, just in case.

I was stunned to find Darren on my doorstep. 'What the fuck do you want, you butt-licking piece of shit?' I blasted at him.

He stepped back in amazement. 'I . . . I just wanted to say goodbye,' he stammered. 'I won't be going back to the office again.'

I gaped at him.

'You wanted to say goodbye after what you did?' I brandished the iron. 'I ought to flatten your face, you twisted little creep.'

'I haven't done anything,' he protested. 'Why are you so angry with me?'

'Are you trying to tell me that you didn't cook up this sexual harassment thing just to get yourself a transfer to France?'

He stared at me uncomprehendingly. 'I have no idea what you're talking about.' His face was such a picture of innocence that I didn't know what to make of him.

'You'd better come in,' I said.

I sat him down on the sofa and, plonking myself in a chair opposite, I told him to tell me exactly what had happened on Thursday.

His face became sullen. 'After you'd made it crystal clear that what we did in the stock room meant nothing to you, I realised my position was untenable. It would be far too embarrassing to carry on working with you knowing that I'd ... that we'd ... that my ...'

'Yes, yes,' I hurried him. 'I know what we did.'

But remembered lust had infiltrated his thoughts, making him obstinate. 'I had my prick in your crack,' he stated daringly. 'I had my hands on your tits. We would have done it if Mr Carson hadn't interrupted us.' He licked his dry lips. 'I couldn't bear the idea of watching you every day, going over and over it in my mind. That's why I asked Mr Carson for the transfer.'

I leaned forward. 'You didn't complain that I'd sexually harassed you?'

He threw up his hands in denial. 'Are you kidding? What kind of nerd would do that?'

I could see that he was telling the truth. I rubbed my forehead in perplexity. 'Then why would he say that you did? Did he question you about what happened in the stock room?'

'He did more than that,' Darren asserted. 'He made me repeat every word and describe every detail. I didn't want to, but he told me that I wouldn't get my transfer otherwise.'

It was slowly dawning on me that Tom had manipulated us both. From the information he'd gained from Darren, he'd concocted a story to blackmail me and keep me suppliant to him. It had never occurred to me that he would go to such devious lengths to hang onto me. And he might have got away with it but for Darren calling round to say goodbye.

'I'm sorry I gave you such a bizarre reception,' I told him. 'I misjudged you, Darren. Tom let me think that you were out to cause trouble for me.'

'But why?' he asked, bewildered.

'Because he's a control freak. He likes to own people. He likes to call the tune and make us all dance like puppets. But I'm not dancing for him any more, Darren. I'm breaking my strings and, just as soon as I'm free, I'm breaking his balls. Or maybe I'll leave that to someone else. Maybe I'll throw him into the path of a certain she-wolf that I know and watch her devour him piece by piece.'

Chapter Seventeen

*I*was still so angry with Tom on Monday morning that, had I been going to work, I would undoubtedly have armed myself with an assortment of potentially harmful kitchen utensils, such as a steak tenderiser or a garlic press. So it was probably just as well that I wasn't going in. He was, after all, still a shareholding director of the company, whereas my own position within it was hardly pivotal. Under these conditions, I considered it unwise to tackle him without first forming an allegiance with someone of equal authority.

It seemed a fortunate coincidence that a man with just these credentials would be delivering himself to my door within the hour.

Whilst I still had reservations about Roger Fielding, I had revised my opinion of him since the conference, deciding that his sexual advances had been more hopeful than predatory and, if starved of encouragement, could be easily deflected. He was a businessman foremost and in this lay the means of currying favour with him in other ways. I reasoned that if I pulled out all the stops to help him win his contract, I stood to gain a vital ally. With this in mind, I put on the skimpiest bikini I owned, which comprised four silver triangles tied together with silver string. I covered the whole thing with a sun dress, applied plenty of waterproof makeup and let my hair hang loose and sexy. When Roger called for me at eleven o'clock, I could see he was impressed.

'You look stunning,' he said. 'I'm quite sure you'll be able to distract Mr Miller from the number of zeros on his quotation.'

'Exactly how many zeros are we talking about?' I asked. 'What's the contract worth, Roger?'

He glanced at me sideways. 'A million and a half, give or take a couple of quid. And that's just the tip of the iceberg. This guy owns a chain of hotels in the Middle East, that's a lot of lifts, lavs and lighting, not to mention our new security system. I'm not suggesting or expecting you to do anything beyond the call of duty, Pam – unless you want to. But it's important to me that you're nice to him and let him down gently if he overreaches himself.'

'I gather he's done that with Janice,' I commented.

Roger shrugged. 'That was a case of her being a little overzealous with her flirting. Miller misread the signals and thought she was coming on to him. He's not the kind of man to be led by a nose-ring and then left to graze on gravel. So – watch your step.'

The pool party was in full swing by the time we arrived at Mr Miller's country home – a rambling mansion with twenty acres. There seemed to be a lot of Arabs present and many of the women were covered from head to feet, some wearing veils across their faces. Conspicuous in my immodest sun dress and with my Scandinavian looks, I attracted a lot of attention.

We were met by an underling of some kind who immediately apologised for Mr Miller's absence, explaining that he'd been detained at the Saudi-Arabian Embassy but would be joining us later. We were invited to circulate among the guests and make ourselves at home.

Waiters carrying drinks and delicacies on silver gilt trays descended on us from all sides as we wove our way to the poolside where a handful of men had stripped to their swimming trunks despite the black clouds and ominous rumbles of thunder in the distance.

Spotting a familiar face, Roger hauled me by the hand to meet a man that he described in an undertone as another potential customer.

'Sal, I'd like you to meet Pamela Roberts. She's standing in for Janice today.'

Sal's dark eyes flickered over me approvingly. 'Where do you find all these lovely girls, Roger?' He lifted my hand to his lips and I couldn't help noticing how pale it looked against his darkly tanned skin. But not so pale as the teeth that flashed with biological whiteness in a face that would have been very attractive but for a long hooked nose. He put his arm around me. 'Shall you be swimming today, Miss Roberts, or taking notes?'

'I hope to do both,' I said, pirouetting out of his grasp. 'But the weather doesn't seem too clever at the moment.'

'Pah,' he threw up his hands. 'Your ruddy English weather is as volatile as a mistress. The only thing that can be said for your climate is its congeniality for growing beautiful and fragrant English roses.' He was delighted when I blushed at the compliment. 'She is charming,' he told Roger.

Roger patted me on the back like a father. 'She's also a very good PA,' he said generously. 'Sal is interested in VoiceCom's shower units, Pam,' he informed me. 'Perhaps you can convince him to buy a few while I go and see who else is here.' Then, leaving me with Sal, he wandered off into the crowd.

I felt awkward and out of my depth. 'I'm not a saleswoman,' I advised Sal, 'but I'll do my best. There are four voice commands: hot, plus hot and cold, more cold. Or is it more hot?' I bounced the thought from eyeball to eyeball. 'I'm not really sure, to tell you the truth.'

Sal seemed more interested in peering down my cleavage. 'What about you?' he asked. 'Are you hot or more hot?'

'I'm quite cold actually,' I said. 'I think it's about to rain. Everyone's going inside.'

'What is the point of a pool party if not to get wet?' Sal speculated, shrugging off his shirt. 'I am going for a swim. Will you join me?'

As the first drops of rain began to splatter on my face, I saw Roger running for cover. He'd abandoned me. 'Is it a heated pool?' I asked Sal.

He was taking off his trousers. 'Probably plus hot,' he answered with a smile. 'Come on,' he urged me. 'There are only two others in there – we shall have it almost to ourselves.'

What the hell, I thought, unbuttoning my sun dress. I was here to make an impression and Sal was a potential customer. But as I shrugged out of my dress to reveal the inadequacy of my bikini, the heated appreciation in Sal's eyes made me doubt my own wisdom.

The two men already in the pool cheered and shouted in Arabic as I descended the steps while Sal dived in. Then they made a beeline for me, splashing me with their hands. I eluded them by diving under the water and swimming to the deep end where, emerging to peer over the side, I saw that, apart from the four of us, the terrace had emptied.

Sal came shearing through the water like a shark and I squealed as he playfully pulled me under.

'Hey, Sal, don't keep her to yourself,' one of the men called out. 'We want to play with her as well.' Then the three of them began chasing me around the pool. Eventually, I held up my hands, exhausted. 'Game over. I'm out of breath.' They circled around me as I trod water, and commented to one another in their own tongue.

'They're saying you're very beautiful,' Sal told me.

'They admire your pale skin and would like to see more of it.'

'I'm getting out now,' I said nervously.

Sal put a restraining arm around my shoulders. 'Don't be shy, little mermaid. We only want to look.'

'We just want to play,' said the older of the other two. He was thickset and swarthy and I didn't like the way he was looking at me.

The younger one, who had a mop of curly black hair, suddenly dipped beneath the water and, grabbing my legs, pulled me under. As I struggled back to the surface, I felt his hands pawing my body.

Wriggling away from him, I swam to the side, hoping to hoist myself out, but they gathered around me, boxing me in. Then Sal caught me round the waist and thrust my hand inside his trunks, pinning it to the slippery snake of his erection. As I fought to free myself, other hands began fiddling at my back, neck and thighs. All three of them were trying to loosen the strings holding my bikini together. Every time I opened my mouth to protest, Sal dunked me under the water and it was all I could do to keep breathing. As my bikini top was dragged from my breasts, I heard him groan, 'Look at her pretty pink rosebuds. Aren't they beautiful?'

'She has blonde pussy!' exclaimed another gleefully as my two remaining triangles parted company. Then, between them, they lifted my naked lower half to the surface where they examined my bush excitedly.

As I threshed to keep my head above water, their fingers prodded and probed, drilling into my sex, poking into my anus. There seemed to be dozens of hands grabbing fistfuls of flesh or slipping and sliding all over me.

'Spread her, boys,' barked Sal.

The two men took an arm and a leg each and split me into an 'x'.

'Wider,' urged Sal, peering lustfully into the open flower of my sex.

'Oh please, oh no!' I cried, as I saw him coming towards me with his cock in his hands.

'Dunk her,' he rasped.

'Wait!' I pleaded. 'I'll play!'

He held up his hand. 'What game, little mermaid?'

'Call off these gorillas and I'll bring you off manually,' I promised.

'Very well,' he agreed. 'Let her go, boys.'

Grumbling and cursing, the two men released me, and then swam to the side to watch as Sal removed his trunks.

'Don't touch me at all,' I dictated, clenching my fist around his prick and glaring into his eyes.

'Let me hold your arse,' he bargained, 'and I won't touch anything else.'

Disgusted by him, I closed my eyes as I pumped his shaft, hating the fingers that dug into my flesh and the grunting sounds of excitement that drove his hot breath blasting into my face.

Then, suddenly, I thought of Flynn and a crazy idea entered my head that, in some parallel universe, I could just as easily be wanking him. I could see his face contorting in ecstasy as my hands slid up and down his cock. I could see his face so clearly, his black eyes fiery with passion, and I groaned at the thought of him loving the touch of my hands.

I was so turned on by my fantasy that when fingers wriggled into my sex, I didn't object. They were Flynn's and I wanted them there. Then Flynn's hands were grasping my breasts and teasing my nipples to tautness as his cock throbbed in my hand. His mouth was kissing me roughly, hungrily, and I was kissing him back as if my life depended on it.

'Oh Flynn,' I gasped, squeezing his cock.

Then Sal climaxed, swearing in Arabic, and I snapped

out of my trance to find all three of them groping me again. As I struggled to get away, the older one grasped my head and pushed it below the water to where the younger one's cock was waiting. Then they both tried to force it into my mouth.

Biting and threshing, I fought my way to the surface and somehow found the breath to holler for help.

To my relief, someone shouted in reply. It was a stern, commanding voice, which had an immediate effect on my assailants who let go of me at once. As I cleared water from my eyes, I heard the voice speaking in English. 'Bitten off more than you can chew again, Pam?'

As I turned round to face the speaker, I heard Sal say, 'We weren't hurting her, Mr Miller. We were just having fun.'

'Mr Miller?' I looked up. The face of my saviour was older but easily recognisable. 'Luke!' I exclaimed. 'Or is Jason?'

Laughing, he lowered his trunks to show me his birthmark. Then he threw me a towel. 'You're the last person I would have expected to find cavorting in my pool.' When I'd covered myself, he hauled me out. 'What are you doing here?'

'Miller.' I shook my head in disbelief. 'It's such a common name. It didn't cross my mind for a minute that it might be you. My God, Luke, is this all yours?'

He gave me a hug. 'I've moved up in the world, as you can see.'

'What of Jason?' I queried.

'He's doing OK. He's an airline pilot. But, never mind about that. Tell me why you're here.'

'I'm here with Roger Fielding. I'm his PA,' I explained.

'VoiceCom? What happened to the busty Miss Becker?'

'She's at a funeral,' I told him. 'I'm standing in for her today but I actually work for Tom Carson in P&P.'

'I don't think I've met him,' he said. 'Look, I'd really love to catch up but there are a lot of people waiting to see me. Could you stick around to the end and we'll talk later?'

'I'd like to,' I said, retrieving my rain-drenched sun dress, 'but my clothes are soaking wet.'

'I'll have someone take you upstairs and kit you out,' he said. 'My live-in girlfriend, Sonia, has a dressing room full of clothes.'

'Won't she mind?' I wondered.

He winked at me. 'She's in Saudi.' He put his arm around my shoulders and steered me inside. Roger pounced on him at once. 'I see you've met Pamela, Mr Miller,' he said.

Luke kissed my cheek. 'We're old friends.' He summoned the man who had greeted us at the door. 'Take Pam upstairs and find her something to wear,' he instructed. Then he told Roger, 'Give me half an hour and I'll take a look at those figures.'

By five o'clock all the guests, including Roger, had left, leaving Luke and me to ourselves and, as we sat reminiscing, he raised the subject of how and why we'd split up.

'I've never forgotten that night,' he confessed, dropping his voice to a husky purr. 'It was some of the best sex I've ever had.' He squeezed my knee over the pedal-pushers I'd borrowed from Sonia's wardrobe, making me suddenly conscious of my nakedness underneath.

'The pair of you behaved like animals,' I reminded him. 'You brutalised me. I could have reported you both for rape.'

'But you didn't,' he said, stroking his hand up my thigh. 'Do you remember how you sucked Jason's cock while I fucked you from behind?' He trailed his thumb over my crotch.

'I remember,' I said, letting his finger rub for a second between my legs as I savoured the memory. Then I plucked his hand from my lap. 'That was a long time ago,' I said firmly.

'Nothing changes though, does it?' he countered. 'How many did you have in my pool? Three of them, wasn't it?'

'Those men were barracuda,' I stressed. 'I don't know what would have happened if you hadn't shown up when you did.'

He laughed. 'It could only happen to you, Pam. You seem to bring out the beast in men. I'd like to ravish you myself, but I'm a respectable businessman these days.'

'That's what I stayed for – to talk business,' I said. 'A contract with Miller Enterprises would mean a lot to VoiceCom.'

'What would it mean to Pamela Roberts?' he wondered.

'Promotion,' I told him bluntly.

He scratched his jaw. 'It seems we both have something the other wants,' he deduced. 'Would you care to negotiate an exchange?'

It was a telling question. Just how far was I prepared to go to secure my promotion? 'I'm not sure,' I hedged. 'I'd like to think about it.'

'Take your time,' he said. 'I won't be seeing Jason until next week anyway.'

I stared at him. 'What does Jason have to do with this?'

He rubbed his hands together. 'That's the deal, Pam. The three of us together, just like the old days. Don't look so surprised, it's a very big contract. Why don't you give it some thought and call me in a couple of days?'

I wanted to tell him exactly where he could shove his proposal, but since I didn't want to ruin VoiceCom's chances altogether, I agreed to mull it over. Content with my response, he dispatched his driver to take me home.

The telephone was ringing as I opened the door. It was Roger Fielding.

'How did it go? Did Miller mention the contract?' he wanted to know.

'It was an interesting reunion,' I replied. 'We talked about old times.'

'But the contract, Pamela,' he prompted me. 'Did you talk about the contract?'

'It's in the bag, Roger,' I answered dully. 'If you're willing to add a new clause.'

'And what's that?' His voice sounded flat, as if he could guess what I was about to say.

'He wants me to sleep with him,' I supplied.

'Oh.' There was a long moment of silence, then Roger said gravely, 'He's a dirty sod. I'm sorry if he's embarrassed you, Pam. Did he say we wouldn't get the contract if you didn't do what he asked?'

I thought back. 'Not exactly but I think that was the implication.'

'Then we'll call his bluff,' Roger decided. 'Let him stew for a few days, then ring and tell him you're not interested. Will you do that for me?'

I was surprised. I had been half-expecting him to try and cajole me. 'Of course,' I agreed. 'But what if he isn't bluffing? I could lose the contract for you.'

Roger chuckled. 'I know you didn't like Sal, but he's a very useful contact. He doesn't often dish out snippets of information but, when he does, they're usually hot off the press. Today, he told me something very interesting: there's a certain oil-rich sheikh who has specifically requested VoiceCom products to be installed in his favourite hotels. We have our Mr Miller over an oil barrel, Pam, and it's all thanks to you.'

I was baffled. 'Thanks to me? How?'

'Sal seemed to think that you earned the information. I don't know what you did, but it's given VoiceCom the edge. I might even be able to add a few zeros. I'll let you know what happens.'

I replaced the receiver with a whoop of joy. I'd not only gained Roger as an ally but my prospects for promotion had soared. I decided to celebrate with a bubble bath and a chilled bottle of wine.

I'd been languishing for almost an hour when the doorbell rang. At first, I ignored it, but when it rang more insistently, I got out of the bath and, throwing on a robe, ran dripping down the hall.

When I opened the door my heart vaulted a double-back somersault as Flynn staggered into my arms.

Chapter Eighteen

'You're drunk!' I exclaimed as he reeled in, reeking of whisky.

'That's right,' he agreed. 'I'm fucking drunk.' He back-heeled the door, kicking it shut and then, rounding on me, stabbed an accusatory finger in my face, narrowly missing my nose. 'You got me fired. You got me roasted, you fucking bitch.' He thumped the palm of his hand against my shoulder, propelling me backward. 'They sent me a fucking e-mail – can you believe that? Nine years I've been working there and they send me a fucking e-mail.'

His drunken wrath scared me. 'Calm down, Flynn. Let me make you some coffee.'

He shoved me again. '"Dismissed for improper conduct",' he slurred. 'That's going to look fucking great on my CV don't you think?' He put his hand over my throat and drove me back against the wall. 'You warned me, didn't you? You said you'd be the one to trip me up. Are you laughing? You said you'd be laughing.'

I couldn't bear the fury in his eyes and looked away. 'I'm not laughing.'

He grasped my chin, forcing me to face him. 'You could have stopped me any time in that lift.'

'I did try to stop you,' I stressed.

'Oh, fuck off, Pam. Your feeble flapping didn't fool me for a minute. The invitation was right there in your face. You double-dared me with your eyes. How could you say I molested you against your will?' He pressed his body into mine. 'You wanted me right from the start.'

'That isn't true. I didn't realise . . .' I stopped myself too late.

'Didn't realise what?' He gloated. 'Come on, Pam, let's hear you say it.'

'You were way ahead of yourself,' I insisted, pushing him to arm's length. 'You should have waited for what you saw in my eyes to come out of my mouth. I didn't give you the green light, Flynn – you assumed it.'

'That colour was flashing long before we hit the ground floor,' he retorted. 'I seem to remember that you came like a fucking rocket. I guess you forgot to mention that when they asked you what I did to you.'

I shook my head slowly. 'I didn't make the complaint. You have to believe me, I didn't ask for any of this.'

He hooked my waist, viciously jackknifing me towards him so that my legs buckled and I had to cling to him for support. 'So you put my head in the noose to save your own neck, is that it?'

I wrenched myself from his grasp. 'It wasn't like that. I told them the truth and they drew their own conclusions.'

'The truth,' he echoed bitterly. 'What is the truth? I think it's time we found out what the truth really is.' Pinning me to the wall with his body, he unfastened the cord of my robe.

'Don't do this,' I pleaded. 'It won't solve anything.'

'Maybe not,' he agreed. 'But at least it'll prove that I wasn't wrong about you.' His hands drove into my robe. 'Resist me if you can, you slut.'

His face was so close to mine that I was breathing in his whisky breath and our lips were almost touching.

'You don't have to do this, Flynn,' I uttered desperately. 'We'll both know the truth if you kiss me.' The plea in my voice was unmistakable.

He pulled back and stared at me in disgust. 'Kiss you? I'd sooner spit in your face. This has nothing to do with what's going on in your head, Pam. This is between me and your body just like it was in the lift.' His black eyes were still discharging venom as his strong hands gripped my haunches. Then, stooping, he scraped his rough-shaven chin across my breasts, the prickling of his stubble instantly shocking my nipples to stiffness.

I trembled as his dark head descended down my body and I felt the pressure of his mouth on my flesh, erotically and deliberately French kissing my skin with all the passion he'd denied my lips. Every cell in my brain screamed to every cell in my body not to respond to this terrible blissful torture of knowing and yet not knowing his kiss: the velvet wetness of his tongue, the sensual movements of his mouth. I hated him for his cruelty. I wanted to hit him, to hurt him, but I didn't want him to stop. To appease myself, I did what I'd been aching to do for so long: I raked my fingers into his midnight hair, moaning his name.

He froze but didn't look up. Then, clawing my hands from his head, he gripped my arms fiercely and yanked me to my knees. 'You're not going to take any pleasure from this,' he warned me, bundling me onto my back and then rolling on top of me. 'I'm here to empty my balls and that's all.'

I didn't move as he wrestled drunkenly out of his trousers. I just lay there looking up at his face, filled with a strange sense of awe and wonder that my fantasy had become a reality. For this really was Flynn's face. Flynn's! And, in a moment, my body would be joined with his. I felt poised on the brink of an incredible discovery.

'Why aren't you struggling?' he growled. 'I'm going to fuck you so damn hard, you'll wish you'd put up a fight.

I'm going to use you like a sex doll and fill you with spunk, just like Tom does. And there's nothing you can do to stop me from taking what's mine.'

'You won't be taking anything,' I told him huskily. 'Because I'm giving it to you. Do you understand? I'm giving it to you, Flynn.'

But he was too drunk to understand. 'Then give it to me, you fucking bitch,' he snarled, plunging his cock deep into me. And, as it entered, a dam of emotion burst inside me, pushing my back into an arch so high that I thought my spine would snap. And, with it, came a long sigh, as if my very soul had been craving this union.

My ecstatic reaction stunned him. 'Look at you,' he uttered contemptuously. 'You don't care how you get it. It's all just cock.'

His words stabbed like daggers. How could he be so blind? This was like nothing I'd ever experienced before. Angrily, I answered, 'You're right – I love sex. But you knew that, didn't you?'

Suddenly his eyes were meltingly soft. 'Yes, I knew that.'

Dear God, don't look at me like that – not without kissing me!

'Get on with it, you bastard,' I urged him, undulating my hips to stir his cock inside me.

'Jesus fuck, what are you doing?' he groaned.

Using every bit of my strength, I tightened the walls of my sex around his cock, jerking him off with upward thrusts of my pelvis and, though he gritted his teeth and screwed up his eyes, his drink-weakened will was no match for my clenching muscles. I wanted him to come. I wanted to capture his sperm inside me and keep it there.

He was swearing and cursing, but he couldn't stop himself and, as I felt the torrential rush of his semen, I gave a final wringing squeeze to milk him dry.

It was more than his whisky-sodden brain could cope

with. His arms buckled, his eyes glazed over and then he passed out in my arms.

I held the dead weight of his body for a long time before rolling him onto his side. Then, cradling his head in my arm, I smoothed his hair and traced his features with my fingers: the black wings of his eyebrows, the feathery cluster of his long eyelashes, the straight line of his nose, the rugged manliness of his jaw.

'Oh Flynn,' I murmured softly and with sudden realisation. 'I love your face.'

I stroked my thumb across his mouth and it felt so warm and soft that I couldn't resist pressing my lips to his. And although they were slack and unresponsive, I kissed them over and over again and then I kissed every one of his features until at last, growing weary, I wrapped myself in his arms and fell asleep.

In the morning he was gone.

As I washed and dressed, I tried not to think of Flynn, but his face kept haunting me and, with it, the memory of the magical moment when he'd tapped into a vein of infinite pleasure that I hadn't even known existed within me. And what astonished me most was that he'd managed to do it whilst drunk, angry and full of hatred. It made me sick to my stomach that I'd made an enemy of a man who had the capacity to thrill me like no other. And it was all due to the interfering machinations of Janice Becker!

As soon as I arrived at work, I stormed into her office. 'I hope you're satisfied, Becker,' I hurled at her. 'Your spiteful meddling has cost Flynn his job.'

She looked up from buffing her nails. 'You seem to have a wasp in your knickers, Pam. I haven't the faintest idea what you're talking about.'

'I'm talking about Flynn,' I snarled. 'He's been fired thanks to you.'

She tilted her head. 'Flynn's been fired? You must be mistaken – the company can't function without him.'

I leaned over her desk to go eyeball to eyeball with her. 'Are you trying to tell me you that you don't know anything about it?'

She waved me away with her hands. 'No I don't. And unless you want this nail-file up your nose, I suggest you sit down and tell me.'

She'd taken the wind from my sails. Deflated, I plonked myself into a chair. 'Somebody put in a complaint about Flynn sexually abusing me in the lift. You were the only one I told, Janice. On Bethany's hen-night. It had to be you.'

She shook her head. 'It wasn't. I wouldn't do that to Flynn. He and I are –'

Like déjà-vu, her telephone rang at this crucial point, just as it had once before. Leaving me with the cliff-hanger: Flynn and I are what?

'No, I haven't seen her,' she said sharply into the phone. 'That was Tom,' she told me, putting it down. 'He's looking for you.'

'What were you about to say?' I prompted her.

'Oh yes . . . Flynn and I are related.' She looked at me archly as I sagged in relief. 'His brother is married to my cousin. You remember, I went to her wedding in Rio de Janeiro. James, his brother, has been trying to persuade him to join the family business in Brazil for a long time. I expect that's what he'll do if he can persuade his fiancée to go with him.'

'Fiancée?' I echoed dully. 'Flynn's engaged?'

'To the redhead,' she told me. 'The one he was with at Matt's Place the other night. I can't remember her name.'

It was like a mule-kick in my guts and it wasn't made any easier by seeing Janice gloating. 'There's always another woman, isn't there?' she said. 'There's always some bitch standing in the way.'

'You've got it all wrong,' I told her. 'I'm not interested

in Flynn. I just think he's been unfairly treated and I want to find out why.'

'How very charitable of you.' She commended me doubtfully.

'So, if it wasn't you who reported him, who was it?'

She spread her hands expansively. 'What difference does it make? What's done is done.'

'Who was it?' I persisted. 'Who did you tell?'

She lowered her gaze. 'I guess it must have been Tom.'

I thumped my fist on the desk. 'What the bloody hell did you have to tell Tom for?'

She gave me a calculating look. 'It was my passport into his pants. I told him what Flynn had done and I don't mind admitting that I suggested you must have enjoyed it or you would have reported him for sexual harassment. I only said it to make Tom jealous enough to get his own back on you by having a fling with me. Either he was angrier than I thought or something happened subsequently. It may interest you to know that Tom seems to think Flynn had something to do with your finding out about us. It looks like he's taken his revenge.'

I clamped my hand to my forehead as I realised what she was saying, for I was gloomily certain that I myself had told Tom that it was Flynn who'd revealed their affair to me.

Janice read the dismay in my face. 'So you're the one responsible for banging the nail into his coffin. That was pretty clumsy, Pam. You ought to know by now what a dirty fighter Tom is. I think we've both underestimated his obsession with you. He didn't do this just to damage Flynn – he's trying to block your promotion bid as well. He's determined to keep you with him, it seems.'

'You've no idea what that bastard is capable of,' I told her. 'You can have him, Janice, although you may not get him in one piece.'

'That's very generous of you,' she responded lightly.

'But after what Roger told me today, I don't think it's likely that Tom will risk an affair with me now.' I looked at her blankly. 'Sheila's pregnant,' she supplied. 'Tom's over the moon about it. They went out for a meal to celebrate last week, apparently.'

I stared at her in disbelief. 'He told me he didn't sleep with her,' I muttered idiotically.

She gave me an old-fashioned look. 'They all say that, Pam. What are you going to do?'

I pulled a grim face. 'I'm going to get Flynn reinstated and then I'll make Tom pay for what he's done.'

'It won't be easy getting Michael Main to change his mind,' she advised me. 'But, like most men, he has a weakness which I'm sure you'll know how to exploit. You'd better think about just how far you're prepared to go to help Flynn.'

As I left her office and made my way to Beryl Parker's, I thought about what she'd said. How much of myself was I willing to give to put things right with Flynn; to keep him from going to Brazil; to give myself another chance with him? The answer was simple: I'd do any-thing – anything at all!

I made an appointment to see Michael Main that after-noon; then I left the building and took a cab into town where I purchased a pair of black hold-up stockings with lacy tops, and a red-satin G-string. After putting them on under my clothes like battle-dress, I returned to the office feeling armed and ready for action.

'Where the hell have you been?' Tom rebuked me as I strolled in, two hours late. But he looked more worried than angry. 'I thought perhaps –'

'That I'd leave you? That I'd resign?' I finished for him. 'It's still an option, Tom.' It was hard keeping the bitter-ness from my voice and he looked at me suspiciously. 'Let me remind you that the taint of scandal will follow you even if you leave this company,' he threatened.

It was on the tip of my tongue to tell him that I knew he'd fabricated Darren's complaint but I'd worked out a plan of revenge that depended on his remaining ignorant of my knowledge. 'Then there's not much I can do,' I said, perching on the edge of his desk. 'Except enjoy your sexual fantasies with you.' He looked at my black-stockinged legs and his tongue slithered over his lips. 'But don't you think it would be fair to indulge me in one of mine?' I requested, stroking my hand over my thigh. 'There's one in particular that I've always wanted to try.'

'And what's that?' he croaked, sliding his own hand under mine. I smacked it from my leg. 'You can find out tonight.' I stood up. 'I've a lot to do. The Frenchman's arriving tomorrow. So, are we working late, or what?'

He nodded. 'You've got me intrigued,' he said. 'I'll ring Sheila and tell her not to expect me for dinner.'

Just to be sure that he didn't forget, I gave my hips an extra wiggle as I walked out of the door, wearing a smile on my face that would have troubled him deeply if he'd seen it.

I worked through my lunch break to make up for the time that I'd lost, but I couldn't seem to concentrate. My mind was firmly fixed on my impending interview with Michael Main and I was relieved when its allotted hour arrived.

His enormous office was dominated by a huge mahogany desk, built like a battleship with him, the commodore, controlling its helm. He was an imposing looking man in his fifties, heavy-jowled and thickset with iron-grey hair sweeping over a high forehead. I'd never liked his eyes: they were ice blue, with the bloodshot whites of a heavy drinker. His gaze, shrewd and frosty, gave nothing away as he looked at me. Though not unattractive, there was something about him that repulsed me. I nonetheless managed to smile flirtatiously as I greeted him.

'Good afternoon, Mr Main.'

He nodded as if banking my smile in his memory, but he didn't return it. He seemed vaguely displeased. 'Take a seat, my dear,' he instructed me.

I sat down and, as I crossed my legs slowly, he lowered his eyelids, covertly observing them in a way that indicated the presence of a red-blooded male beneath the icy exterior. The discovery encouraged me. 'I'd like to talk to you about Flynn Faraday,' I ventured.

'An unfortunate incident,' he remarked. 'I was rather hoping we might bury it.'

'I think he should be reinstated,' I declared.

He lifted his silvery eyebrows. 'I'm surprised to hear you say that.'

'He didn't deserve to be fired,' I went on. 'It was a stupid misunderstanding and it shouldn't have gone this far.'

'Confidentially, I agree with you,' he said. 'But the law is quite specific: when a charge of this nature is brought, the company has an obligation to examine it and then act on the findings.'

'But it wasn't serious enough to sack him,' I insisted.

He leaned back in his leather chair, tapping his fingertips together as he scrutinised me carefully. He seemed to be weighing something up in his mind. 'I gather you're rather fonder of Mr Faraday than you admitted in your statement.'

Colour flushed in my cheeks. I didn't know what to say. 'I . . . um . . . I wouldn't have wished this on anyone.'

He leaned forward. 'But we're discussing Mr Faraday in particular. Wouldn't you say that you're going out on a limb for him by making this appeal? You're asking the most senior executive of this company to reverse a decision. Why should I listen to you?'

I realised it was time to make my move. I pouted my lips. 'Because I'm asking you nicely.'

He drew a deep breath. 'I see.'

'Surely there must be something I can do to persuade you to reconsider?' I offered suggestively.

He looked at me sternly. 'Let me be clear about this,' he determined. 'Are you volunteering sexual favours in return for Mr Faraday's reinstatement, Pamela?'

It was the crunch moment. If I'd misjudged him as a man then I might as well have offered my own resignation. But as he waited for my answer, I saw a glimmer of anticipation flicker in his eyes. I stood up and, moving round to his side of the desk, slowly and provocatively lifted my skirt up one side to expose my white thigh above the black lace of my stocking top. 'This is the limb that I'm prepared to go out on,' I murmured seductively. 'Is that clear enough for you, Mr Main?'

Without taking his eyes from my leg, he reached out and pressed the intercom. 'Hold all my calls, Beryl,' he commanded, 'but let me know when my visitor arrives.' Then he looked at me with an expression of naked lust on his face. 'Very well, my dear,' he said lasciviously. 'You have my undivided attention.'

Chapter Nineteen

*I*f *the shudder inside me should permeate outwards, I will transform it into a tremble of desire with a moan so loud and ecstatic that his ego will persuade him he is turning me on. But nothing could be further from the truth.*

His hands disgust me: they are hot and clammy and I can feel their dampness through the sheer fabric of my stockings as, with agonising slowness, they crawl up my outer thighs, raising my skirt as they progress – inch by slithering inch.

Hurry up, hurry up, I am thinking. Slip your hand inside my panties and let my libido come to my rescue. My clit doesn't care who you are. Finger my trigger. Rub my nub. Get the endomorphs firing in my brain.

But he is taking forever and I swallow a lump of revulsion as he spreads his fingers so that his hands sprawl like starfish on my naked rear.

Hours seem to pass before he pulls the G-string from the crack of my arse and drags my panties to my feet. His lower lip is quivering wetly as I step out of them. Then, with tongue flicking like a lizard's, he buries his face in my bush. My moan sounds unconvincing and comes a fraction too late for the shudder that precedes it. But he doesn't notice – the bastard is deceived.

* * *

'I love eating pussy, especially blonde pussy,' he grunted into my sex. I didn't want to touch him but I was forced to grip his shoulders as he pushed my thighs apart and plunged his tongue between them.

I was angry with myself. I should have been responding by now. After all, he was only trying to pleasure me – I wasn't being flayed alive or burned at the stake for God's sake. Where was the cock-crazy slut that Flynn had identified? And it wasn't as if Michael Main didn't know what he was doing. The man was a clit-licking genius whose remarkable skill ranked him way above average.

My body suddenly shrieked at me: hang on a fucking minute! I'd felt these sweaty palms and the craftsmanship of this tongue before.

'It was you!' I exploded, jumping back from him. 'You were the one!'

He plucked a pubic hair from his lip and examined it casually. 'I wondered if you'd recognise me.'

'You tricked me, you dirty old man,' I raged. 'You and Tom . . . the pair of you set me up.' That Michael Main of all people should have seen me tied up and naked and then tongued me like a dog was so abhorrent that I heaved with nausea.

'It seems that we needn't have bothered to deceive you,' he said, sitting back. 'But how was I to guess that in a matter of days, you'd be handing me your pussy on a plate. At the time it seemed like a golden opportunity . . . if you'll forgive the pun.' He looked longingly at my thatch.

I yanked my skirt down. 'It was a horrible thing to do to me.'

He smiled lewdly. 'You didn't seem to think so at the time, my dear. You certainly didn't think so when you were coming all over my face.'

My blushes were spared by Beryl's voice crackling over the intercom. 'Mr Main, Mr Faraday has arrived.'

I was stricken with panic: Flynn? What was Flynn doing here?

'Send him in,' Michael Main said calmly. He looked at me sideways. 'You should find this interesting, Miss Roberts. I suggest you take a seat.'

I slunk back into the chair I'd vacated and clutched my stomach to still the swarm of butterflies that had just taken flight within. It would be the first time I'd seen Flynn's face since I'd smothered it with kisses last night.

I heard the door open and was surprised to see Michael Main rise to his feet and hold out his hand like he was greeting an old friend. 'Faraday, dear boy, I can't apologise enough for this ridiculous misunderstanding.' Flynn shook his hand but his eyes were looking at me. 'Take a seat, dear boy, take a seat,' Michael urged him.

Flynn shook his head. 'I'll stand, if you don't mind.'

I was puzzled by the look of concern on Michael's face. 'I trust Beryl's explained everything?'

'I'd like to hear it from you.' I couldn't believe that Flynn was speaking to the managing director like this. He seemed gloriously defiant and I felt fiercely proud of him for no logical reason I could fathom.

'First let me assure you that my view hasn't altered since our chat yesterday morning,' Michael said. 'I made it clear then that I wouldn't be taking the matter any further and I meant what I said.'

'I must admit that I was a little surprised to receive the e-mail,' Flynn replied warily. 'I assumed you'd had second thoughts.'

'No, no, no.' Michael waved his hands emphatically. 'It was Beryl's fault, as I'm sure she's explained. The poor dear woman has an exaggerated belief in this company's moral values and had prepared the e-mail in advance under the misguided belief that I would want to dismiss you. By sheer chance I was called away immediately after our interview and omitted to inform her of my decision. Convinced, as she was, of what my judgement would be, she dispatched it anyway. Naturally, I had her call you the minute I found out what she'd done.'

My jaw was hanging open. 'Just a moment,' I interrupted. 'Are you saying that he was fired by mistake?'

'A serious mistake,' he confirmed. 'If the old dear wasn't already retiring, she would have been dismissed herself for pre-empting me. The fact is, Miss Roberts, as I'm sure Mr Faraday knows, he is indispensable to this company. Ninety per cent of our products would fail were it not for his expertise. He's a technological wizard.'

And I'd thought he was just the maintenance man! I couldn't believe I'd been so stupid, thinking him arrogant when, instead of flaunting his power, he'd concealed it. It made me cringe when I remembered that I'd once insisted on his calling me Miss Roberts.

'If I were to fire Mr Faraday, the board would have my head,' declared Michael.

'But you told me –'

'I don't believe I told you anything, Miss Roberts,' he intercepted. 'But you assumed a great deal. I would have explained things to you, given half a chance.'

'Oh, I'm sure you would have ... eventually,' I seethed.

Michael turned his attention to Flynn. 'You will, of course, be immediately reinstated and I will personally ensure that you're compensated.'

Flynn dipped his head in my direction. 'What about her? Doesn't she have something to say about this?'

Michael smiled, displaying teeth that might have been dentures. 'Miss Roberts has made it abundantly clear to me that she wishes your reinstatement and bears you no ill will whatsoever.'

Flynn looked at me searchingly. 'Is that true?'

I nodded. 'I tried to tell you that I didn't bring the charge. You and I were the victims of a malicious attempt to discredit us both.'

I saw the pained expression on his face, remorse for

what he'd done to me sparkling in his eyes. 'Pam, I'm sorry.'

I stood up with dignity. 'I have nothing more to say, Mr Main. May I leave now?'

'Certainly, Miss Roberts.'

Sensing that they were both watching me walk to the door, I held my head high.

'Just one more thing, Miss Roberts,' Michael called after me. I turned and, to my chagrin, saw him dangling my red G-string from his finger. 'Best not leave this lying about. I can't have Beryl thinking that I'm a dirty old man now, can I?'

My face flushed redder than the garment as I sheepishly crept back to his desk and snatched the G-string from his finger.

He looked at Flynn with a boys-will-be-boys grin on his face. 'Moral values,' he huffed, 'who gives a fuck about those? I'm in this game for profit.'

I didn't want to look at Flynn but I wasn't going to slink out with my tail between my legs. Confronting the cold condemnation in his eyes, I shot him a look that dared him to despise me.

An acrid smile curled the corners of his mouth as he muttered in Portuguese.

'Was that an insult?' I challenged him.

He shrugged his eyebrows. 'It wasn't a compliment.'

'Neither is this: stick your ingenious cock up your ingenious arse and go fuck yourself,' I snapped. Then I stormed out of the room to the sound of both men's laughter.

As I ran down the corridor, I imagined them swapping stories about me. I felt like a crude joke and barely managed to contain my tears as I hurried to the ladies where I let them all come flooding out. In the middle of the torrent, Asia walked in.

'What's the matter, Pam? You're ruining your make-up.'

I couldn't tell her about Flynn, so I sobbed, 'I've just called Michael Main a dirty old man to his face.'

'That doesn't strike me as being very sensible,' she said. 'Dare I ask why?'

'It doesn't matter,' I sniffed. 'I'm more upset about blowing my promotion.'

'You've nuked it,' she agreed. 'But you can't be sacked for having an opinion, especially if it's accurate. One assumes that he must have done something dirty or you wouldn't have said it. In any case, it's hardly the end of the world. You still have a good job with Tom.'

'I hate Tom,' I fumed. 'He's ruined everything for me.' Grabbing a paper hand-towel, I blew my nose furiously. 'I'm going to teach that bastard a lesson he won't forget.'

'Well then, what if Janice moves up? You could side-step into her job,' Asia reasoned. 'Failing that, there's always France. You've a director coming tomorrow. It'll be a great opportunity to make an impression.'

But in France there would be no Flynn and I hadn't given up on him yet. 'I'll give it some thought,' I said.

'Let me help you fix your make-up,' Asia offered and, after fifteen minutes of her expert ministrations, I came out of the toilet looking better than when I'd gone in. But I was in a grim mood and more than ready to wreak my revenge on Tom.

Walking back to my office, I mulled over the catalogue of wounds that he'd inflicted on me: betraying me with my arch-enemy, blackmailing me with a false threat of exposure, sabotaging my career, lying to me about his relationship with Sheila and, even worse, getting her pregnant! Then, on top of all this, he'd conspired with the managing director to degrade me in the most devious and disgusting way. The punishment I'd planned for him was more than warranted and I considered that I owed it to my own sex to get even in a way that would deter him from ever wielding his power over a woman again.

But I let none of this bitter resolve reflect on my face as I walked into my office. The precaution was unnecessary: Tom had gone out and there was only Georgia, my stand-in during Monsieur Planquet's stay. I didn't care much for this matronly pudding of a woman who'd worked in P&P for countless years without progressing beyond assistant. Yet despite having no ambition, she was supremely efficient and could have stood in for Tom himself if need be.

'I've been going through the literature stock,' she advised me. 'We're short on brochures for VC blinds and drapes. Have you ordered more from the printer?'

I looked wistfully at the VoiceCom module for the blinds on the wall. It seemed ages ago that Flynn had fixed it while I'd watched him, barely conscious of how attractive he was. How much had changed since his kiss had taken the lid off the pot of sizzling sexual chemistry between us.

'Miss Roberts,' Georgia prompted me. 'The brochures – did you order them?'

'Oh yes,' I uttered dreamily. 'They'll give us a kiss when they're ready ... I mean ring, they'll give us a ring.'

She cast me a dubious look. 'Are you OK?'

'Yes I'm fine. When is Tom coming back?'

'He said around five,' she informed me. 'He wants you to wait for him.'

I was still waiting patiently when he returned at six o'clock. He swept me into his arms. 'I've been longing to do this all day.'

I avoided his lips. 'Let's go into your office. I'm anxious to get started.' Disengaging from his embrace, I took hold of his tie and led him through our connecting door. It was like leading a calf to an abattoir.

He chuckled excitedly. 'You sexy bitch. I have a feeling I'm going to like this.'

'Trust me, you're going to love it,' I said. 'Take your trousers and pants off and sit in that chair.'

Still smiling, he stripped off his lower garments and sat down. 'Now what?' he wondered eagerly.

I went over and stood in front of him then, like a human flagpole, raised my skirt for the second time that day. The black magic of the stockings had immediate effect. 'Bloody hell,' he groaned as his prick wanged upright. 'You're not wearing any knickers.' Actually, I'd forgotten to put them back on, but I judged it a fortunate oversight in view of his turgid response.

His hands snapped open and shut as he reached out to fondle me, but I wagged my finger in front of his face. 'No touching.'

His features contorted in frustration. 'Oh God, let me just slip my cock inside your stocking-top,' he pleaded.

'This is my fantasy. Remember?' I told him. 'Just sit back and do as I ask.'

He shrugged. 'Whatever you say.'

To titillate him further, I ran my hands up and down my legs with my eyes half-closed as I writhed in front of him like a table dancer. My hooded gaze witnessed a line of drool dribbling from the corner of his mouth as steamy lust snorted from his nostrils. I lifted my leg onto his desk, exposing my thigh and the plump swell of my buttock then, hooking my thumbs into the clinging black lace, I rolled the stocking slowly to my ankle. I removed my shoe, slipped the stocking from my foot and then repeated the entire process with the other leg. Tom watched, spellbound.

'Here comes the fun bit,' I said. 'Put your hands behind your back.'

He was way ahead of me now, holding out his wrists to be tied as I moved to the back of his chair. I secured his hands with one stocking and then used the other to fasten his feet to the pole of the chair, trussing him like a chicken.

His cock was straining at the leash so I ran my hands over its purple head and then up and down its rigid column. It was a handsome critter in its own right: a magnificent thing that didn't deserve a pig like Tom for an appendage. This cock had given me considerable pleasure in its day. I had nothing against it personally.

'Sit on it,' he growled. 'For fuck's sake sit on it, or suck it, or shove it up your arse. I'll settle for anything.'

I stepped back, enjoying his exasperation. 'Be patient,' I instructed him. 'There's something I need to fetch from the other office.' Then I left him to stew, half-naked, tied-up and vulnerable.

As I was bending over my desk, unhurriedly searching through a drawer, a sudden voice behind my ear made me jump like a cricket. 'I was hoping you'd still be here.'

As the deep voice identified itself to my brain, the muscles in my legs, and in the arm I was leaning on, seemed to collapse like a set of punctured tyres.

'Flynn!' I exclaimed, lurching round to face him. I'd misjudged his proximity and as I stumbled against his chest the unexpected contact jarred us both. We sprang back from each other as if the magnetic attraction between us had somehow reversed its polarity.

He made a joke of it. 'I was expecting you to throw *some*thing at me but I never guessed it would be you.'

'You made me jump,' I uttered lamely. 'What do you want?'

He rubbed his jaw. 'I came to thank you for trying to get my job back for me. The boss told me how convincingly you'd pleaded my cause.'

I gulped. 'He did?'

'But was it really necessary to show him what you were wearing that day?' He scratched his head. 'The funny thing is – I don't recollect that it was a G-string.'

'I felt the story needed embellishment,' I said quickly,

flushed with relief that Michael had come up with a viable explanation for my panties being on his floor. 'I figured that if I showed him my sauciest underwear, he'd write me off as a temptress. But I wouldn't have gone to so much trouble if I'd known that you were VoiceCom's answer to Superman.' I looked at him gravely. 'Surely you knew that you were indispensable?'

He shook his head. 'I didn't know last night, if that's what you're asking.'

'Didn't you?'

We stared into each other's eyes, erotic memories of our savage coupling bubbling to the surface of our thoughts. 'I shouldn't have done that,' he uttered thickly. 'I was drunk. I wasn't thinking straight.'

'But you were right,' I admitted. 'I did put your head on the block to save mine. You made me realise how callous I'd been. And I wouldn't have been able to sleep at night knowing that I'd ruined your career. That's why I went to see Michael.'

His eyes grew soft. 'I misjudged you, Pam. Can you forgive me for what I did?'

'I can forgive you,' I murmured softly, gazing longingly at his mouth. 'But please don't ask me to forget because . . . I really don't want to.'

He caught his breath and took a step towards me. 'Baby, if that isn't a green light flashing this time, I must be colour-blind. Tell me that you . . .' He broke off, suddenly noticing my bare legs. '. . . That you haven't left your stockings in someone else's office,' he amended. 'Or are there bits of your underwear festooned all over the building?'

Just at this moment, Tom's voice bellowed out, 'Hurry up, Pam, I've got a hard-on in here as big as the Apollo eleven and I'm waiting to take you to the moon.'

My heart sank like a soufflé as Flynn shot me a look of utter disbelief. I was cringing as he strode to the door and opened it a fraction, but almost giggled when his eyes rolled heavenward and he gave his head an incredulous shake. It seemed a laughably muted reaction from someone who'd just seen a half-naked man tied to a chair with black stockings.

He closed the door and, turning to me with a thunderous expression on his face, uttered darkly, 'You say you wouldn't have been able to sleep at night, huh? You'll never need to worry about insomnia, Pam. All you have to do is count the notches on your bedpost.'

'It's not what you think,' I told him.

'You've no idea what I'm thinking,' he growled. 'I guess that green light was just a "go for launch" signal after all. You'd better get aboard that rocket, Pam, while it's still pointing towards the stars.' Then he spun on his heel and, in a few angry strides, was gone.

'Pam!' wailed Tom. 'What are you doing out there?'

I blinked back the tears that were scratching at my eyes and grabbed what I needed. 'I'm coming, Tom,' I shouted. 'Get ready for the biggest surprise of your life!'

Chapter Twenty

This is the moment that I still like the most: his cock in my mouth, his legs trembling, his eyes glazing over with euphoria. My power over him is absolute. He knows no fear and his trust in me is childlike. I am the vehicle of his pleasure and it does not enter his mind that I could harm him. Poor Tom – poor unsuspecting Tom.

'Fantastic,' he groaned ecstatically. 'You're the best, Pam, the best.'

'I'm glad you enjoyed it,' I said, standing up to untie his necktie. 'I wanted to give you a final taste of what you'll be missing.'

'What are you talk . . . umph.' I choked off his question by gagging him with his own tie. 'You've been a very naughty boy,' I said, taking the red G-string from my pocket and flicking his face with it. 'A very naughty boy.'

He nodded, warily participating. I flicked him again. 'You made it all up, didn't you? You told some nasty little lies.' This time, I slapped him hard across his face with the back of my hand. After a moment's shock, he strained at his bonds, snarling muffled expletives.

'Poor Tom,' I crooned, stroking his reddened cheek

with the satin panties. 'You thought you'd get away with it, didn't you?' His face was a mask of confusion. If he thought this was still a game, he had no idea how to play it.

'You tried to discredit me by bringing a complaint against Flynn,' I accused him. 'You lied about Darren.' A worried look entered his eyes. 'You lied about the celebration meal you had with Sheila. Oh yes, I know about the baby, Tom. Janice told me. You remember Janice, don't you? Lastly, in my own home, you let Michael Main take advantage of me. I've decided to put you on trial for these crimes. How do you plead, Tom?'

He babbled furiously into the gag. 'Guilty?' I queried. 'Have you nothing to say in your defence?' He threshed in his chair. 'In that case, I sentence you to be tortured.' I reached into my pocket and withdrew a pair of bulldog clips the size of my thumbs. 'If I knew how to wire these to the mains, I would.' His eyes bolted from their sockets as I squeezed the clips to demonstrate their snapping jaws.

'You do understand, don't you Tom?' I continued equably. 'I have to ensure that you never abuse your power again.'

Ignoring his dampened shrieks and the wild convulsions of his body, I gently lifted his balls, one after the other, and attached the bulldog clips to his scrotal skin.

'Don't be such a baby,' I scolded him, wiping wincing tears from the corners of his eyes. 'If I really wanted to hurt you, they'd be biting into your plums. And, think about this, Tom: just a few minutes ago I had your cock between my teeth. Things could have been a lot worse for you.' His face turned ghostly white and he looked nauseous.

I smiled reassuringly. 'Don't worry, Mr Carson. The cleaners will be here in a couple of hours. You won't have to suffer long.'

He flung his head back in obvious despair at the

prospect of being discovered like this. 'I'll make it easier for you,' I chuckled, slipping the scarlet panties on his head so that the triangular crotch-piece sat on his brow like an arrowhead. 'You can tell them you're a freemason!'

I ran a final check on him to ensure that the stockings were holding and that the clips were gripping securely and, when I was satisfied, I walked over to the VoiceCom by the door. 'Lights out,' I purred into it. 'Goodnight Tom.'

On the way home, I felt curiously light-headed as if I'd been drinking champagne. And every time I thought of Tom, I burst out laughing, attracting some strange looks from my fellow commuters. Oddly, I didn't feel any remorse at all; just a joyous sense of freedom as if I'd been released from some dark dungeon of desire where Tom had held me captive for the past year. I had conquered my Svengali at last.

I wasn't surprised when he didn't turn up for work the next day or when his wife, Sheila, telephoned to report that he'd had an accident.

Endeavouring to sound concerned, I said, 'I do hope it's nothing serious.'

'It's more embarrassing than serious,' she explained. 'It seems he fell against his desk last night and hurt himself in a rather personal place.'

I sucked in my cheeks to stop myself giggling. 'How awful,' I sympathised. 'But a couple of days rest might do him some good. He's been overworking himself lately, don't you think?'

'It's funny you should say that,' she remarked. 'He's just been telling me that he won't be putting in so many late nights in the future.'

'Give him my regards,' I told her. 'And be sure to tell him that I'll be happy to tie up his loose ends for him.' Oh yes, I'll tie them into a reef-knot, I thought, chuckling as I put down the phone. It rang again immediately. It was reception ringing to advise me that Monsieur Planquet had called from the airport and would be arriving in half an hour.

'You have the reins,' I told Georgia, collecting my bits and pieces. 'Don't worry if you get stacked up with Tom away. I'll be popping in and out as much as I can.'

Nodding curtly, she handed me my agenda. 'I'm sure I shall cope,' she said stiffly, with a look of abject disapproval on her face. I had a horrible feeling that somehow she blamed me for Tom's absence.

I was still thinking about Georgia's animosity as I stepped into the lift and mumbled a greeting to the occupant without looking up. It only hit me as the doors closed that I'd just said hello to Flynn.

He didn't speak – he didn't need to, his dark brooding countenance and the muscle working in his cheek said it all. I couldn't bear his silent criticism and, after a few seconds, exclaimed, 'Oh, for goodness sake, say something, even if it's another of your snide comments in Portuguese.'

'You'd consider my opinion irrelevant in any language,' he said. 'So, if you don't mind, I'll keep it to myself.'

'Who the fuck are you to judge me?' I raged at him. 'You're the one who, stinking drunk, barged into my home, verbally abused me, forcefully screwed me, passed out on top of me, and then buggered off in the morning without a word!'

He suppressed a smile. 'The way I remember it, you were the one doing all the screwing.'

I flushed furiously. 'I only did that to get it over with as quickly as possible.'

He blinked his long eyelashes. 'Look, I've already apologised for what I did. What more do you want me to say?'

I heaved a deep sigh then, crossing the space between

us, curled my hand around his arm. Squeezing his biceps, I stood on tiptoe and uttered breathlessly into his ear, 'I want you to say "maintenance override twenty-one" into the VoiceCom. I want us to start again.'

He sagged for a second, but then swung his head away from me. 'That was a mistake,' he rasped. 'If I'd known where it would lead, I wouldn't have done it. I can't handle you, baby. You're too hot for me.'

I put my hand to his cheek and turned his face towards me. 'If you can't stand heat then why start a fire in the first place?'

His black gaze travelled over my hair. 'For no better reason than I wanted to add your pretty blonde scalp to my collection. I wasn't thinking beyond a one-night stand. If you'd fucked me instead of Tom that night, it would have made things a whole lot easier.'

'Do you honestly think that once would have been enough?'

He shrugged. 'Maybe.'

'Then let's do it once and see if it is.' I moved my hand from his cheek to his hair. Then, tilting up my face, offered him my lips. He looked at them for a long moment but then gripped my shoulders and pushed me back. 'You little fool. You don't even know what it is that you want from me.'

'I don't understand you,' I cried. 'You went out of your way to make me want you and now that I do, you won't even kiss me. Why won't you kiss me, damn you?'

He clenched his jaw. 'I have my reasons. Ground floor,' he stated gruffly as the doors slid open. 'Or were you planning on going to the basement?'

'Are they red-headed reasons?' I demanded. 'I hope your ginger freak girlfriend knows what she's letting herself in for marrying a bastard like you. You're a pig and I hate you.'

His lips twitched and for a second I thought I saw a glint of humour in his eyes. But his words were callous and cold. 'Do you know something? I'm sick of hearing you say that. And, if you want to know the truth, I hate you right back!' Then he shoved me out into the corridor, turning his back on me as the doors closed.

I walked away, smarting. How could he hate me? Why did he hate me? Damn you Flynn! I scratched at my arms, wishing that I could remove him from under my skin as easily as that. I couldn't understand why I felt so wounded by his rejection. It was only sex after all; only a physical attraction that would have burned itself out anyway. Suddenly, I wanted to get away from him, as far away as I could. I wondered if France would be far enough. Lifting my chin, I strode purposefully on to reception.

I was surprised to find Janice waiting there. 'Roger thought it would be a nice touch to send someone from sales to greet Mr Plonker,' she informed me.

'Monsieur Planquet,' I corrected her, looking critically at her tight yellow sweater. 'Don't you think he might mistake you for the English butter-mountain in that?'

She sniffed. 'You never could stand competition.'

'What makes you think there's going to be one?' I asked her. 'I thought you'd made up your mind that it was Tom you wanted.'

She looked at me scornfully. 'Is that a joke? You've made bloody damn sure that I'm never going to get him.'

'What do you mean?'

She narrowed her gaze. 'Don't play the innocent with me, Pam. There's a rumour going round that the cleaners found Tom trussed up and naked in his office.'

'How ridiculous,' I declared. 'You ought to know better than to listen to silly gossip, Janice.'

'I don't believe *everything* I've heard,' she asserted. 'Rumours get distorted like Chinese whispers and there's talk that he was wearing women's underwear. I don't see Tom as a transvestite somehow.'

I sniggered. 'Absolutely not.'

'This smacks of revenge,' she said shrewdly. 'If it's true and you've smeared Tom with scandal, it'll be impossible for him to have another affair.'

'Don't underestimate his sex drive,' I told her. 'He'll be back sniffing for pussy as soon as this blows over. But he'll never get his nose anywhere near mine again, I can assure you of that.'

'Somehow that makes him less attractive,' she acknowledged. 'I only seem to want what's yours.'

We fell silent until a cab drew up outside the glass reception doors. 'This will be our visitor,' Janice said, jostling me aside. I jostled her back and we were still shoving each other as the tall dark Frenchman came through the door.

Pierre-Nanu Planquet had all the trappings of the 'ladies' man' that Tom had described: dark brown hair streaked with grey, strong chiselled features, and liquid-brown eyes like pools of melted chocolate. He was attractive in a way that ordinarily would have had my sex twitching by now and I could only assume that the reason it wasn't had something to do with Flynn.

His smile flashed white in a deeply tanned face and his sexy eyes strolled lazily over our bodies. I could see Janice drooling, so I jumped in quickly with a speech that I'd prepared, taking his lean brown hand in my own.

'I am enchanted to meet you also, Miss Roberts,' he responded in English. 'Your accent is very good.' The soft rich tones of his own delicious accent would ordinarily have made my pubic hair stand on end. Damn Flynn!

'Bon jovi, Mosher Plonkette,' mumbled Janice, nudging me aside. 'Me nom de plume esta Janice Becker. Je suis mucho pleased to meet you.'

He laughed. 'How charming.'

'She's the sales director's PA,' I muttered contemptuously, as if referring to a piece of dog shit on my shoe. I hooked his arm possessively. 'I've been assigned as your personal assistant during your stay with us. Would you care to come with me?'

Janice shot me a poisonous look but smiled sweetly at my charge. 'I'll look forward to seeing you later,' she said, tossing her hair so that, beneath her tight sweater, the rolling landscape of her breasts threatened to avalanche from the inadequate restraint of her half-cup bra.

She wiggled her bum as she walked away and I noticed the Frenchman flex his fingers instinctively. 'She seems like a nice girl,' he commented.

'Don't let the arse-wiggle fool you,' I advised him. 'She may wriggle like a grass snake but she's all viper.'

'I see that you're looking out for my interests already,' he said. 'What is your first name?'

His gaze was so intense that, ordinarily, I would have felt like I was drowning in a vat of creamy chocolate. 'Pamela,' I told him. 'What would you like me to call you?'

'Pierre-Nanu or just Pierre,' he supplied. 'In France, a man's personal assistant is even closer to him than his wife or his mistress. Is it so in England?'

The directness of his question took me by surprise. After a brief hesitation, I said, 'I want you to feel at home, Pierre. I want to make your stay as enjoyable as possible.' I didn't add 'whatever it takes' but I made sure that my eyes carried the footnote.

He seemed content. And so was I. I'd launched my offensive and, if I played cards right, my transfer to France was in the bag. The only fly in the ointment, as usual, was Janice Becker. I'd seen the way she'd looked at him and, knowing her, she'd find any and every excuse to flaunt her fat tits in his face or wag her arse like a duck to draw his attention from me. I would have to use every trick in the book to make sure that he wasn't distracted.

Since I had the advantage of being assigned to him, I spent the rest of the day exploiting it: flirting with him as boldly as I dared and notching up points for personality and efficiency. But it wasn't easy to gauge his reaction to me. I knew that he found me attractive but he was surprisingly conscientious and it was almost impossible to divert him from the purpose of his visit. Nonetheless, by the end of the day, his smiles and glances had become more frequent and he'd advanced to pinching my rear now and then, confirming himself as an 'arse man'. But whether he would prefer my shapely hips to Janice's wobble-butt remained to be seen.

Thursday 11 a.m. Meeting with Tom Carson in Promotions and Publicity.

I crossed it off the agenda. 'I'm afraid Mr Carson is on sick leave at the moment,' I explained apologetically to Pierre, after showing him around the department. 'That leaves you with a couple of hours free.'

'In that case, I would like to make some correspondence with France and some personal phone calls.'

'You can use Mr Carson's office,' I proposed. 'I regret that my French isn't good enough for dictation but, as you know, VoiceCom's Electro-Sec software is multilingual.'

He nodded. 'It will suffice. But before I commence, Pamela, there are two things I wish to ask you. Firstly, will you lunch with me today?'

'I'd be delighted,' I said. 'And the other?'

He pointed to my computer screen. 'What is the meaning of these words "Flynn sucks"?'

'Er . . . it's a sort of joke.'

Although I'd passed it off as such, I didn't find Flynn's screen saver the least bit amusing any more. And I didn't see why I should have to be reminded daily of the man who'd not only refused point blank to kiss me but had declared to my face that he hated me.

It was like ants in my pants, fidgeting me as I tried to

work. Eventually, I couldn't stand it any longer and, snatching up the phone, rang through to maintenance.

A young lad answered. 'Sorry, Miss, they've all gone down to the Duck and Feather. It's Harry the programmer's birthday.'

I glanced at my watch. I hadn't realised it was lunchtime. 'I'd like to leave a message for Mr Faraday,' I said. 'This is Pamela Roberts in P & P. I have a problem with my computer and I'd be grateful if he could send someone up to deal with it as soon as possible.'

I felt a throb of disappointment as I put the phone down. There was no sense in kidding myself. I'd been hoping to speak to Flynn.

'Are you ready for lunch?' asked Pierre, coming out of Tom's office. I nodded. 'Where shall we eat?' he enquired.

An idea popped into my head and jumped out of my mouth before I had a chance to think about it. 'Have you ever tried a traditional English pub lunch?'

Half an hour later, as we entered the public bar of the Duck and Feather, I spotted Flynn among the rowdy VoiceCom crowd who were gathered around the dartboard. He was concentrating on the game and didn't notice me come in.

Pierre looked dubiously at his surroundings. 'Is this where we eat?'

'We can eat in the lounge,' I said. 'But it's traditional to have a drink at the bar first.'

'Then let us be traditional,' he said. 'What will you have to drink?'

While he was being served, I drilled my gaze into the back of Flynn's head, willing him to sense my presence. But he didn't turn round.

'Your English customs intrigue me,' Pierre remarked, handing me my vodka and tonic. He took a sip from his own glass of cognac. 'What other traditions do you have?'

As Flynn noticed me at last, I flicked my eyes away, pretending not to notice him. Pierre looked at me strangely as I laughed flirtatiously. 'Did I say something funny?'

'I was just thinking of a custom we have, which might appeal to you as a Frenchman,' I said, clinging to his arm. 'It goes like this: when a girl wants to let a man know that she likes him, she sips from his glass.' I lifted the tumbler from his hand and gulped a mouthful of its fiery content. 'If an English girl does this, she's inviting you to kiss her,' I explained. It was utter bollocks but he had no reason to doubt me.

'You just did it,' he pointed out.

'So I did,' I answered demurely.

'No Frenchman could refuse such an invitation,' he declared, taking my glass and placing it alongside his on the bar. Then, under the watchful eye of Flynn, he scooped me into his arms and kissed me. It was a scorching French kiss: hot, wet and sexually explicit. My passionate response encouraged him to keep going and, as the kiss went on, I locked eyes with Flynn who unconsciously bit into the cigarette he was smoking.

I knew what he was thinking just as he'd known what I'd been thinking when he'd kissed Mel in front of me. He wanted my kiss for himself and only stubbornness stopped him from claiming it.

Breathless, I pulled back from Pierre. 'Let's not get carried away,' I warned. 'This is England after all. Perhaps we should eat now.'

He licked his lips. 'As you wish. But I fear that the sweetness of your kiss may have jaded my palate.' I couldn't help wishing that Flynn had heard that one!

Over lunch, Pierre squeezed my knee as we talked and when his fingers foraged under the hem of my skirt, I parted my legs invitingly, letting him probe me as I probed him. 'What is your PA like in France, Pierre?'

'She's not as –' he searched for a word '– obliging as you, Pamela.'

'I've always wanted to go to France,' I said bluntly.

'Is that so?' His fingernails scraped down my thigh as he withdrew his hand to let the barmaid clear our table. 'Have you asked for a transfer?'

'I was thinking about it. How do you rate my chances?'

He leaned forward and his sultry brown eyes flicked over my face before dipping to the swell of my bosom. 'It's possible,' he said.

I trailed my fingers over my breast. 'A lot of things are possible. But what does it take to make a certainty?'

He put his head to one side, considering. 'Gratitude perhaps. If I were to help you, how grateful would you be?'

I lifted his hand and, putting his finger into my mouth, let my lips glide over it suggestively. 'Very grateful,' I said, returning his hand to his lap.

He smiled knowingly. 'I believe this gesture means the same in both our countries. Very well, Pamela, I will see what I can do. What is my schedule for this afternoon?'

'My research on you revealed that you enjoy playing golf. So I've arranged an informal meeting with Roger Fielding on the golf course. He'll be picking you up at your hotel in forty-five minutes.'

He glanced at his watch. 'That should give me enough time to get changed.'

'Then, this evening you'll be dining with Michael Main and his wife at their home,' I concluded.

He spread his hands. 'You have done your job too well, Pamela. You have left me no time for recreation.'

'You'll be free after the party tomorrow,' I hinted.

He winked at me. 'C'est bon.'

When I arrived back at my office, I was astonished to find Flynn seated at my desk.

'What do you want?' I barked to the back of his head.

As he swivelled round to face me, he avoided my eyes. 'I got your message,' he growled. 'I've just checked your computer and there's nothing wrong with it.'

'You needn't have come yourself,' I said woodenly. 'Monsieur Planquet asked me the meaning of your screen saver today. It's an embarrassment to me and I want it removed.'

'The Frenchman,' he muttered, turning back to the screen. 'You don't seem to have wasted any time getting to know him.'

'He's a useful man to know,' I remarked, watching his clever hands rattling over the keyboard. 'And a girl has to think of her future.'

He glanced up sharply. 'A future in France?'

'Maybe.'

'That figures,' he pronounced, stabbing the return button.

'What figures?'

He laughed sardonically. 'I hope the Frenchman was hanging onto his balls while you were kissing him.'

'What's that supposed to mean?'

He leaned back in my chair. 'I let my curiosity get the better of me Tuesday night and sneaked back here to see what you and Tom were doing. I found him as you'd left him.'

I swung away from him so that he wouldn't see my burning cheeks. 'I should have known you'd do something like that. You just can't stop spying on me, can you?' He didn't answer. 'Did you let him go?'

'I removed his gag and took the clips off his bollocks . . .' he whistled through his teeth '. . . that was nasty! But after he'd confessed what he'd done to you, I decided to leave him where he was. Oh, and I left the panties on his head – I thought that was a nice touch.'

I turned back to him. 'Do you think I went too far?'

He shrugged. 'I don't think you did your career any favours. That's why it figures that you're sucking up to

229

the French guy. And when I say "sucking", that's exactly what I mean.'

'What if I am?' I retorted. 'It's only cock. You said it yourself – it's all the same to me. One man's meat is much the same as another man's meat. You don't think I'm capable of discriminating, do you?'

'Probably not,' he agreed, tapping in a final command. 'I'm done here.'

I stepped up behind him and ran my fingers over his hair. 'I know what you're doing, Flynn,' I told him. 'You're trying to hang on to your scalp. It was OK when you were the hunter. But you don't like being the prey.'

He leapt to his feet and, snorting like a bull, grabbed hold of me. 'Is this what you want?' he snarled, crushing his mouth viciously and cruelly on mine. I was too shocked to do anything but hang limply in his arms as, brutally kissing me, he plunged his hand inside my jacket and spitefully squeezed my breast like he was juicing an orange. Then, with a judder of violent emotion, he thrust me away from him. His dark eyes blazing as he wiped his mouth with the back of his hand.

'Don't look at me like that,' he raged. 'You wanted my kiss and you got it. I threw in the grope as a bonus. I hope you're satisfied.'

He strode out without waiting for my reply, so I whispered it to myself. 'Not like that, Flynn. Not with hate.'

I was still nursing my bruised and swollen lips when Georgia came in to announce that Mr Carson had telephoned to say that he would be back tomorrow and wanted to see me.

'I'll be in Research and Development with Monsieur Planquet for most of the day,' I advised her. 'Tom will have to wait until I'm free.'

But Tom wasn't prepared to wait. On Friday morning, he turned up in R&D and introduced himself to the

Frenchman. 'I hope you don't mind if I borrow my secretary for an hour this lunchtime,' he requested.

'Not at all,' Pierre replied. 'I am lunching myself with Miss Becker today.' Seeing my crestfallen look, he added, 'She's going to fill me in on some of the clients who will be attending the party this evening.'

Tom turned to me, his face expressionless. 'I'll see you in my office, Pam.'

I didn't know what to expect. Would he rant at me? Would he fire me? There had been nothing in his face to prepare me for what he might do.

I nonetheless walked boldly into his office, ready to tough it out. For a long time, he sat without speaking. Then, suddenly, he laughed. 'I must have looked pretty stupid with those pants on my head.'

His tone was conciliatory. Relieved, I sat down. 'I was angry, Tom. I wanted to hurt and humiliate you. But I went too far.'

'No,' he said firmly. 'No, you didn't. I had it coming to me, Pam. You were right to be angry. I treated you like a possession. I tried to control your life. You made me realise what it feels like to be abused by someone you trust; to be diminished by someone else's power. I was shitting myself when you snapped those clips in front of me. But I deserved far worse.' He reached out his hand to me. 'Let's not hate each other, Pam. We've had too many good times for that. Can we call it quits?'

I shook his hand. 'We can forgive each other, Tom, but we can't continue working together after everything that's happened. I've decided to request a transfer to France.'

He nodded slowly. 'You're right, of course, and I'll help you all I can. But I've lost a lot of my influence with Michael after the Flynn fiasco. In all honesty, your best chance is Planquet.'

'I already know that,' I said.

Chapter Twenty-One

I dressed with care for the evening: a chic designer suit in virginal white, with just a silver top and a white G-string underneath. I'd already tinted my skin all over with expensive fake tan the night before, adding a golden glow to my complexion. And, with my hair in a soft French pleat, I looked cool and classy, like something from the pages of a Parisian magazine.

As I entered the boardroom where the function was being held, I was pleased to see Pierre hurrying towards me with the gleeful look of a hunter who'd just seen his trap sprung. 'You look beautiful,' he said, sweeping up my hand to plant a less than papal kiss upon my chunky silver ring. I basked in his admiration for all of five seconds, then, 'Janice!' he exclaimed, looking over my shoulder. I knew without turning that I'd made a mistake. His eyes were practically standing out on stalks.

With a sense of dull expectancy, I twisted my head to face her. Bugger! She looked stunning in a clinging red jersey silk dress, slashed deep at the front and high at the sides. There seemed to be masses of soft white flesh erupting out of the flimsy garment but her free-flowing mane of yellow hair revealed only tantalising glimpses of it.

Everything was red, from her tinted stockings with their scarlet tops, which flashed saucily as she walked, to the visible lace edge of the bra that was manfully holding her cleavage together. With red shoes, red lips, red nails and sluttish false rubies in her jewellery, she'd gone way over the top with the red and, in my opinion, looked like one of the victims out of a *Scream* movie. Nevertheless, I felt colourless beside her and was conscious of my presence diminishing, like a snowman next to a raging fire.

She eyed my white outfit critically. 'Did someone call for a doctor?'

I scowled at her. 'It was a novel idea for you to come in *period* fancy dress,' I remarked. She nodded grimly, waiting for the punch line. 'Whose period have you come as?'

'I think you both look charming,' Pierre said quickly, sensing the antagonism between us. 'Can I fetch you both a drink? Er . . . red or white wine?'

As soon as he'd gone, Janice rounded on me. 'You're wasting your time,' she said, tossing her head. 'Pierre prefers me. I should have thought it was obvious even to a thick cow like you.'

'You're the only thing that's obvious,' I retorted. 'Why didn't you write "fuck me" in scarlet paint on your forehead while you were at it?'

Her pupils diminished to pinpricks. 'It's pretty obvious what your own game plan is, Pam,' she countered. 'In that white suit you can suck off Pierre without worrying about getting splatters of spunk on your clothes.'

'Bitch!' I snarled at her.

'Cock-gobbler!' she swatted back.

At precisely this moment, Pierre returned with the drinks and, overhearing her insult, looked at me with renewed interest, his lustful eyes considering the contours of my mouth. Irritated, Janice flicked back her hair to reveal more of her bulging bosom, but I held his eyes captive with a snaky movement of my tongue.

'Your drink,' he murmured huskily, barely looking at Janice as he handed over hers.

She was fuming and upped the stakes by sliding her hand across his buttocks. 'It's time you met some of the clients,' she insisted. 'There are lots of people waiting to meet you.'

'But of course,' he agreed. '*A bientôt, ma belle*,' he said, squeezing my hand.

Janice's eyes sparkled with malevolence – even *she* knew what 'belle' meant – but her face was gloating as she steered him away.

Tom suddenly materialised at my side. 'You seem to be enjoying your assignment,' he observed. 'Only natural, I suppose. He's a good looking guy.'

'But he's leaving tomorrow,' I moaned. 'I don't think I've had enough time to make a lasting impression.'

'You've got some stiff opposition,' Tom remarked. 'And I mean stiff. If my balls weren't still sulking, I'd get a hard-on just looking at that girl.'

'You haven't missed the point of that dress then.'

'Miaow,' he purred. 'Be careful, Pam, your claws are showing.'

'When we were talking earlier, you offered to help me get my transfer,' I reminded him. 'Is that offer still open?'

He looked at me wistfully. 'I used to demand a price for such favours.'

I shook my head. 'Forget it, Tom. Not even for old time's sake.'

He shrugged his shoulders. 'You can't blame a man for trying. Of course I'll help – it's the least I can do. But I don't see how.'

'It's Janice,' I emphasised. 'She's getting in my way and I need a diversion for her. Do you think you could commandeer her when the dancing starts?'

'I wouldn't mind that at all,' he speculated. 'But what if she won't be commandeered?'

'She likes you, Tom,' I assured him. 'And, besides, you're management. How could she refuse?'

An hour later, I watched my plan unfurl as Tom swung a proprietary arm around Janice's shoulders and manoeuvred her onto the dancefloor.

I took a step in Pierre's direction but my progress was halted when a man's hand alighted on my own shoulder. It was Roger Fielding and I realised the bitch had pre-empted me when he said, 'Janice has just reminded me that I haven't yet thanked you for helping me land the Miller account. Can I buy you a drink?'

'I can't accept any credit for that,' I insisted. 'I didn't do anything.'

But he was adamant. 'Nonsense, Pam. Sal's information clinched the deal. Now, about this drink – you're not turning me down, are you?'

How could I? He was management. I allowed him to steer me to the bar and, as he talked to me, I kept a watchful eye on Pierre who was circulating freely among the guests. News of his charm must have spread around the boardroom because every time he stopped, a bevy of women clustered round him. Yet none of them seemed to draw his attention away from Janice and me for long. His eyes kept seeking us out and I knew it was a two-horse race.

As Roger droned on, I could feel my impatience mounting. But I couldn't think of a way to get rid of him without causing offence until, suddenly, I hit on an idea. Jogging his arm with my elbow, I deliberately slopped his wine over my silver top.

'Oh dear,' I bleated woefully. 'I shall have to do something about it.'

Believing himself to be responsible for the accident, Roger handed me the key to the executive loo. I was pleased with my cunning. For not only had I managed a nifty escape from Janice's boring boss, but I'd also contrived the perfect excuse to rearrange my appearance.

Off came the wine-sodden top, to allow the plunging 'V' of my jacket to expose almost all of my bra-less breasts. I softened my hair by teasing out wispy curls to frame my face and then replaced my pale lipstick with a rich strawberry red that made my mouth look luscious.

My reflection in the mirror had dramatically altered. I'd substituted chic for a look that was far more sexy and inviting. Now I felt properly armed for a battle with Miss Becker.

Heads turned as I moved back into the throng and Pierre's face was a picture as he sprinted nimbly over to claim me.

'What have you done?' he asked, pulling me into his arms for a dance.

'I had an accident with some wine,' I replied. 'Do you think anyone will notice?'

He dipped his eyes into my jacket. The advantage of height gave him a bird's-eye view of my dusky pink nipples. 'I shouldn't think so,' he answered cheekily.

I coiled my arms around his neck. 'Are you having a good time?'

'It's getting better by the minute,' he said.

I laid my cheek on his and rubbed myself against him. 'I could make it better still,' I whispered.

I felt his cock stir against my pubis. 'How so?' he uttered hoarsely.

But I had no chance to answer. Someone was peeling me from his body. The bitch was back again!

'Look who's here, Pam. It's a very good friend of yours,' she announced, taking stock of my transformation. She had Luke Miller standing next to her. 'Mr Miller is one of our most important clients,' she explained to Pierre as the two men shook hands. 'I'm sure you won't mind if he steals Pam away from you. They're intimate friends from way back.'

'Not at all,' Pierre responded, letting her take his hand and draw him away. I watched irritably as she wrapped herself around him like an anaconda.

'So, Pam,' Luke said, 'I'm sorry that you didn't take me up on my offer. I'm sure you would have enjoyed revisiting the past with Jason and me.'

I glowered at him. 'Maybe your bait wasn't big enough,' I suggested.

'You never used to think so,' he refuted.

'It took two of you, didn't it?'

'Hey, I didn't come over here to be insulted,' he protested. 'I was hoping that we might be friends again. I know it was wrong of me to dangle that contract over your head. But, fuck it, Pam, you should have seen yourself in that pool with all those guys groping you! It reminded me of the past and I wanted it back. Can you blame me?'

I softened. 'It wouldn't have been the same, Luke. Nothing ever is. Besides, I wasn't the key person in that threesome. What really turned you on was watching Jason. I think you derived some form of narcissistic pleasure in observing your identical twin's performance. It must have been like an X-rated out-of-body experience.'

His eyes glazed over. 'You're right, Pam. You can't imagine how horny that was.'

'Then why don't you persuade him to do it again with someone else?'

He shook his head. 'I don't know; the subject never came up. I daresay he would, if I could find the right girl.'

'What about her?' I suggested slyly, pointing to Janice.

'Well, I've always had a bit of a thing for the busty Miss Becker,' he admitted. 'But I don't think she likes me.'

'Oh, but she does,' I assured him. 'And when I told her

about my experience with you guys, she said she loved the idea of fucking twins.'

'Is that so?' He looked at Janice speculatively.

'Why don't you ask her to dance?' I urged him. 'Don't be put off if she doesn't seem interested. She likes to play hard to get.'

'That doesn't seem to be her game at the moment,' he said, observing Pierre's finger exploring Janice's stocking top through the slit in her dress. How I hated that pissing red dress!

'He's merely checking out her cellulite,' I said petulantly. When the music stopped, I thrust him towards her. 'I'd get in quick if I were you.'

Janice's face looked like I'd thumped it with a mallet as, once again, she was forced to relinquish Pierre. But she could hardly refuse to dance with such an important client.

Pierre responded to my beckoning summons but approached me more diffidently than before. 'Is something wrong?' I asked him.

'Janice told me that you and Luke Miller are lovers,' he revealed.

I put him straight. 'That was a long time ago. I was just a kid of nineteen.'

'Ah, I must have misunderstood.'

'I doubt it.' Clearly, she'd misled him on purpose. But she'd have to be good deal craftier than this, I thought, watching her battling to keep Luke at arm's length.

Realising that it was time to move in for the kill before she had a chance to retrench, I put my hands on either side of Pierre's face and kissed him full on the lips. But he was tapped on the shoulder before he could respond. 'Sorry, Planquet. I must have a word with Pam.' It was Tom.

'What do you want?' I snapped, as Pierre wandered off again. 'You're supposed to be taking care of Janice for me.'

From the way he was swaying as he stood there, it was obvious that he'd been drinking heavily. 'I've just heard that Beryl Parker is retiring at the end of this month,' he said. 'I thought you might be interested.'

With such blistering news, I forgave him the intrusion. 'She's leaving early? What brought that on?'

He looked at me squarely. 'You probably know the answer to that better than I do.'

'Do you know who's taking her job? Is it Janice?' I probed.

He shook his head. 'No, it isn't Janice. I think this may come as a bit of a shock to you both. But I have it on good authority that the promotion is going to a little brunette from accounts – the girl who just got married.'

'Bethany!' I exclaimed. 'It can't go to Bethany. She has hardly any secretarial experience at all.'

Tom smiled sagely. 'Listen, Pam, you can't blame Michael for wanting a pretty young thing to brighten up his office. He's been stuck with that old crab for as long as I can remember.'

'But Bethany isn't qualified,' I stressed.

'I've heard that she gives good head,' Tom cackled. 'What better qualification could she have?'

I stared at him. He had to be joking. Bethany! Sweet innocent Bethany – a cock-sucker? Why, the scheming, conniving two-faced hypocrite! I thought of all the times that she'd scolded Janice and me for being outrageous, and of all those smug self-satisfied lectures about foetal rights, animal rights, and the fucking ozone layer.

'Does Janice know?' I asked him.

Tom shook his head. 'No. Shall I tell her?'

Over his shoulder, I saw Janice and Pierre drawing together again like magnets. If I was going to make any headway with him, I realised that I'd have to come up with a more effective means of diverting her. Tom's information had given me an idea.

I drew his head forward and spoke to him clandestinely. 'I want you to tell Janice about Beryl leaving but don't mention Bethany. On the contrary, I want her to think that Michael's about to offer her the job.'

'What are you up to, you devious minx?'

'Just do it, Tom,' I pleaded. 'You said you'd help me. And I'm not asking you to lie exactly – just bend the truth a little. Her ego will do the rest.'

'Fair enough,' he agreed, leading me by the hand to where the other two were deep in conversation. 'Sorry, Planquet,' Tom apologised. 'I need to speak to Janice now.'

'You English,' moaned Pierre, throwing up his hands. 'I wish you'd make your bloody minds up.' But, as I pulled him onto the dance floor, he seemed content to have me back in his arms.

'I've missed you,' I said. 'But you seem to be keen on Janice.'

'She's very nice,' he conceded.

'Nicer than me?'

'Different to you. Like strawberries and cream.'

I followed his gaze from her red dress to my white suit. 'Don't get any ideas,' I cautioned him.

'In France *les trois* is quite common,' he remarked.

I balked at the idea. 'Forget it,' I advised him.

He shrugged as only a Frenchman can. '*Il n'y a pas de quoi.* It matters not.'

I let my hands creep over his bottom. 'I don't want to share you with anyone.' He smiled and let his own hands creep over mine. Then we squeezed each other like we were checking out peaches.

I wasn't sure if it was the wine or the fact that Janice wanted him, but I was beginning to warm to his charms. One of his charms was rubbing itself against my pussy when, out of the corner of my eye, I saw the burly frame of Michael Main approaching. Straightening up, I greeted him with a manufactured smile, which he accepted with a nod.

'I see you're looking after our visitor, Miss Roberts.' He turned to Pierre. 'Learning how the English operate, Planquet?'

'It has been most enlightening,' Pierre said.

'And what has impressed you most on your visit?' Michael enquired.

Pierre flicked a look at me. 'Your female personnel, of course,' he quipped, then added more seriously, 'but I would trade them all for one Mr Faraday. He strikes me as being someone capable of constructing the first voice-controlled woman.' Bizarrely, I felt a warm glow of pride to hear him speak so well of Flynn.

'Which of us men wouldn't give their right arm for an invention like that?' cackled Michael.

'Could I have a word in your ear, Mr Main?' I requested.

'Certainly, my dear.' He drew me to one side. 'What is it?'

'I've heard that Beryl's leaving,' I said.

'Well, yes,' he responded awkwardly. 'But I'm afraid, my dear, that –'

I intercepted him. 'I just wanted to put in a word for Janice. I know how desperate she is for the job, Mr Main. She told me that she'd do anything to get it – anything at all. There's a rumour going round that you've already made your choice, but don't you think it's only fair to give Janice a chance to persuade you otherwise? She can be much more persuasive than I am and I'm sure you'd appreciate her enthusiasm. Why not let her give it her best shot before you reject her out of hand?'

A sly look entered his eyes. 'More persuasive than you?'

'Much more.'

'And is she also a blonde, Miss Roberts?'

I winked at him. 'That's for you to find out.'

He ran his hand over his chin. 'You could be wrong. If

I made an improper suggestion, she might think that I'm a dirty old man.'

'Confidentially, it's my guess that she's counting on it,' I said.

A crafty smile played around his lips as his bloodshot gaze flickered towards Janice. 'In that case, I think you're right, my dear. I should at least give her a chance to exhibit her credentials.'

As he headed off in my rival's direction, I slithered back into Pierre's arms and, while we danced, I watched my plot unfold, smiling to myself as Janice, animated by Tom's news, threw herself at Michael. Giving it everything she had: eyes, tits, wiggling hips. And all to no avail!

'You're smiling,' observed Pierre. 'What are you thinking?'

'I was thinking how fickle Janice is,' I declared. 'A minute ago she was climbing all over you like ivy on a trellis. Now look at her!'

'I don't want to look at her,' he said, peering into my eyes. 'I want to look at you, Pamela.' I could feel his hands under my jacket, caressing my bare skin. 'I want to look at your naked body.'

'How grateful would you be if I were to let you look?' I teased him.

'Profoundly grateful,' he answered with a smile.

'In that case . . .' I was about to lead him from the dancefloor when I saw Beryl Parker coming towards me with a look of disapproval on her pinched face. 'A word please, Pamela,' she commanded. Looking past her, I saw Janice watching.

'Mr Main's just called me over,' Beryl said. 'It seems that Miss Becker has brought to his attention that you've been monopolising our guest of honour this evening. She quite rightly pointed out that a number of our female clients are hoping for a dance with Monsieur Planquet.' She smiled frostily at Pierre. 'I'm not sure how it works in France, but in England we tend to put business before pleasure at these sorts of functions.'

He flashed his most charming smile. 'Ah well, we bloody French – we like to mix them up. But I am at your disposal, Miss Parker.'

As she steered him away, I skewered Janice with my eyes and received a grin like the Cheshire cat's. She must have thought it was her birthday: promotion in the bag, Michael's nose between her cleavage, and now Pierre had been delivered from my clutches. But little did she know that her bed of roses had been planted in manure that I'd put down myself.

Something of my satisfaction must have shown on my face because, as soon as the dance was over, she joined me at the makeshift bar where I was downing another glass of wine.

'What are you up to?' she asked me accusingly.

I looked at her innocently. 'I don't know what you mean.'

'I've seen that look before, Roberts. You're up to something.'

'Oh piss off, you paranoid pork ball,' I grunted sourly. 'You're not as clever as you think. I'm not up to anything.'

'You're a lying cow,' she confronted me.

'And you're a scheming bitch.'

We exchanged evil glares. My hand was itching to slap her. 'I hope you realise, Janice, that because of your meddling, Beryl will be keeping a beady eye on Pierre to make sure that he doesn't fraternise with either of us. You couldn't stand that you were losing him to me, could you?'

'Losing to you? That'll be the day,' she scoffed.

'Pierre's mine,' I insisted. 'Didn't you see us together? We were practically fucking on the dancefloor. Admit defeat, Janice.'

She gave her head an obstinate shake. 'The show's not over till the fat lady sings,' she decreed.

'The fat lady isn't going to sing with her teeth rammed down her throat,' I growled.

'Is that a threat?'

'You bet your fucking life.'

We squared up to each other, just as we had at school.

'How's it going, ladies?' slurred Tom, staggering in between us. 'It's nice to see you chatting together. Like I said once before, we're a team here and we should all be happy, happy friends.' He was obviously drunk. 'You two have a lot in common.'

Like wanting to scratch each other's eyes out, I thought. 'Janice and I understand each other perfectly,' I said.

'Good,' he announced, plonking his arms around our shoulders. 'Let's all have a drink.'

We had a drink with him and then, leaving him propped at the bar, headed off in different directions. We spent the rest of the evening avoiding each other.

Eventually, as the guests were beginning to leave, Pierre returned to my side. 'I am yours again,' he said, steering me to the bar for a last glass of wine. The hired staff had gone so we helped ourselves. 'A toast to Michael Main,' he said, sweeping his glass to his lips. 'May he continue to hire the most beautiful women.'

'Fuck him,' muttered Tom, lolling across the table. 'That dumb bastard thinks he's the boss.'

'He is the boss,' I said.

'No, no he isn't,' giggled Tom. 'He only thinks he is.'

'You're soused, Tom,' said Janice, joining us.

'I know what I know,' insisted Tom, grinning like a fish. 'He thinks he's the boss, but she's the boss and she's the boss.' He stabbed his finger towards Janice and me. Janice shrugged and walked away.

'What does he mean?' Pierre asked.

'He's drunk,' I explained. 'Take no notice. I think we should go now. Everyone else has left.'

'Beware of British bulldog bitches,' bellowed Tom. 'They'll truss you like a turkey and then decorate your balls with items of office stationery. I'm warning you, arsehole.' Then he dropped to his knees and keeled over.

Pierre looked at me anxiously. 'Does he mean you?'

'No, of course not,' I denied swiftly. 'He means Janice. They were having a torrid affair but he dumped her rather cruelly and rumour has it that she stapled his balls together.' I hadn't realised that she was standing behind me until I felt her nails digging into my shoulder. Then I heard her say, 'I've had just about enough of you and your lies, Pamela Roberts.'

Chapter Twenty-Two

Spinning me round, she launched herself at me so violently that I fell backwards onto the floor where she jumped gleefully on top of me. I half-expected Pierre to break us up, but a quick glance in his direction revealed that he had seated himself to watch.

Janice was tearing at my hair, so I grabbed a fistful of hers and pulled her head back sharply. Yowling, she smacked my face, and I retaliated with a stinging slap to her cheek that knocked her head sideways. Then we lunged at each other, vicious and spiteful as wildcats. Our tempers were erupting in a volcanic explosion of fury after years of hatred, jealousy and frustration.

We rolled on the floor, clawing and spitting; tearing at each other's clothes. I shredded her bastard red dress and she shrieked with glee as the sleeve of my designer jacket ripped from its seam and came away in her hand. Then, grasping my lapels, she gave a mighty wrench so that my buttons burst from their moorings and my jacket flew open.

I punched her in the stomach and, when she doubled up, I lifted her tattered dress and sank my teeth into the wobbling half-moon of buttock that was bulging from her high-cut briefs. She lashed out with her foot, clipping my calf with her stiletto heel and drawing blood.

'You fucking bitch!' I screamed, raking my nails into her exposed shoulder, leaving vivid red tramlines.

'You skinny-arsed slapper!' she cried, tugging at my skirt with all her strength and then grinning hysterically as the side seam split. I could feel it ripping all the way to my waistband but I didn't care, for I was single-mindedly attacking her wispy red panties with the wicked intention of revealing her black bush and thereby exposing her bottle-blondeness. I hooted in triumph as I held aloft my scalp of red lace. 'Black as a crow, you fucking fraud!'

It was then that I noticed Pierre. He was sitting back with his fly open and his eyes half-closed, wanking himself as he watched us. His cock was as stiff as a baseball bat.

Dodging Janice's flailing fists, I shouted, 'He's getting his rocks off on this!'

Her blazing eyes darted towards him. 'The filthy French pig,' she panted, dropping her arms to her sides. 'Mind you, I can hardly blame him. Look at the state of us.'

I surveyed the wreckage of her dress. Her wiry black thatch peeked rudely through a yawning gap. One of her tits was hanging loose from her scarlet bra. Her stockings were torn and two of her suspenders had snapped.

Looking down at myself, I saw that both of my sleeves were detached, my jacket was gaping and my breasts were bared. The split in my skirt was revealing my saucy G-string.

We were covered in scratches and teeth marks and bruises. My hair, pulled from its chignon, was hanging in tatty clumps. Her ear was bleeding where I'd torn off an earring.

Pierre's eyes were raw with lust. 'Don't stop girls,' he

urged, pointing to his rampant prick. 'To the winner – the spoils!'

I felt wildly excited. Adrenalin was pumping through my veins. And I could tell from Janice's face that she felt the same. We both wanted his tumescent cock with an urgency that now surpassed our desire to kill each other.

Laughing lustfully, Janice went over to him, unclasped her bra and dangled her heavy breasts in front of his face. 'What do you think of these, Frenchie?'

He sighed ecstatically as he hefted them in his hands and buried his face between. They were almost as big as his head. My sex throbbed hungrily as I watched him pulling her large rubbery nipples like he was milking a cow. He saw the longing on my face and beckoned me over.

Unwilling to compete with her massive breasts, I unbuttoned my skirt and, stepping out of it, bent over in front of him, offering him the alternative of my G-stringed arse.

'*Mon Dieu*,' he groaned, his hot hands frenziedly caressing my silky flesh. 'You have a perfect *derrière*, *ma petite*. And you, Janice, have the most wonderful breasts.'

The sound of him sucking and slurping on her nipples made my own stand up, demanding attention. Removing my jacket, I turned round and cupped myself invitingly.

'Come here, *cherie*,' he croaked, pressing one of my breasts together with one of hers. They were an ill-matched pair but he moulded his hands into a D and a G cup respectively. Then he flicked his tongue from her nipple to mine.

'Feels good,' Janice moaned, nodding towards me.

'Feels great,' I agreed, nodding back.

'Christ, I'm horny as hell,' she grunted, fingering the black pelt between her legs. 'Lick my beaver, lover boy.'

I untied my G-string and, whipping it from my crotch, invited him to, 'Kiss my pussy.'

A creaking groan rumbled from his throat. 'You are both so adorable. What is a man to do?'

In unspoken agreement, we each took one of his hands and guided them to our furry mounds, quivering in unison as he rubbed and fingered us both. 'You English girls – you like this?'

'You'd better believe it,' Janice said hotly.

We held onto each other for support as his fingers frigged us furiously. I noticed that her legs were trembling as much as mine.

'Enough!' cried Janice. 'Let's fuck.'

Pierre reached into his pocket and, withdrawing a condom, held it out. 'Who wants to be first?'

Janice and I looked at each other. 'Stone, scissors, paper?' she suggested.

We played and I won. 'You can have his tongue,' I consoled her.

She smiled. 'Sounds reasonable. Let's get him.'

Working as a team, we dragged him onto the floor and stripped off his clothes. Then Janice held the base of his cock as I smoothed the condom over its bulbous head.

We laid him flat on the floor and, as I straddled him, I impaled myself gently onto the rigid pole of his cock. When I'd seated myself to my satisfaction, I signalled to Janice who knelt above his head.

'Don't suffocate him,' I beseeched her as she lowered her crack onto his face.

It felt strange riding his disembodied cock with Janice's fat arse rippling in front of me. But curiously arousing to watch his brown fingers digging into her flesh. It felt stranger still when I had to grip her shoulders to raise and lower myself. It was the first time we'd played any kind of game together and I was surprised to find myself enjoying it.

'Jesus almighty, he's good with his tongue,' she exclaimed. 'What's happening back there?'

'It's weird,' I said. 'Your jiggling butt reminds me of

two bouncing bombs heading for a dam. I certainly won't be kissing him now.'

'Don't be so squeamish – just think of it as lip gloss,' she giggled. 'Oh, shit, I think my dam's been breached,' she groaned. 'Yes, oh yes, I'm coming.'

'Don't drown him,' I pleaded.

Her oohs and aahs put me in the mood for my own modest orgasm. Pierre's followed almost at once. 'Chocks away,' I told Janice.

'Bugger,' she moaned, crawling from his head. 'He might have held something back.'

I flopped from his body. 'He's a spent force.' I stated.

As he collected his clothes, we both noticed his hairy arse for the first time. 'That's put me right off,' confided Janice. 'I'm glad I didn't see it earlier.'

'Me too,' I agreed. 'Not that it would have made any difference. I would have screwed him if he'd had hair on his prick just to get my transfer.'

'To France?' she queried. 'You shagged him to get a transfer?'

I nodded. 'Go ahead, condemn me. I wouldn't blame you.'

'I'm hardly in a position to criticise,' she admitted, glancing up at the clock. 'I have an appointment of a similar sort with Michael Main in half an hour.'

I felt a sudden rush of guilt. 'Don't go,' I pleaded earnestly. 'The wily old bastard has already picked Beryl's replacement. If you sucked him off all night, you still wouldn't get the job.'

'The sly old dog,' she uttered peevishly. 'So, who did get it?'

'Bethany,' I announced. 'And before you query her qualifications, she gives good head, I've been told.'

She was just as shocked as I'd been. 'Bethany!' she exclaimed. 'The cunning, conniving, two-faced cow!'

'That was pretty much my own reaction,' I said.

'Well I'm gobsmacked,' she said. 'It just goes to show

that you can't trust friends. I guess that's one thing about being enemies, Pam – we know each other inside out.'

It was an oddly intimate moment, sitting there cross-legged on the floor, vulnerable without clothes but relaxed because we'd seen each other's bodies so many times in the showers at school.

'Do you know something, Pam,' Janice said. 'I'd miss our fights if you went to France. You've been part of my life for so long that I'd feel I was losing a rotten sister.'

'We've had some great scraps, haven't we?' I chuckled. 'But I really don't have any choice.' I sighed. 'I can hardly carry on working for Tom. You heard what he said. What we did to each other was unforgivable.'

'We could always swap jobs,' she suggested. 'Roger isn't as bad as you think. He'll certainly try it on with you, but if you give him a knock-back, he'll leave you alone. Would it surprise you to know that I've never slept with him?'

It did. 'You're kidding!'

'You'd know if I was.'

'Then why do you let people think that you do?' I asked curiously.

'Because it's good for his ego,' she replied. 'Didn't you know that balling one's secretary gives a man status at VoiceCom? He likes to think he's a wolf but, actually, he's a lamb. You could do a lot worse, Pam.'

'Tom's all pig,' I warned her. 'He's a control freak.'

As we both looked across at Tom's body on the floor, I noticed Pierre sprawled in a chair beside him. They were both fast asleep and snoring in harmony.

'I can guess what you mean by the way he dictated the pace when I was sucking him off,' said Janice. 'But I still fancy him: that body, those shoulders and, especially, that cock. What's he like in the sack?'

'Dominant,' I decided. 'He'll go the distance but he's not bothered if you're with him or not, if you know what

I mean. He likes to call the tune and he'll have you dancing for him if you're not careful.'

'Interesting,' she mused. 'He sounds like a challenge. I still want to have a crack at him, assuming that you haven't permanently discouraged him from playing away from home.'

'What about *him*?' I asked, pointing to Pierre.

She yawned. 'We've been there and done that, haven't we? It was fun but nothing special. And as for that hairy arse!' She shuddered. 'Sometimes I think I'll never find a man who'll mean anything more to me than just a casual fuck. I've never met anyone yet who can make my toes curl just to look at him. Have you?'

I thought of Flynn and just the image of him made my toes curl. 'Yes,' I answered gravely. 'But he's engaged to someone else.'

She looked at me intently. 'You're talking about Flynn,' she guessed. When I nodded, she hung her head. 'Since we're being honest with each other, I have a confession to make. What I said about him having a fiancée – I made it up.'

My heart fluttered wildly. 'Then ... who was that redhead?'

She shrugged. 'Some girl he picked up, I guess. As far as I know, he's as free as a bird. I just said it out of spite because I knew you liked him. But if you really want him, Pam, then go and get him.'

I shook my head doubtfully. 'He hates me.'

She rolled her eyes. 'After all these years you're still that silly little freckle-faced cunt, do you know that? I've seen the way he looks at you and, believe me, it isn't with hate! Don't let the grass grow under your feet, kid. Take some sisterly advice – swallow your pride and go get him.'

I sighed. 'Maybe I'll speak to him tomorrow.'

'Why wait till tomorrow?' she stormed at me. 'He'll be downstairs now working overtime on these wretched security cameras.' She pointed up at the ceiling. 'See how the smoke in here has turned the stupid thing on again?'

When I saw the red light blinking my hands flew to my face. 'Oh my God!' I cried in despair. 'He'll have seen everything!'

'So what?' she said nonchalantly. 'You're a red-blooded woman. Are you ashamed of it?'

'No,' I answered decisively. 'I'm not ashamed of it. He'll have to get used to the idea that this isn't just a man's world we're living in. I happen to like having sex a lot.'

She stood up and helped me to my feet. 'Perhaps it wouldn't be wise for you to confront him in the nude. Best put some clothes on.'

I retrieved my silver top from my handbag and put it on. Then I fastened my skirt with a couple of safety pins but I couldn't find my G-string anywhere.

'He'll never know,' Janice said, trying to pin her own panties together. I helped her, then loaned her my jacket. 'You've lost weight,' I acknowledged as she squeezed herself into it.

She looked up and smiled. 'That's the nicest thing you've ever said to me.'

'Don't let it go to your head,' I chuckled, heading for the door. 'You're still a fat arse.'

'Hey, tit head!' she called after me. 'See you on Monday!'

I was shaking like a leaf as I stepped into the lift. What would I say to Flynn? What would he think of me now? Was I right to trust the advice of my old enemy? Oh, what the heck! There was only one way to find out.

The basement was eerily quiet and, with minimal lighting, gloomy. I trod the corridor rattling with nerves, half-expecting something horrible to jump out at me. But it wasn't half as nerve-racking as opening the door to maintenance.

My heart was beating like a drum as I went inside. He was alone and sitting at a console in front of a bank of wall-mounted screens. He glanced up as I entered and didn't seem the least surprised to see me.

'What do you want?' he asked. I expected him to remark on my dishevelled appearance, but he didn't say anything more. There was no longer any doubt in my mind that he'd been watching me.

I strode up to him boldly. 'I have a fault to report,' I declared.

He lifted an eyebrow. I loved the way he used the raven wings of his eyebrows to pose questions. 'Where is it?'

'What?' I was distracted now by his smouldering dark eyes.

'Where's the fault?' he prompted me.

'In my head,' I replied. 'I can't seem to get you out of it, Flynn.'

'I see.' His delectable mouth twitched in a barely perceptible smile. 'I'm not sure that I want to fix that.'

I moved round to the back of his chair, clenching my fingers to stop myself from thrusting them into the jet-black mane of his hair. I leaned over him to look at the monitors and I loved that he caught his breath and that his shoulders flexed as I laid my hands on them.

'You've been spying on me again,' I murmured softly, observing the screen displaying the interior of the board-room where I could see Janice trying to rouse Tom.

I moved to the front of his chair, tutting as I spotted his unfastened fly. 'You just can't keep your hands from yourself when you're watching me, can you?'

He shrugged and held my gaze unashamedly. 'That fight was better than porno,' he said. 'But the fuck afterwards – I've seen more convincing performances from you.'

'Maybe "just cock" isn't enough for me any more,' I suggested. 'If my lack of enthusiasm spoilt your entertainment, it's your own damn fault.' I grazed my fingers over his mouth. 'Am I really too hot for you, Flynn?'

'What do you think?' His sexy eyes told me that no woman on earth could ever be too hot for him.

'I think you lied,' I said.

He slipped his fingers between my legs. 'You're damn right about that.'

I closed my eyes as he fondled the tight curls of my pussy. 'Then why did you say it?'

'Call me old-fashioned,' he said, 'but I don't like sharing my women.' He drove his fingers into my sex. 'Do you get it?'

'Yes,' I gasped, whimpering as he withdrew his hand from my skirt. 'Don't stop. I love it when you touch me.'

He put his head to one side. 'I'm waiting.'

'Waiting for what?'

He leaned forward to consider me. 'For you to wake up to what it is you want from me.'

I gripped his thigh. 'You know what I want. Don't torture me, Flynn.'

He lifted my hand and, without taking his eyes from my face, ran his tongue across my palm. 'Spell it out for me, baby.'

'I want your body, I want your kiss. I want you to take me in your arms and make love to me. I want you to bury your cock inside my body. But, more than anything, I want you to tell me that you don't hate me,' I begged him.

He gripped my waist roughly and pulled me onto his lap. 'I don't.' He stroked my hair, then ran his finger down my cheek. 'Let me tell you something,' he said. 'When I kissed you in the lift, I knew right away that I wanted more than just a one-night stand. But you kept on telling me you hated me. I wanted you to know what it felt like.'

'Oh, Flynn.' I wrapped my arms around him, pressing

my face to his. 'How could I hate you? I'm crazy about you. Is that why you wouldn't kiss me?'

He stroked his thumb across my lips. 'You've been so hard to resist.'

'Won't you kiss me now?' I implored him.

A mischievous twinkle entered his eyes. 'Let me think about it – I'll get back to you.'

'Damn you!' I exclaimed, jumping up in frustration.

He caught my wrist and pulled me back down. 'Just kidding,' he said. 'Come here.'

'Maybe I don't hate you any more but you're still an infuriating bastard!' I scolded him.

'And you're still a cock-hungry bitch,' he returned. 'It should make for an interesting relationship.'

'I'm glad you're a bastard,' I decided, cuddling up to him again. 'There's no danger of my falling in love with you.'

He tilted his head. 'Is that what you think?'

'Oh, don't start that again,' I groaned. 'You can't possibly know anything I don't.'

He quirked his chin. 'Do you want to bet on that?'

Somehow I knew that if I bet against him, I'd be throwing my money away: he'd always been light years ahead of me.

Sighing, he took my face in his hands. 'I guess I'll have to show you what I know.'

'Oh yes,' I whispered, closing my eyes as his mouth descended on mine. 'Please show me.'

Then, suddenly, he was kissing me, and I was in heaven. I'd never known a mouth so blissfully sensual as his. I clung to him fiercely, desperate for more. And, as the pressure of his lips increased, violent shock waves of pleasure sizzled through my body and gasps of sheer ecstasy exploded in my lungs.

I could feel him shuddering with me, as his kiss, growing hot and hungry, became an act of penetration with the rolling caress of his tongue.

He was driving me wild and I couldn't get enough of him. The honey of his kiss was pouring into my veins, turning me into liquid, and I could feel myself melting into a black hole of tenderness deep within myself.

Then, in the midst of my rapture, came the sudden realisation that, at last, I knew what he knew.

Visit the *Black Lace* website at

www.blacklace-books.co.uk

Find out the latest information and take advantage of our fantastic **free** book offer! Also visit the site for . . .

- All *Black Lace* titles currently available and how to order online
- Great new offers
- Writers' guidelines
- Author interviews
- An erotica newsletter
- Features
- Cool links

Black Lace – the leading imprint of women's sexy fiction.

Taking your erotic reading pleasure to new horizons

BLACK LACE NEW BOOKS

Please note that publication dates given here are for UK only. For other territories, check with your retailer.

Published in December

GOING TOO FAR
Laura Hamilton
£6.99

Spirited adventurer Bliss van Bon is set for three months travelling around South America. When her travelling partner breaks her leg, she must begin her journey alone. Along the way, there's no shortage of company. From flirting on the plane to being tied up in Peru; from sex on snowy mountain peaks to finding herself out of her depth with local crooks, Bliss doesn't have time to miss her original companion one bit. And when brawny Australians Red and Robbie are happy to share their tent and their gorgeous bodies with her, she's spoilt for choice.

**An exciting, topical adventure of a young woman caught
up in sexual intrigue and global politics.**

ISBN 0 352 33657 9

COMING UP ROSES
Crystalle Valentino
£6.99

Rosie Cooper, landscape gardener, is fired from her job by an over-fussy client. Although it's unprofessional, she decides to visit the woman a few days later, to contest her dismissal. She arrives to find a rugged, male replacement behaving even more unprofessionally by having sex with the client in the back garden! It seems she's got competition – a rival firm of fit, good-looking men are targeting single well-off women in West London. When the competition's this unfair, Rosie will need all her sexual skills to level the playing field.

A fun, sexy story of lust and rivalry ... and landscape gardening!

ISBN 0 352 33658 7

THE STALLION
Georgina Brown
£6.99

Ambitious young horse rider Penny Bennett intends to gain the sponsorship and the very personal attention of showjumping's biggest impresario, Alistair Beaumont. The prize is a thoroughbred stallion, guaranteed to bring her money and success. Beaumont's riding school is not all it seems, however. Firstly there's the weird relationship between Alistair and his cigar-smoking sister. Then the bizarre clothes they want Penny to wear. In an atmosphere of unbridled kinkiness, Penny is determined to discover the truth about Beaumont's strange hobbies.

**Sexual jealousy, bizarre hi-jinks and very unsporting behaviour
in this Black Lace special reprint.**

ISBN 0 352 33005 8

Published in January

DOWN UNDER
Juliet Hastings
£6.99

Priss and Diva, 30-something best friends, are taking the holiday of a lifetime in New Zealand. After a spell of relaxation they approach the week-long 'mountain trek', brimming with energy and dangerously horny. It's Fliss's idea to see if, in the course of one week, they can involve every member of the 12-person trek in their raunchy adventures. Some are pushovers but others present more of a challenge!

A sexual relay race set against a rugged landscape.

ISBN 0 352 33663 3

THE BITCH AND THE BASTARD
Wendy Harris
£6.99

Pam and Janice, bitter rivals since schooldays, now work alongside each other for the same employer. Pam's having an affair with the boss, but this doesn't stop Janice from flirting outrageously with him. There are plenty of hot and horny men around to fight over, however, including bad-boy Flynn who is after Pam, big time! Whatever each of them has, the other wants, and things come to head in an uproar of cat-fighting and sexual bravado.

Outrageously filthy sex and wild, wanton behaviour!

ISBN 0 352 33664 1

ODALISQUE
Fleur Reynolds
£6.99

Beautiful but ruthless designer Auralie plots to bring about the downfall of her more virtuous cousin, Jeanine. Recently widowed but still young, wealthy and glamorous, Jeanine's passions are rekindled by Auralie's husband. But she is playing into Auralie's hands. Why are these cousins locked into this sexual feud? And what is the purpose of Jeanine's mysterious Confessor and his sordid underground sect?

A Black Lace special reprint of a cult classic of the genre.

ISBN 0 352 32887 8

LOOK OUT FOR THE NEW-STYLE BLACK LACE BOOKS COMING IN FEBRUARY!

GONE WILD
Maria Eppie
£6.99

At twenty-six, Zita's a babe on the way up: live-in cameraman lover, urban des-res, stupendous media job. It seems she can do no wrong. But somehow the volume gets turned up a little too loud and she ends up wrestling naked one night with her girl pal and now they're not just pals anymore. She is also becoming obsessed with Cy, the beautiful tai-chi naturist. And then the nude rave scene in the music promo she supervises gets totally out of hand! And what's her boyfriend up to in Cuba? If Zita thinks she has all the rules sussed, how come everyone else is playing a different game?

A hot and horny story of urban girls on the move.

ISBN 0 352 33670 6

RELEASE ME
Suki Cunningham
£6.99

Jo Bell is a feisty journalist with just one weakness – her boss, Jerome. When he sends her on an assignment to a remote stately English home, she finds herself sucked into a frenzied erotic battle of wills with the owners of the mansion. The decadent Alicia will go to any lengths to prove her sexual superiority and her seemingly shy brother is keeping his own proclivities too quiet for Jo's liking. Jerome becomes a pawn in the siblings' games, too, and boundaries are pushed to the limit as degradation and punishment are firmly fixed on the agenda.

Past and present mingle in this compelling tale of modern-day aristos up to no good.

ISBN 0 352 33671 4

JULIET RISING
Cleo Cordell
£6.99

Nothing is more important to Reynard than winning the favours of the bright and wilful Juliet, a pupil at Madame Nicol's exclusive but strict 18th-century ladies' academy. Her captivating beauty tinged with a hint of cruelty soon has Reynard willing to do anything to win her approval. But Juliet's methods have little effect on Andreas, the real object of her lustful obsessions. Unable to bend him to her will, she is forced to watch him lavish his manly talents on her fellow pupils. That is, until she agrees to change her spoilt ways.

This sophisticated, classic novel is a Black Lace special reprint of one of the earliest titles in the series – by an author who pioneered women's erotic fiction.

ISBN 0 352 32938 6

To find out the latest information about Black Lace titles, check out the website: www.blacklace-books.co.uk or send a stamped addressed envelope to:

Black Lace, Thames Wharf Studios,
Rainville Road, London W6 9HA

Please note only British stamps are valid.

BLACK
lace

BLACK LACE BOOKLIST

Information is correct at time of printing. To avoid disappointment check availability before ordering. Go to www.blacklace-books.co.uk

All books are priced £5.99 unless another price is given.

Black Lace books with a contemporary setting

THE TOP OF HER GAME	Emma Holly ISBN 0 352 33337 5	☐
IN THE FLESH	Emma Holly ISBN 0 352 33498 3	☐
A PRIVATE VIEW	Crystalle Valentino ISBN 0 352 33308 1	☐
SHAMELESS	Stella Black ISBN 0 352 33485 1	☐
TONGUE IN CHEEK	Tabitha Flyte ISBN 0 352 33484 3	☐
INTENSE BLUE	Lyn Wood ISBN 0 352 33496 7	☐
THE NAKED TRUTH	Natasha Rostova ISBN 0 352 33497 5	☐
ANIMAL PASSIONS	Martine Marquand ISBN 0 352 33499 1	☐
A SPORTING CHANCE	Susie Raymond ISBN 0 352 33501 7	☐
TAKING LIBERTIES	Susie Raymond ISBN 0 352 33357 X	☐
A SCANDALOUS AFFAIR	Holly Graham ISBN 0 352 33523 8	☐
THE NAKED FLAME	Crystalle Valentino ISBN 0 352 33528 9	☐
CRASH COURSE	Juliet Hastings ISBN 0 352 33018 X	☐
ON THE EDGE	Laura Hamilton ISBN 0 352 33534 3	☐
LURED BY LUST	Tania Picarda ISBN 0 352 33533 5	☐
LEARNING TO LOVE IT	Alison Tyler ISBN 0 352 33535 1	☐

THE ORDER £6.99	Dee Kelly ISBN 0 352 33652 8	☐
ALL THE TRIMMINGS £6.99	Tesni Morgan ISBN 0 352 33641 3	☐
PLAYING WITH STARS £6.99	Jan Hunter ISBN 0 352 33653 6	☐
THE GIFT OF SHAME £6.99	Sara Hope-Walker ISBN 0 352 32935 1	☐
GOING TOO FAR £6.99	Laura Hamilton ISBN 0 352 33657 9	☐
COMING UP ROSES £6.99	Crystalle Valentino ISBN 0 352 33658 7	☐
THE STALLION £6.99	Georgina Brown ISBN 0 352 33005 8	☐

Black Lace books with an historical setting

PRIMAL SKIN	Leona Benkt Rhys ISBN 0 352 33500 9	☐
DEVIL'S FIRE	Melissa MacNeal ISBN 0 352 33527 0	☐
WILD KINGDOM	Deanna Ashford ISBN 0 352 33549 1	☐
DARKER THAN LOVE £6.99	Kristina Lloyd ISBN 0 352 33279 4	☐
STAND AND DELIVER	Helena Ravenscroft ISBN 0 352 33340 5	☐
THE CAPTIVATION £6.99	Natasha Rostova ISBN 0 352 33234 4	☐
CIRCO EROTICA £6.99	Mercedes Kelley ISBN 0 352 33257 3	☐
MINX £6.99	Megan Blythe ISBN 0 352 33638 2	☐
PLEASURE'S DAUGHTER £6.99	Sedalia Johnson ISBN 0 352 33237 9	☐

Black Lace anthologies

CRUEL ENCHANTMENT Erotic Fairy Stories	Janine Ashbless ISBN 0 352 33483 5	☐
MORE WICKED WORDS	Various ISBN 0 352 33487 8	☐
WICKED WORDS 4	Various ISBN 0 352 33603 X	☐
WICKED WORDS 5	Various ISBN 0 352 33642 0	☐

Black Lace non-fiction

| THE BLACK LACE BOOK OF
WOMEN'S SEXUAL FANTASIES | Ed. Kerri Sharp
ISBN 0 352 33346 4 | ☐ |

------✂------------------------

Please send me the books I have ticked above.

Name   ....

Address ....

           ....

           ....

        .... Post Code ....

Send to: Cash Sales, Black Lace Books, Thames Wharf Studios, Rainville Road, London W6 9HA.

US customers: for prices and details of how to order books for delivery by mail, call 1-800-343-4499.

Please enclose a cheque or postal order, made payable to **Virgin Books Ltd**, to the value of the books you have ordered plus postage and packing costs as follows:

   UK and BFPO – £1.00 for the first book, 50p for each subsequent book.

   Overseas (including Republic of Ireland) – £2.00 for the first book, £1.00 for each subsequent book.

If you would prefer to pay by VISA, ACCESS/MASTER-CARD, DINERS CLUB, AMEX or SWITCH, please write your card number and expiry date here:

....

Please allow up to 28 days for delivery.

Signature ....

------✂------------------------